THE WEATHER
MAGE

LINDA SMITH

THE WEATHER MAGE

Book Three of the TALES *of* THREE LANDS *trilogy*

Edited by Barbara Sapergia.
Cover painting by Aries Cheung.
Cover and book design by Duncan Campbell.
Typeset by Karen Steadman.
Printed and bound in Canada by Tri-Graphic Printing Inc.

Library and Archives Canada Cataloguing in Publication

Smith, Linda, 1949-
    The weathermage / Linda Smith.

(Tales of three lands ; bk. 3)
ISBN-13: 978-1-55050-352-4
ISBN-10: 1-55050-352-9

   I. Title. II. Series: Smith, Linda, 1949- Tales of three lands ; bk.3.

PS8587.M5528W43 2006   jC813'.54   C2006-903832-5

10 9 8 7 6 5 4 3 2 1

COTEAU
BOOKS

2517 Victoria Avenue
Regina, Saskatchewan
Canada S4P 0T2

Available in Canada & the US from:
Fitzhenry and Whiteside
195 Allstate Parkway
Markham, Ontario
Canada L3R 4T8

The publisher gratefully acknowledges the financial assistance of the Saskatchewan Arts Board, the Canada Council for the Arts, the Government of Canada through the Book Publishing Industry Development Program (BPIDP), the Association for the Export of Canadian Books, and the City of Regina Arts Commission, for its publishing program.

Canada

To all the idealistic young people I know,
especially my nephews and niece.

PROLOGUE

SHE WAS A CHILD OF THE STORM, BORN ON A day of wind and rain that swept out of the sea surrounding Rork and slapped the small island with an angry hand.

The day had not *appeared* threatening. Mala had thought it perfect for gathering oysters and mussels and the salty, chewy zaca plants that her children loved. The air was as mild as cows' eyes, the sky a robin's egg blue. The few clouds that troubled it looked like soft lamb's fleece. Nor was Mala worried about the child in her womb, which wasn't due for a few weeks yet. She smiled when she felt the baby kick.

It did slow her, though, as she made her way around the rocks and kelp that littered the shore and bent to her task. Perhaps she should have brought the younger children with her to help. But no. They were better occupied learning their letters and numbers from old Fara. There was no hurry. She walked slowly, her eyes intent on the sand, the knife at her belt ready to dig out oysters or cut zaca fronds free of their cord-like stems.

A sudden gust tugged at her skirt. She glanced up. The lamb's fleece had turned into black ram's wool that raced across the sky. Mala looked out to the sea. Wind whipped the waves into white foam.

Atholl and their two oldest children, out on the water with a storm brewing...

No. They would be safe. Lynneth had accompanied the fishers today, and she had been taught by the Wise Women of Atua to sense the patterns of wind and rain. She would give warning.

Mala took another glance at the sky and gasped. The clouds had changed again. Between one breath and another, it seemed, they had become a solid blanket of black. She started to run.

With a savage roar, the storm pounced. Wind swooped across the land and tore the sky. Clouds opened to torrents of rain. In a moment, Mala was drenched.

She strained to see through the sheets of water. There. A large boulder crowned by fallen branches. Half-blinded by the rain, she hurried towards it.

She saw the rock, partly buried in the sand, too late. Tripped. Fell.

Stinging pain, on face and arms and legs and distended belly. Mala breathed deeply, then scrambled forward and huddled by the boulder, like some lost lamb seeking comfort from a strange ewe.

Pain. Sudden. Stabbing.

No! Mother, no! Not now. Not here.

The pain ebbed. Mala lay still. But soon – too soon – it came again.

Mala was used to childbirth. Not only had she had five babies of her own, she had helped other women in their childbearing. She counted the intervals between spasms and, after a while, knew that her child would be born here, in the middle of wild wind and battering rain. She would do what she could, and pray to the Mother for help.

THE CHILDREN RETURNED from their lessons to find the house empty. It worried Peris and Cai, but ten-year-old Arlan reassured them. "Mama will come home as soon as the rain dies down. And Father and Reanna and Corven will be back when it's calmer."

But the rain kept on, while the fire in the hearth smoked and wind lashed the building. Arlan whistled, as much to cheer himself as the others, but his whistling was as wobbly as the flames. Eventually, the rain petered out into a thin trickle, like a child exhausted by its tantrum, though the wind continued to shriek. But Mala did not return. The fear that had been nibbling at Arlan's stomach leapt into his throat.

"Stay here," he told the younger ones. "I'm going to look for her."

"I'm coming too," announced seven-year-old Peris. Little Cai nodded. His thumb had crept into his mouth, where it had not been for a year or more.

"No. If Father gets home and finds no one here, he'll worry."

After a moment, Peris settled back and placed her arm around Cai.

The stones were slippery against Arlan's bare feet. He inched his way along the shore, peering through rain-speckled greyness and calling, "Mama! Mama!" His voice seemed to lose itself in the rushing wind.

She must be here somewhere, among the rocks and sand and kelp and shells tossed up by the sea. She couldn't be lost. Not Mama, with her brown hair and bubbling laugh. Mama, who comforted his hurts and soothed his fears and told him stories on winter evenings when mist sealed them in like so many caterpillars in a cocoon. He called again, a cry that was more sob than shout.

And heard...something. Not his mother. But a human wail, above the shriek of the wind, the surge of the waves. He stood and listened. The wind moaned, gusted, tugged his shirt free of his trousers and tossed his hair about like black crow feathers.

There it was again. A human cry answering the cry of the wind.

He half ran, half leapt up the beach to where a large boulder crouched like a wary sea lion.

On the rocky sand beneath the boulder was a body. Legs outstretched. Brown skirt pulled high. Brown hair tumbling all about. Eyes closed. It looked like Peris's rag doll, tossed aside and forgotten.

The howl came again, from the other side of the still form. The woman's eyes opened.

Arlan wanted to cry then but couldn't, for the breath was trapped in his throat.

His mother's eyes found his face. "Arlan."

Her voice was a mere thread of sound, but it revived him. "Mama. Oh, Mama!"

Pale lips moved in a waxen face. "Don't...sound so, my love. I'm all right." Her eyes moved to one side. "So is your sister."

"My sister?"

Mala smiled. "She arrived early. Come see."

Arlan took a couple of steps forward. Then he was looking at the red, crumpled face of a tiny creature, naked except for a tight cluster of dark curls crowning her head. Her mouth opened again in a cry unbelievably loud for one so small.

"Hush," Mala said softly. "Yes, I know. You wish to be fed. And so you shall be. You have strong lungs, my daughter. You cry as loudly as the wind." She laughed, the memory of pain fading from her face. "You are a true child of the storm. Galia, you shall be called." She looked up at her son, now kneeling beside them. "Is she not beautiful?"

Arlan gazed down at the scarlet face, at the umbilical cord, roughly cut by Mala's oyster knife, at the tiny hands. He touched one. It curled around his finger as though it belonged there. "Yes," he breathed. "She is."

GALIA'S BROTHERS AND SISTERS accused their parents of spoiling her, and they were right. Child of the storm she might be, but her tempests were brief, and were followed by such rainbow-tinted sunshine that it was impossible not to forgive her. She danced through life as joyously as she clambered over rocks on the shore, and sang as naturally as a lark – though not, her brother Cai informed her, as tunefully.

To be truthful, her sisters and brothers tended to spoil Galia too. Especially Arlan. He took her sailing when her head could scarcely bob above the prow, and taught her to swim and dive while she was yet a minnow. In turn, Galia worshipped Arlan, following him about as a seal pup follows its mother, and repeating his every word.

Galia's childhood was spent playing with other village children, gathering shellfish with her mother, cavorting like a porpoise in the sea, and following Arlan. It was good that she was quick to learn, for old Fara found it difficult to keep her at her lessons, especially on days when the sun rippled the water like a mischievous child begging to be chased, or the wind drove black clouds before it and made waves pulse with anger. Then, Galia could *not* be kept indoors.

When she was ten, Arlan announced that he was going to be married. His bride, Brianne, a round-faced, rosy-cheeked girl with a shy and beautiful smile, was a neighbour whom Galia had always known and liked. She refused to like her now.

"But Galia," Arlan said. "This makes no difference between us. I'm still your brother. Nothing can change that."

But things *had* changed. For months now, Arlan had worn the face of a silly sheep. Half the time, he failed to hear what she said. Once he had even shooed her away, as though she were a bothersome fly. And now he would leave home, as Reanna and Corven had when they married. Oh, he and Brianne would be nearby. But it wouldn't be the same. Nothing would ever be the same again.

"Don't spoil things for Arlan," Peris snapped.

She didn't want to spoil things for Arlan. She *didn't*. But oh, the misery that was in her. It was like dense fog, blotting out all the light.

The wedding was held on a day laughing with sun and wind. Arlan and Brianne made their vows to the Mother and to each other on the cliff above the sea, as had villagers for countless generations before them, their union echoing the union of land and sea and sky that was Islandia. Galia was there. She even smiled. But afterwards, while others celebrated with food and song and dance, she slipped away. Kicking off her shoes, worn only on feast days and weddings, she ran down to the shore.

A curlew perched on a rock. A gull floated lazily overhead, the sun silvering its wings. Waves curled onto the shore, then withdrew, over and over again. The world was happy. Like Arlan and Brianne.

The dark fog descended. She wanted to push it away. Strike it away. But she couldn't. It only pressed closer. Swallowing her. Smothering her.

No! She would not be swallowed. She would not be smothered. It was not fair, not *right*, to be so miserable. Anger rose in her like a white-hot flame, like a twisting fork of lightning.

7

And the lightning came, searing the cloudless sky, followed almost immediately by a crack of thunder. Wind came, boiling the sea into a frenzied froth of foam. The gull squawked its protest, but Galia laughed. There was no room for a smothering fog amidst this rage of wind and weather.

The wind and lightning chased the wedding party home. Soon, the only people to be seen on that part of the island were a short, slight girl with dark curls who stood, eyes upturned to the thunderous sky, and the woman who approached her.

"Galia."

The voice was quiet, but there was strength in it that could not be ignored. There was also something else that Galia had never heard there before. Fear? She turned.

Mala stood close to her. The skin on her face was stretched tightly over its bones. For the first time, Galia knew what her mother would look like when she was old.

"Let your anger go."

"Anger?" Galia blinked.

"It is right that Arlan marries. It is time."

Galia stared at her.

"Let your anger go," Mala repeated.

"I'm not angry."

Her mother said nothing.

"I'm *not*. At least..." Galia faltered. She *was* angry. But not at Arlan. Not even at Brianne. Just angry. Angry because of the fog.

"You must come home."

Galia's shoulders slumped. She felt very tired suddenly,

achingly tired, as though she'd used all her muscles in some new and arduous task. Slowly, she walked towards her mother. The two climbed the steep dirt path that led to the house on the headland. Behind them, the sea resumed its gentle rocking rhythm. The sky was quiet.

ARLAN'S MARRIAGE *did* make a difference, but not as great a one as Galia had feared. It helped that now, young as she was, she was allowed to go with the fishers sometimes. She delighted in every moment, from their departure when the sun was only a promise on the horizon, to their return, when she helped haul the boat onto shore, then hauled her own weary body up the path to home and the welcoming smell of fish stew or oyster pie. But the greatest joy of those excursions was being with Arlan.

He and Brianne spent much of their time in his old home, too. Brianne felt closer to Mala than to her own mother, a widow who brooded over the wrongs done her by an unkind fate and seemed happiest forecasting doom.

When Brianne said she was going to have a baby, Galia smiled. She was sure that she and this child would share a special bond, just as she and Arlan did. And always would.

The baby was a girl with Brianne's round face and Arlan's crow-feather hair. Her parents named her Mala. Galia touched her petal-soft cheek with an awed finger, and wondered how Arlan's marriage ever could have made her miserable.

It happened two years after the wedding, on a day as sparkling with promise as that one had been. Arlan had just reached the top of the cliff, home from a day's fishing. Galia, who had climbed the path before him, turned to laugh at his slowness. A hawk screamed overhead. Arlan twisted his head to see it. At that moment, two small boys erupted from behind a rock to his left, shrieking with laughter as they chased one another.

Arlan was sure-footed. The twist of his head, the swerve of his body, shouldn't have mattered. Nor should the loose stone beneath his foot. There were many such stones on Rork.

But they did matter. That day, they did.

Galia saw him teeter. She opened her mouth to call — what? A warning? A taunt at his clumsiness?

He grasped at the air for balance, for support. Then he fell.

If he'd still been on the path, the worst that would have happened would have been a bruising tumble down the dirt track to the beach below. But he had stepped beyond it. Just beyond. He fell down the cliff.

Galia knew there was no hope even as she tore down the hill faster than anyone should have run. She was the first to see his body, though others soon arrived, to gape in shock and bewilderment and pain. Eventually, strong arms carried him back up the path.

"It's not the children's fault," Mala told their white-faced mothers, while Brianne held the sobbing boys to her.

"It just...happened," Atholl said, his face grey and slack, as though blood had fled from it, and taken with it the strength of the underlying bones. "These things do. Sometimes. I don't know why."

At the funeral, Galia envied Brianne, who held little Mala tightly in her arms. But Brianne needed comfort too, she supposed.

There was no storm. She had no spark of anger to ignite one, to lift the heavy darkness that lay on her. Not fog this time. More like earth, the earth that covered Arlan.

It rained. Day after day, grey skies emptied their tears onto the land and sea. Finally it stopped, as though the skies were too tired to cry any more.

THE WOMEN CAME SIX WEEKS after Arlan died. Galia wondered, when she saw the unfamiliar boat drawn up on shore, but she didn't join in the buzz of speculation as she helped beach their own boat. Villagers clustered on the cliff. They fell silent as Galia passed.

Cai was ahead of her. She saw him stop in their doorway and hesitate before entering. Curiosity stirred in Galia, like the embers of a fire that had almost died.

A woman she'd never seen before sat in a chair by the hearth. Another stood beside her. Like Cai, Galia stopped. Strangers were rare on Rork.

The seated woman smiled at her. "Come in, child. We won't bite."

Galia inched in and stationed herself in front of the window. She glanced around. Cai, at sixteen as bumbling and bumptious as an overgrown pup, perched on the edge of a chair. Mala, interrupted in her dinner preparations, stood wiping her hands on her apron. A streak of flour smudged her chin. Peris sat, needle and thread in one hand and the shirt she was mending in the other, darting glances from Galia to the strangers and back. Galia felt like a rare type of jellyfish swept up on the beach for village children to gawk at. She turned her attention to the women.

Both wore grey, serviceable dresses that bore the marks of sea spray and much darning. At first glance, one might take them for fishers or farmers, but authority rested on the seated woman as easily as a long-worn cloak.

The standing woman, in her twenties perhaps, was tall and angular like a heron. Even her nose was long and narrow under light brown eyes.

The other woman was ageless. Her hair was swan-feather white, but her skin, drawn tightly over perfect bones, bore only a fine network of lines around the mouth and eyes. Her beauty and small bones gave her an air of fragility. Galia's eyes dropped to her hands. They were reassuringly normal, the hands of someone used to work.

Atholl entered. "Ah. I was told that two Wise Women from Atua had come to our house. You are most welcome. To what do we owe this honour?"

Wise Women from Atua! Wise Women weren't unknown, of course, even on this smallest and most westerly of the islands that made up Islandia. Galia had seen others – the Plant Helper, the Animal Helper, and the Healer who was, surprisingly, not a woman at all but a man. They came at least twice a year to help growing crops, newborn animals, ailing humans. But this was not the time they usually arrived.

The seated woman inclined her head. "We will explain."

Atholl sat. He looked, Galia thought, as wary as a sheep waiting to be sheared.

"My name is Rona. I am the Mother of the Wise Women." Galia's eyes widened. Everyone knew that the Mother on Atua was the representative of the Mother's wisdom. "This is Sandis." The younger woman smiled. "We have come to take your daughter back to Atua with us."

The words hit Galia like a fist striking her throat.

Cai gasped and Atholl's back stiffened, but neither Mala nor Peris reacted. They must already know.

"I have three daughters," Atholl said. "Which one are you talking about?"

"I think you know." Rona's eyes moved to Galia. "I'm sorry. I don't know your name, child."

Galia stared at her, dumb.

"Galia is young," Atholl said carefully. "Only twelve. Too young to leave home."

"Young, yes. But she already possesses great power."

"Power?" Galia whispered.

"Power in changing the patterns of wind and rain. In calling up storms."

"But..." She had never called up a storm. Never changed the patterns of wind and rain.

Atholl cleared his throat. "You didn't even know her name. How can you be so sure that she is the one you seek?"

"Two years ago, our Weathermonger realized that magic had been used to create a storm over Rork. This interested us, but we did nothing, only waited. This summer, the same power brought weeks of rain to the island. We were concerned. Untaught power can be dangerous. Our Dreamer dreamed of a young girl who lived in a house on the headland overlooking the western sea."

Had she created the storm? Made the rain? Surely not. Even if she had...

"I won't do it again," she whispered. Why should she? She would never be so angry again. So sad.

"Oh, Galia," Mala said. She wrapped her daughter in her arms.

"She's too young," Atholl said loudly. "I won't let you take her."

"No, Atholl," Mala said. "They are right."

Galia jerked as though she'd been stabbed. Mala's arms dropped.

"Galia, you *do* have power. You use it without even knowing that you do so. If you do not learn how to control it, you might hurt yourself. And others."

Galia stared at her. Mala's brown eyes were steady on her face.

The room was still. The sun, slanting in through the window, flared red.

"Does this mean that Galia will be a Wise Woman?" Cai asked. "The next Weathermonger?"

The younger woman laughed. "I hope not. The present Weathermonger is old, but the Dreamer has dreamed me as her successor. Galia will only become Weathermonger if I meet an early and unexpected end."

The other woman smiled. "And we would not wish that.

No. It used to be thought that only one person in each generation possessed one of the Mother's nine gifts, but we no longer believe that, just as we no longer believe only women are born with the gifts. Galia will be trained as all Wise Women are, but she will not, as far as we know, become one of us. Nor will her life on Atua be unpleasant." She smiled at Galia.

"There will be hard work," a voice said from inside her head. It held the gentle laughter of a breeze on a hot summer day, the music of the sea. "There will be discipline. And challenges. But you will be among friends."

But to leave home, everything she knew, everyone she loved...

"May I...May I say goodbye to little Mala?" She needed to hold Mala's small body close to her before she left. She *needed* to.

"Of course," Rona said. "We will not be leaving until morning. There will be time to make all your farewells." She looked around the room, at all their faces, then back at Galia. "And you *will* return to Rork. That I promise."

It was a promise Galia held to her heart in the years that followed.

CAT

THERE WAS NO LETTER.

Cat watched the boat from Freyfall glide to the middle of the river and then, oars flashing in the sun, head downstream. The sails caught the breeze and billowed out.

Above her, the voices got fainter, though she could still hear Bettina chattering and laughing. Bettina was happy. She had received word from her sweetheart.

It would be a fortnight before the next boat from Freyfall. Would there be news from Garth then?

Slowly, Cat turned and climbed the dirt steps dug into the side of the cliff. By the time she reached the top, the others had vanished. Good. She didn't want to talk to any of them. Especially Bettina. She would purchase the items she'd come to town for – or, rather, used as her excuse for coming – then leave.

She really hadn't needed an excuse. Neither her mother nor Kenton would dream of hindering her from meeting the boat from Freyfall. If she'd been sure she'd hear from Garth today, she would not have fabricated one.

She walked down the one long street that made up Frey-under-Hill, stopping to buy thread, bootlaces, buttons. She hesitated in front of a small shop that sold paper as well as a few tattered books, then walked on. Her supply of paper was almost gone, but why buy more? She only used it to write to Garth, and he had yet to respond to her last two letters.

Wizard Weaver's house leaned over the street, casting a tall shadow. She glanced up to the room on the top floor. A year ago, she had entered that study and asked Master Weaver to cast a finding spell to locate her father. That spell had led her to Freyfall and, eventually, to another wizard's house and to an apprentice wizard who only wanted to be a musician. Garth.

She quickened her step. It was cool, despite the brightness of the spring sun. The river valley was sheltered, but up here the wind still bit.

The sound of hammering drew her eyes to the open door of the forge. The large young man inside waved. She waved back and smiled. She had been hot with resentment, a year ago, when Aunt Dalia sold her deceased husband's smithy and moved to Ashdale with her son. How she had smarted over the fact that Morty would inherit Ashdale when her grandparents died.

Since then, she had come to like living on the Herd farm with her mother and stepfather. Oh, she still missed Ashdale, with its row of ash trees and wandering brook. But it no longer bothered her that it would never be hers. At least, not much.

Cat swung past the last house and began her six-mile trek home. Kenton had offered her a pony for the trip, but she had declined. She had wanted to walk home with Garth's letter safe in her pocket, Garth's words dancing through her mind.

Perhaps Garth was too busy with his studies to write.

He'd been studying music ever since she left Freyfall. That had never prevented him from writing before. His letters had arrived as punctually as the winds and currents that sped or slowed the boat from Freyfall would allow. Sometimes they were just a hasty scrawl – or so he'd claim as he began them, though they usually turned into page after page of cramped writing as he poured out all that he'd learned and done and thought and felt. She'd feared her replies were dull, but he'd seemed as interested in the daisy-filled hollow she'd discovered, the funny sayings of old Clem the cowherd, and the way Bedelia's new calf followed her about, as she was in the activities of the Spellman household and his life as an apprentice musician. She had even, shyly, hesitantly, sent him a copy of a song she'd composed, and caught her breath at the enthusiastic praise in his reply.

There had been another song in the note she'd sent a month ago. Was it painfully bad? Was that why he had not responded?

No. She didn't believe that.

Then why?

Had he lost interest? Had some girl in Freyfall caught his

eye? His heart? But the only girl he had ever mentioned was Talisa, the red-haired Uglessian who was a fellow student. And Talisa had left Freyfall last fall, fleeing with a boy who was suspected of setting fire to the barracks and killing two soldiers.

Was Garth in trouble? Was that why there'd been no word?

Nonsense. Garth had given money to Talisa and her friend to help them escape to Uglessia, but Cat was the only one who knew that. There was no reason anyone should suspect Garth. Anyway, he was the grandson of a rich and powerful wizard. No. If Garth hadn't written, it wasn't because he was in any danger from the authorities.

She stared ahead. The tree-dotted fields rolled away gently. Did waves riding into shore look like that? Garth had talked about the ocean in one of his letters. Some day, he had said, they would sail downstream to Frey-by-the-Sea and cross the ocean to the mist-enshrouded isles of Islandia.

That had been three months ago. After that...

"Cat!"

She jumped, then grimaced. That voice was all too familiar. Slowly, she turned.

"Freyn's Day, Morty."

Her cousin grinned down at her from his superior height on the dun-coloured horse. "How come you're walking? Won't Kenton let you use one of his horses?"

"I'd rather walk."

Morty laughed. He had a donkey's bray of a laugh, but resembled a frog in other ways, although he looked less pale and puffy than he had before, now that he'd had a year of work on the farm, Cat admitted. But his green eyes still bulged out. "You expect me to believe that?"

She opened her mouth to protest, then closed it. Morty wasn't worth the effort. She turned her back on him and resumed walking.

"So what do you think of the news?"

She ignored him.

"I don't imagine it makes you very happy."

What news? Why should it make her unhappy?

She strode on. The dun horse kept pace by her side.

"How will you like having a brother or sister?"

What was he talking about?

"Whoever it is will inherit the Herd farm, Mother says. But maybe they'll let you stay there if you ask nicely enough."

"I have no intention of remaining in Frey-under-Hill."

"No? What will you do? Wander the roads like your father?"

She said nothing. The horse's hooves were large. Small clouds of dust eddied around each foreleg as the horse plodded along. If she raised her head, she knew she would find Morty's eyes on her face, as hungry as a starving child's.

"Or is it that boy you met in Freyfall, the one who came here at Midwinter?" Morty sniggered. "Mother says he'll never marry you. She says he's the only heir of a wealthy wizard."

She stopped. She knew she shouldn't, but she did. "Do you repeat every word your mother says, Morty Black? I'd have hoped you were old enough to have a thought or two of your own."

Her jibe stung, as it was meant to. Her cousin's voice, long since deepened to a man's register, quivered into falsetto. "I have lots of thoughts of my own. You think you're better than the rest of us, now that you've met this wizard's brat. Well, you're not. You've never been anything, and you're nothing now!"

Morty kicked his horse, which blew out its breath in an exasperated snort and quickened its pace to a brisk walk. Morty called back over his shoulder. "At least my mother tells me things. I bet yours didn't even let you know she was expecting."

THE KITCHEN SMELLED OF LAMB STEW and freshly baked bread when Cat entered the house. Lianna smiled at her daughter. "Dinner will be ready in a few minutes." Her face was pink from the heat of the stove, and glowing with health.

Cat went to the washing alcove, poured water into the basin, and scrubbed her hands. She took her time.

"What's the news from Freyfall?" Kenton greeted her when she emerged.

"I don't know."

"You don't? But –"

"If any of the sailors spread any gossip, I didn't hear it."

"But –"

Cat saw Lianna frown at her husband. He closed his mouth. They ate in silence.

"Great food," Kenton said at last.

"It will be better when we have fresh vegetables again."

"True. But nothing can make the bread better." Kenton's large hand reached for a third slice. "Your mother makes the best bread in Freya," he told Cat.

Cat felt Lianna's eyes on her. She forced herself to nod and smile. They relapsed into silence.

When the meal ended, Cat took the kettle from the hearth and poured hot water into the basin. She washed each dish carefully, trying to ignore the heavy silence behind her. With the dishes were dried and stacked, she wiped the cherry-wood table. The slanting evening sun warmed the wood to a rich reddish brown.

"Cat," Kenton began, "your mother and I –"

"Not now, Kenton," Lianna said quietly.

Cat shook the cloth out and folded it over the side of the basin. She wiped her hands on her dress. "If you were about to tell me that you're going to have a baby, you needn't. I've already heard." She kept her back to the room.

"You heard?" Lianna exclaimed. "How...Who told you?"

"It's true, then?"

"Yes. But I don't understand. How did you hear?"

"Why didn't you tell me?" Her back was still to them.

"We haven't known for long ourselves. Not for sure."

But long enough to tell others.

"Who told you?" Kenton asked.

"Morty."

"Morty?" Lianna echoed. "But how...Unless Dalia...She was here a couple of days ago and was looking at me strangely. I suppose she guessed. But she didn't *know*. To spread the story as though it were true –"

Kenton laughed. "Don't sound so indignant. It *is* true, thank Freyn."

"But she didn't know that. And it's not right that Cat learned this from someone else."

Cat turned. Her mother's hands were clenched, her grey eyes angry. Lianna rarely showed anger, even towards her interfering older sister. Cat returned to the table.

"I'm sorry, Cat."

"It's all right."

"We would have told you earlier, but I thought we should choose a good time. We planned to tell you tonight."

After I'd received a letter from Garth and was in a good mood.

"Do you mind?"

"No."

"It won't make a difference, you know."

"No crying babies, you mean? No dirty underclothes?" Cat felt a smile quivering at the corners of her mouth.

Lianna laughed. "I can't promise that." She sobered. "But it won't change how I feel. It won't mean I love you less."

"That *we* love you less," Kenton corrected softly.

The dust motes were a golden shimmer in the evening light. Cat blinked rapidly, and they grew less misty. "I know."

Lianna covered her hand with her own. "You really don't mind?"

"No." Cat thought about it for a minute, then smiled. "In fact, I'm glad. When is it due?"

"In seven months."

"At harvest time. *Our* harvest," Kenton said. Cat looked away, embarrassed by the way they were gazing at each other.

The silence this time was warm. Comfortable. If it hadn't been for Garth...Cat stared down at the table.

"Cat..." Lianna's voice was tentative. Cat looked at her.

"I don't want to interfere, but you seem...Is something wrong? Was there bad news in Garth's letter?"

"No."

"That's good." Uncertainty hovered in Lianna's voice.

Cat gazed out the window, to where the sun splashed gold onto the leaves of the lilac bush. "There was no bad news. Nor good news. There was no letter."

"Oh." After a moment, Lianna added softly, "I'm sorry."

"He must have missed the boat," Kenton said. "I imagine he's kicking himself."

"Then he'll be sore by now. He missed it last time too." It was amazing how golden the leaves looked.

"There's sure to be a good reason," Kenton said. "He wouldn't not write if he could. Not the boy I met last summer. Not the one who was here at Midwinter."

"People change." The sunlight was too bright. She closed her eyes. "I was thinking..." Her voice wobbled. She cleared her throat, tried again. "His last three letters were different."

"In what way?" Lianna asked.

"They...It was as though he wasn't really thinking about what he was writing. As though his mind was on something else."

"Perhaps a song had broken into his thoughts," Kenton suggested. Cat glanced at his broad, concerned face. He was trying so hard to make her feel better.

"Maybe. But that's happened before, and he always told me when it did, and included bits of it, or the whole thing." Sometimes the words to the songs were about her. "And that doesn't explain why he hasn't written for over a month." The tears were very close now.

"Was something on his mind? Did he say anything at Midwinter?" Lianna asked.

Garth had arrived three days before Midwinter, on a day filled with soft, lazy snowflakes. Cat remembered how the snow had clung to his dark hair and planted a large dot, like a flour smudge, on the tip of his nose. His hands had been cold and wet when they grasped hers.

Had Garth said anything at Midwinter that might explain his present neglect? He had talked about music, the words tumbling over themselves in his eagerness. He had told her how his teacher, Master Coyne, could play any instrument he wanted to, and play it with a purity and passion that made Garth's throat ache. He had told her how he and his grandfather were getting along so much better, now that Konrad Spellman had accepted his grandson's desire to be a musician.

He had already poured out all this in his letters, but she had listened patiently, enjoying the excitement in his voice, the light in his eyes.

And he had told her about Talisa Thatcher's search for a Freyan youth suspected of arson and murder, and how that search had led to a flight through the night, and his gift of money to aid their escape. This news had never been relayed in a letter. Garth said he hadn't dared. He only told her about it when they were walking alone in the fields, their fingers intertwined, their breaths making white puffs in the air.

Had he said anything else about that night?

He had talked about the man in whose house Talisa's friend was hiding. A musician. Swan something. Swansong? Swanson? Something like that. Garth admired his songs. Cat had smiled inwardly, listening to him. How typical that, in the middle of telling her about danger and flight, Garth had broken off to talk about music. He had said –

Cat drew in her breath.

"What is it?' Lianna leaned forward.

"Garth said he had met a man who…Well, he might be involved in something dangerous."

"Not another conspiracy!" Kenton said, alarm sharp in his voice.

"No, nothing like that." At least, she hoped not. "Garth met him because he was the friend of a friend of someone Garth knew."

They were both staring at her. Kenton frowned. "And you think Garth might be mixed up in this too?"

"I don't know. But…" She took a deep breath. "I just remembered. Garth said he went back to see this man. I don't know whether that has anything to do with…with anything. I don't know *anything*."

The tears came then, not the silent tears of misery that had been threatening, but loud sobs that released her pent-up frustration and anger. Anger at Garth for not writing. Anger at herself for not *knowing.* She laid her head on the table and cried like a child. She felt her mother's hand stroking her hair, Kenton's resting gently on her shoulder. They helped. A little.

The storm subsided at last. Raising her head, she reached for a handkerchief, wiped her face, then blew her nose firmly.

"I must go to Freyfall."

She blinked, surprised at her own words. But of course she must go. If Garth had lost interest in her, it was better to know than to wonder. And if something was wrong...

The sun had set, leaving the room in dim twilight. Cat wished she could see her mother's and stepfather's expressions better. She knotted her fingers together, readying herself for their arguments.

"Yes," Lianna said slowly. "I think you must."

Cat stared at her. So did Kenton. Then he sighed. "You're probably right, Lianna. But she can't go by herself. I'll go with her."

"No!"

"Cat –"

"No. I do appreciate...But you can't leave at planting time. I'll be all right on my own. All I plan to do is go to the Spellman house and talk to Garth. Then I'll return. I promise."

"You can't go alone. You yourself said Garth might be mixed up in something dangerous."

"I don't know that. It's just a possibility."

"I'll go with you," Lianna said.

"It's not necessary. Really it isn't."

"Perhaps not," Lianna conceded. "But it will make Kenton and me feel better."

Cat opened her mouth to protest. She didn't think she could bear Lianna's sympathy, should Garth no longer want her as...as a friend. As someone important in his life. Then she looked at the two faces across from her and closed her mouth. "All right."

"Good," Kenton said. He rubbed a hand across his face. "The next boat going upriver will be here in six days. I suppose you'll want to take passage on it."

Cat nodded. Even six days seemed like an eternity.

TALISA

TALISA EDGED HER URSELL PAST A CART AND almost bumped into a small, bald-headed man who stood examining the leather saddles displayed on a stall. He glared at her and yelled something she couldn't catch above the rumble of carts and cries of vendors. Just as well, perhaps.

Her ursell's ears were twitching uneasily. "Don't fear, brave heart," she murmured in Uglessian. Terrin was placid, almost nerveless at home on the mountains, but the jumble of sights and sounds here must jangle his senses. The smells, too. Talisa wrinkled her nose. In the six months she'd been gone, she'd forgotten not only how crowded and noisy Freyfall was, but also how it *reeked* of frying onions and sausages, raw fish, horse dung, and unwashed human flesh. What must it be like for poor Terrin?

"I will have you off these streets and into a quiet stable as quickly as I can," she promised, then grimaced. That would not be soon. She'd decided to rent a room in the small inn where she'd stayed last summer. It was cheap, and clean, but it was on the central island, and she had to travel through the whole east side to get there. Unfortunately, she'd arrived at midday, when Freyfall was at its busiest. She threaded her way past a group of youths holding a spirited discussion – or argument – in the middle of the street, and prayed to the mountain spirits for patience.

Perhaps she should go to the Spellman house before seeking lodging. It was somewhere on the east bank. But no. Garth would be studying music at the Coynes' house at this time of day. Even with her grandparents' letter, she'd need Garth's help to convince Konrad Spellman to use his influence to gain Cory's freedom.

A hand touched her leg. She looked down, first at the small and dirty hand, then at the equally small and grubby face peering up at her.

"What's that you're riding?" He practically shouted to make sure he was heard.

Talisa raised her voice too. "An ursell."

"Ursell." He screwed up his face in fierce concentration, his hand still on her leg, his bare feet skipping sideways to keep pace with Terrin. "Is it a goat?"

A cart delivering wood was parked horizontally in front of her. She stopped.

"No. Not a goat. Nor a horse. Ursells live in Uglessia and are very good on mountain tracks."

He absorbed this. "You're a Uglessian then."

"Yes."

"I thought Uglessians was giants." Disappointment clouded his face.

"I'm quite tall," Talisa pointed out.

"Not a giant though."

"No."

"Gammer said all Uglessians was giants. He's allus telling tales."

"I do have six fingers," Talisa offered.

His eyes moved to her hands on the reins, verified the number of fingers. When he looked up, she saw wonder. He flashed her a gap-toothed grin, then darted away, presumably to tell his friends that he'd seen a real live six-fingered Uglessian. Would she grow into a giant in the telling?

Well, she might be a curiosity to him, but at least he had shown neither suspicion nor fear, which was more than could be said for some of the adults she had met on her way here. Talisa winced, remembering wary looks, muttered obscenities, the villagers who had shooed their children indoors at her approach. Ancient enmities died hard.

Her eyes followed the boy's disappearing back as he wriggled like an eel through the crowd. No more than six or seven. Cory's fingers would have itched to carve his image.

Cory.

How many days ahead of her were Cory and his captors? Four? Five? They had left Uglessia before her, and horses were bigger and faster than ursells, if less sure-footed. When would Cory's trial be held?

Spirits of the mountains, let it not be soon. Not until her grandparents' letters had been read. Not until those who read them had a chance to act. *If* they acted.

They would. They *would*.

The cart still blocked the way. Her lips tightened. Dismounting, she led Terrin around it. They just managed to squeeze past.

"You've been here before, haven't you? Last Midsummer, as I recall."

"Yes."

The innkeeper, a brown squirrel of a woman with bright, inquisitive eyes, nodded. "Glad to have you back. We've only the one free room at the moment, mind, the one at the top of the stairs. It's a mite small, but I'm sure you'll find it comfortable enough. And clean. If there's one thing I pride myself on, it's keeping the inn clean."

"I'm sure it will be fine. How much is it?"

The price had risen by five coppers since last year. Talisa sighed. Still, it was cheap by Freyfall standards. She could only hope that her money would last.

The room had barely enough space to inch around the narrow bed. But it *was* clean, and a dormer window let in plenty of light. A basin and pitcher perched on the window ledge. Gratefully, Talisa poured water into the basin, stripped off her tunic and leggings and washed herself, then took a wrinkled dress from her saddlebag and pulled it on. Her hair, too long confined under her travelling cap, was tangled. She ran an impatient comb through as much of it as could be straightened without a fight.

Retrieving her precious letters from her bag, she spread them on the bed. One was addressed to Kerstin and Jem Brooks, far away in Frey-by-the-Sea, one to Konrad Spellman. There were five others, to wizards Talisa had never heard of. But her grandparents knew them. They must believe that these people would help Cory. *Could* help Cory.

Two of the letters, as well as the one to Konrad Spellman, had Freyfall addresses. She didn't want to waste money on a messenger, but neither did she want to waste time fumbling her way through Freyfall's twisting streets. Perhaps after she talked to Master Spellman, he would take the letters to his fellow wizards. He'd be better at convincing them of Cory's innocence than she would, anyway. Of course, first she'd have to convince Konrad. But surely, with Garth's help, she could do that.

She looked out the window. The street below was narrow, but even it was thronged with stalls. A plump woman stood in front of one, inspecting meat pies. A man in a swirling black cape strode by. Had it been a nine days' wonder when the soldiers brought Cory in, as it had been last autumn when the barracks went up in flames? Was he here, or had he been taken to Freybourg where the Freyan queen and her court lived?

Her only tools were her letters, her acquaintance with Master Coyne and, through him, the Musicians' Guild, and her song. Her song for Cory. *About* Cory.

Too few. Too frail. Talisa closed her eyes, saw Cory, face etched by the light of a campfire, arms bound behind his back. Heard his voice saying goodbye. She drew in a breath that shuddered through her whole body and opened her eyes again.

Her tools might be few. They might be frail. But they would have to do.

She gathered the letters and put them in a pouch that she slung over her shoulder. To the docks first, to send the letter to the Brookses in Frey-by-the-Sea. Then back to the east bank and the Spellmans' house. Garth would be home by then.

It was easier to weave her way through people and stalls on foot, and she was soon at the broad quay, facing a long line of boats. Some looked like fishing craft, but most were bigger and fitted with a dozen or more seats for rowers. Were they all sailing as far downriver as Frey-by-the-Sea? Were they all equally fast? When would they leave? Talisa gazed around, feeling as bewildered as a bird lost in a storm.

A broad-shouldered man stood in front of one of the boats. She approached him.

"Excuse me, sir. Is this boat sailing to Frey-by-the-Sea?"

He looked at her from under beetling brows. "Eventually."

"When?"

"We just got into port today. I wouldn't have any rowers left if I didn't give them a few days to spend the money they've made."

"Oh." Talisa glanced at the other boats. "Are any of them leaving sooner?"

"In a hurry, are you? You'll want a boat that goes directly there, rather than one that stops on the way." He surveyed those tied up at the wharf. "There's The Blue Swan and The Frey Rapids. They both go direct. Don't know when they're leaving, though, having just arrived myself."

"Thank you."

She picked her way over the rough cobblestones to where The Blue Swan was docked. No one was in sight. She hesitated. But the gangplank was down. *Someone* must be on board. She started to walk up the plank. A head poked out of the cabin at the top. Talisa took a few more steps, then stopped and called, "I have a letter I want to send to Frey-by-the-Sea. You're going there, I understand."

"Yes." The head remained stuck out of the door, but its owner didn't bother to join it.

"When do you sail?"

"Day after tomorrow."

"Oh. Well, thank you." She turned to leave.

"You won't find a boat that will get there faster."

"The Frey Rapids —"

"Leaves the same day as us."

She turned back, walked the rest of the way up the plank and onto the deck. Even moored as it was, the ship swayed under her feet. The sailor, a small, wiry man, finally stepped out of the cabin. Talisa held out the letter.

"That'll be twenty coppers."

More than she'd expected. Was she being cheated? Or

possibly he expected her to bargain. Talisa bit her lip. But she had never bartered, and the message was too urgent to haggle over. She counted out the coins.

"How long will it take you to get to Frey-by-the-Sea?"

"Fortnight more or less, depending on the winds."

She gulped.

"Won't find a boat to get there faster."

She nodded and walked away.

A fortnight for her letter to get to the Brookses, and at least another fortnight for them to get here. Would they arrive too late?

It was a long walk to the Spellmans'. Once on the east bank, Talisa began to ask directions. "Gotham Street?" people asked. "That way." They pointed, or told her to go this way, or that, then turn left, or right, then...She smiled and kept walking – and asking. It was so much easier to find one's way in the mountains.

Gradually, the busy commercial thoroughfares gave way to quieter avenues lined with tall houses. They're like elegant cats, Talisa thought. They know they are impeccably groomed and deserve the best of the cream. She could imagine Cory's scathing reaction to this discreet display of wealth.

The sun was halfway down the western sky by the time she reached 6 Gotham Street, which was distinguished from its neighbours only by an unobtrusive gold plaque that hung beside the door and stated simply, "Konrad Spellman, Wizard." She hesitated. It must be dinnertime. She didn't want to interrupt their meal. Nor did she want them to think themselves obligated to invite her to share it. Perhaps she should wait.

No. Cory's need was too urgent. She lifted the brass knocker and tapped.

After a minute, the door opened. A tall woman, with a face as tight as the grey-brown bun behind her head, confronted her.

"Mistress Spellman?"

"Mistress Spellman is at dinner."

Of course. In a house like this, there would be servants. "Is Garth home?"

The woman's face went even tighter. "No."

"Oh. When do you expect him?"

"I don't."

Talisa blinked at her. "You don't? Do you mean... Doesn't he live here now?"

"No."

She felt as though she'd stepped onto what she took to be a solid ledge only to have it crumble under her feet. She swallowed. "Could you tell me where he lives?"

"I have no idea."

The ledge crumbled some more. She swallowed again. "Could I please speak to Mistress Spellman?"

"Mistress Spellman doesn't know where Master Garth is any more than I do." Was there a note of triumph in the woman's voice? Surely not. "Now, if you'll excuse me..." She made to shut the door.

It was almost closed when Talisa cried, "Wait!"

It stayed open a crack.

"May I see Master Spellman?"

"Master Spellman is away from home." The door started to close once more. Frantically, Talisa put her foot in the crack.

"I must see him. When will he be back?"

"In a week's time or more."

A week. A week before she could talk to him, ask him for help. Talisa felt sick.

"If you'll excuse me, I would like to shut the door." The woman's voice was as warm as water edged with ice.

"Yes. Yes, of course. I'm sorry. I...I have a letter for Master Spellman." Talisa reached for her pouch, fumbled for the envelope. "Here. From my grandparents. He knows them."

She held out the letter. The woman took it. Then the door closed, leaving Talisa staring at it while the wind, which had risen with the coming of twilight, sighed and moaned and wrapped itself around her legs.

GALIA

ABOVE HER, A GULL MEWLED.

Galia's head jerked up. She watched the bird hover on outstretched wings, then tilt its body and wheel away from the tree-shadowed common, the hall and dormitory and stables of the college. It headed into the sun. Headed west. Towards the sea. Towards home. She followed its flight till she could no longer see it.

"You look sad."

Galia started. She glanced sideways, then up again. She had to look a long way up to see Thannis's face.

It would be Thannis. Of all the students at the College of Wizards, he was the only one who sought her out. Perhaps that was because they were both outsiders.

She smiled but said nothing. Thannis didn't press her. She was glad. She liked the big Uglessian, but sometimes he could be too determined to get answers.

As though something in her gaze had awakened longings

of his own, he said, "The snow will be melted in the hills now. It would be possible to go home."

"'Are you going, then? To Uglessia?"

He had been looking into the distance. Now his eyes flew back to her face. "No! Oh, no. I wouldn't leave the college. Not until I've learned...Well, not everything, maybe, but a great deal more than I know now."

She nodded gravely. Thannis's desire to learn was a great hunger in him that eclipsed all other needs. Sometimes she envied him that hunger.

"It's different for you," he said. "There's nothing these Freyans can teach you that you don't already know."

"Raven says we can learn as much from them as they from us."

"Mmm." His doubt was obvious.

She sighed. "He is probably right. He *is* right. But their magic is so different. All these words. These spells. They are hard, in a language not my own. But it is not just that. They seem so, so..." She groped for the right word. "*Unnecessary.*" It wasn't that she hadn't listened when Master Clark explained Freyan weather spells. It wasn't that she didn't respect his knowledge or that of the other teachers at the college. But it was so much easier just to feel the air around her, its moisture, its movements, its electricity.

She had tried to tell Master Clark how she did this. He had listened, and asked questions. Most she couldn't answer. How could she explain how she became part of the air? At first, she had thought he was angry when he frowned and said he didn't understand. Later, she realized he was only frustrated. She could understand that. She was frustrated too.

"You'll be going home this summer," Thannis said, watching her.

"No."

"No? But I thought...At the council last year, it was decided the exchange of wizards from the three lands would be for one year. That's how it is with us, anyway. Branwen and I will be here this year only." Regret weighed down his voice. "And it's the same with the Freyans who went to Uglessia. In fact, I've heard that Master Granton and Master Ford have already returned, since there's no point in remaining in Uglessia once spring planting starts. I hope they'll come here soon and bring news." He was silent a moment, then asked, "Won't you Islandians be leaving when the college closes?"

"Yes."

"Then –"

"We will return to Atua. Atua is not my home." And never would be, she thought. But at least it was close to the sea. In Freybourg, she was so far inland that only the occasional gull brought tidings of it. And at least in Atua she *belonged*. Oh, not the way she did at home. Never that. But it didn't seem strange to be part of that quiet, hard-working circle of women – and some men – who lived simply and dedicated their lives to the gifts given them by the Mother. Here...

It wasn't that anyone was unkind. There had never been a history of enmity between Freya and Islandia, as there had been between Freya and Uglessia, and Islandian magic was viewed with awe. But few people approached her. Was it because she looked different, with her brown skin? Because she sounded different, with her accented Freyan?

Thannis crouched down beside her. "Perhaps you can go home soon."

Galia bent and plucked a blade of grass. "Perhaps."

Come summer, it would be three years since she had seen the house on the headland, her parents, her sisters and brothers, little Mala. Mala wouldn't even know her when they next met.

She understood why she had been taken to Atua. She *should* understand. The reason had been explained often enough. "You must know your power thoroughly before you leave. You must be able to control it." And she had tried. She had been diligent. Obedient. The only times she called up winds or brought rain were when she was ordered to do so. If storms occasionally battered Atua's shores and hills, it wasn't because she had summoned them. She hadn't even wanted to. All she wanted was to go home.

Instead, she had been sent here.

When she'd been told that she was to accompany the Islandian delegation to the council, she'd been surprised and excited. What an adventure, to sail across the ocean, visit Kerstin and Jem Brooks in their house in Frey-by-the-Sea, then travel upriver to Freyfall, where water fell from the cliff above the city like a thousand waves crashing into shore, and shops and stalls held so many wonders that she had to keep scolding herself for gawking like a witless fool.

It was only at the conclusion of the council that she had been told she was to be one of the two Islandians who remained in Freya.

"Why me?" she had asked.

"Because the Dreamer saw you at the college."

It was unthinkable not to do what the Dreamer foretold. But *why*? She couldn't explain Islandian weather magic to the teachers and students at the college. She herself had gained little from the Freyan magic that was taught here.

"We have a couple of hours before the bell rings for dinner. Why don't we head into town?" Thannis asked.

Galia looked up, surprised. If she drew sideways glances, Thannis drew stares. His long flaxen hair and unusual height – he was tall even for a Uglessian – attracted not only curiosity but fear or a challenge. It wasn't only his dedication to his studies that kept him on college grounds.

Thannis was smiling at her, his pale blue eyes kind. Galia stiffened. She didn't need kindness. She didn't need pity.

"It's too beautiful to stay inside or even study outside."

It was. The sun was warm and the breeze soft. At home, the waves would be dancing. And Thannis was as homesick as she was. "All right."

The gatekeeper was busy greeting two newcomers who he seemed to know. Galia glanced at them. They were strangers to her. As though feeling her gaze, the shorter man turned his head to look at her. His eyes were very blue and very intense. She felt like a bug, pinned down for his inspection.

Unlike Freyfall, Freybourg didn't take Galia's breath away with bustle and noise. There were no stalls or vendors, only shops with discreet signs to beckon customers inside. The broad streets all radiated out from the hill in the centre of the city, where the palace stood like a graceful white swan poised for flight.

Thannis and Galia walked along quietly, gazing at grey stone houses behind their screen of trees, and at the goods in shop windows. They didn't enter any of the shops. Galia would have felt as out of place as a herring in a school of salmon.

"It's so...so *rich*," Thannis said.

Galia nodded. She couldn't imagine anyone in Islandia wearing the satin trousers, fur-lined capes, and lacy dresses she saw displayed. How could you work in such clothes? Most people they passed were neatly but plainly dressed, but not all. She couldn't help staring at a rider who cantered past, his feathered hat so broad that she wondered he could see. When a carriage clattered by, her eyes rested in fascination on its occupant, whose hair looked like an elaborate beehive threaded with jewels.

"I think we should go back." She might not be at home at the college, but at least she didn't feel quite so much like a swimmer who has ventured into unknown waters.

"Yes," Thannis agreed. "The bell will soon ring for dinner."

They started retracing their steps. Clouds had appeared and the wind picked up. Galia shivered and quickened her pace. Even so, she found it difficult to match Thannis's long strides, slowly as he tried to walk.

Behind them, someone snickered. "Have you ever seen such an outlandish pair? That short little brown-skinned girl from the Islands and that lout of a long-haired Uglik?"

Laughter.

Heat burned in Galia's cheeks.

Thannis whirled. Took two steps. Dove. A tall young man wearing a blue waistcoat, jewels on his fingers, and a sneer on his face, went sprawling. So did his two nearest companions, mowed down by the Uglessian's winnowing arms. Galia heard a thud as a head hit cobblestones. She shuddered. There were other sounds. Grunts. Groans. Down the street, a woman screamed.

The two men left standing glanced at each other. One tried to lift Thannis by his collar. The other made a half-hearted swipe at his head. Galia took a quick step forward. It wasn't fair, five against one.

Thannis needed no help. Without glancing up, he reached out. A long arm wrapped around the knees of one attacker. An elbow jabbed into the stomach of the Freyan bending over him. Both men fell, one on his back, one to his knees.

Shoppers and shopkeepers crowded into the street, like hornets drawn by the smell of rotting meat. No one ventured into the forest of pounding fists and flailing legs.

The clatter of hooves jerked Galia's attention away from the fight. A troop of men in uniforms trotted briskly down the road. It halted. The captain barked a command. Within minutes, the soldiers had pushed their way through the onlookers and hauled the combatants to their feet. Four soldiers held Thannis.

One man still lay on the ground. Blood puddled beneath his head.

Galia wasn't a healer, but anyone who had lived on Atua for two and a half years knew something of the body and its ailments. She walked towards the man. A soldier blocked her way. She stared at his green-clad chest. It looked massive.

"Please..." Her voice croaked. She cleared her throat. "Please let me by. That man needs help." The soldier glanced from her to the still form, then stood aside.

For a moment, the figure on the ground blurred and she saw her brother Arlan, bruised and broken on the rocks at the foot of the cliff. She pushed the memory aside and knelt. As gently as she could, she moved brown hair away from a crack that was oozing blood.

She glanced at the man's face. It was pale. Too pale, surely.

Voices babbled around her. She ignored them. Slowly, carefully, she extended fingers of thought, tendrils of perception.

Bleeding. Bruising. At the back of the skull, among the masses of nerves and tissues. Growing.

He needed more help than she could give. She withdrew.

As she did so, she heard a cold voice state, "I don't care that you're at the college for this exchange of wizards. No one has a right to attack others on the streets of Freya."

Galia scrambled to her feet. The captain stood, gloved hands on hips, confronting Thannis. The skin beneath Thannis's right eye was bruised and his face bore several scratches. The four soldiers still gripped his arms tightly, but they didn't need to. Thannis looked as limp as a beached fish. The man in the blue waistcoat held a blood-smeared handkerchief to his nose. Good.

"It was not the fault of Thannis."

No one looked at her. She clenched her hands and spoke louder. "It was not the fault of Thannis."

This time the captain's head turned. He had thick fair hair, a ruddy complexion, and a squashed pug nose. His blue eyes were angry. "Not his fault? He jumps on these men without provocation and –"

"There was prov...provo...what you said."

"Oh? And what was it?"

They were all staring at her now, all the soldiers, all the spectators. She wished they wouldn't. She swallowed. "This man –" she gestured towards the one with the bloodied nose – "he said mean things."

The captain glanced at the young man, eyebrows raised. The man shrugged and removed his handkerchief. "I said something about the two of them looking strange together, he being so tall and she so small. If they took it as an insult..." He shrugged again, then replaced the handkerchief hastily as blood spurted from his nose.

"Scarcely justification for an attack," the captain said.

"It was the way he said it," Galia protested. And the way he laughed, she thought. The way they all laughed.

"Still, to take umbrage at such a comment is excessive. Dangerous. How is *he*?" The captain nodded towards the unconscious man.

She had forgotten him. She should not have done that. "He needs a healer."

A brown-haired youth with a cut lip and blood on his satin jacket started. "Casper? I didn't think..." He came over and gazed down at the white face and blood-stained hair.

The captain's lips tightened. He glared at Thannis. "I'll send for one."

Galia brushed a damp strand of hair off her forehead. "I think the injury is bad. Can you send for Raven? He is the Islandian Healer and he is at the college."

The blue-waistcoated man removed his handkerchief again. His nose was beginning to swell. "So you think Freyan healers aren't good enough?"

Galia stared at him, shocked by the venom in his voice.

The boy beside her turned to him. "Maybe we should send for him, Denys. I've heard he's teaching all the wizards at the college."

"Freyan wizards are good enough for me."

"But –"

The captain interrupted. "We'll send for the nearest healer. If he wants help, that's up to him." He nodded to one of his soldiers who left, then glanced at the injured man's companions. "I trust you'll stay with your friend until the healer arrives." They nodded. One was nursing his hand. Another looked green.

Galia watched as the soldiers made Thannis mount a horse. There was a dazed look about him that she didn't like. She stepped forward. "Thannis."

He raised his head and looked at her. After a moment, his lips moved in what was probably meant to be a smile. Then the troop, with Thannis in the middle, trotted off.

CAT

THE SMELLS BROUGHT EVERYTHING BACK. They were even more familiar than the wall of noise and the waterfall dropping like a shimmering curtain from the cliff above the city. Smells of fish and onions and frying sausage and horses and dust and people. So many people. It was ten months since she'd been in Freyfall, but she felt as though she'd never left.

She wasn't the same person as the runaway girl who had landed here before, Cat reminded herself as she walked down the gangplank, carrying her small bag. There was no chance that she would wander through the streets with no coins in her pockets, no food in her belly, and no place to lay her head. True, she was alone now too. A day before Cat's departure, Lianna had come down with a fever. After anxious discussions, it was decided that Cat could come by herself. But this time she had money. She had letters to win her acceptance from friends of Kenton's if...

If an invitation to stay at the Spellman's was issued only from politeness and obligation, not because Garth wanted her there.

"Like a ride, Mistress?"

Cat stopped and looked at the man in front of her, a short, bright-eyed fellow with muscular forearms and callused hands. He gestured towards a horse and carriage waiting in line. "Best, smoothest ride in town."

Cat hesitated. But her bag was heavy, and she *did* have money. "Yes, thank you."

"Where to?" the driver asked, opening the door of the carriage.

"6 Gotham Street."

His eyes widened a trifle before he nodded and closed the door. Cat looked at her plain brown dress. Not the clothes for Gotham Street. No wonder the man was surprised.

"Mother says he'll never marry you. He's the only heir of a rich wizard."

Morty's words jounced in her mind, as rough as the cobblestones she was riding over. Cat stared out the window at the busy street, the stalls piled high with clothes or pots or food. One held bouquets of tulips and daffodils.

The carriage stopped, blocked by a crowd gathered around a juggler. Balls circled his head in a smooth red stream. The cloak at his feet was speckled with copper coins. It would have been better, last year, if she'd been able to toss balls rather than sing.

The driver was shouting at the spectators. Cat saw them

glance at the carriage then slowly move aside. Others filled the gaps. The carriage inched forward. It would have been faster to walk.

Never mind. She was in no hurry to reach the Spellman house. What was she going to say to Garth anyway? Why haven't you written? Are you in trouble? Don't you want to be friends anymore?

It was even more congested as they crossed a bridge into east Freyfall. Cat closed her eyes.

When Garth saw her, what would he say?

He wouldn't need to say anything. Garth was not good at keeping his emotions secret. As soon as she saw him, she would know.

There wasn't enough air in here. It was hard to breathe.

The carriage went faster once over the bridge, but then stopped again, barred by a large cart. Cat fumbled with the handle, opened the door, and jumped out, pulling her bag after her. "I'll walk the rest of the way."

The driver looked down at her, surprised, then shrugged. "That's fourteen coppers."

She handed him the money and walked around the cart. Once past it, she halted. She didn't want to go to the Spellmans'. She didn't want to see Garth. Not yet.

Could she find out from someone else how Garth was? How he felt?

Who?

Musicians. Garth had always frequented the taverns where they met to play and laugh and talk. He felt at home there.

The Laughing Lute was close. She would go there.

Her feet were more accustomed to dirt roads than cob‑
blestones. She walked carefully, shifting her bag now and
then from one hand to the other, glancing around to make
sure she was going the right way. Once, at a crossroads, she
asked for directions.

The woman she'd stopped looked at her sharply. "The
Laughing Lute? That's a tavern. No place for a girl on her
own. Why do you want to go there?"

"For the music."

The woman sniffed. "The music, or the musicians?"

Cat's face burned. She turned and walked away. A few
blocks later, she decided she'd taken the wrong turn and
retraced her steps.

She heard The Laughing Lute before she saw the sign,
swaying gently in the breeze. Music and laughter rang from
behind the propped-open door.

She halted on the threshold, dismayed by the number of
people squeezed into the tavern. She had forgotten how
crowded it could be. How noisy.

What if Garth was here? Her heart thudded once, then
began to race.

Compared to the brightness of the sun outside, the can‑
dlelit room was dim. Clutching her bag, Cat advanced a few
steps, then stopped, waiting for her eyes to adjust.

The benches on both sides of the long trestle tables were
jammed with men and a few women. Other people wan‑
dered from table to table, some with mugs in hand. It took
a long time to scan all their faces. Cat caught a few curious
glances and stepped back into the shadows by the wall.

Garth wasn't there.

But someone else was, someone she recognized from her last visit here. A young, brown-haired man with a merry face and a gift for drawing laughter. He sat in the middle of one of the benches, surrounded by eager listeners who bent towards him to catch the words of his song. What was his name? She bit her lip, trying to remember, but nothing surfaced. Hesitantly, she walked forward and stood behind him, waiting till his song ended.

Amidst the roar of laughter that greeted the conclusion, Cat tapped his shoulder. "Excuse me."

The curly head turned. Bright brown eyes surveyed her. "Freyn's Day, Mistress. What can I do for you?"

"My name is Catrina Ashdale. You know Garth, don't you? Garth Spellman?"

The singer managed, with some difficulty, to swing his legs over the bench and face her. "I certainly do. But how do you know that?"

"I've seen you before. With him, I mean."

Mobile eyebrows lifted. "Oh? I'm sorry, I don't recall meeting you."

"No. I...Well, I..." Cat stopped. How to explain that, when they'd last met, she had worn a cat's body?

The man sitting beside the brown-haired singer must have heard the last few sentences. He turned his dark head to reveal the dramatically handsome features of a young man a few years Cat's senior. "What, Mel? Not remember a lovely girl like this? I'm shocked. Let me assure you, Mistress, my memory would not fail in such circumstances." He flashed her a charming smile, revealing strong white teeth.

She smiled faintly at the compliment, then turned back to the other man. Mel. Yes. She should have remembered. "I'm a friend of his. Have you seen him lately?"

"No," Mel said slowly. A burst of laughter at the next table drew his eyes for a moment. When he looked back at her, he was frowning. "No, I haven't. Which is strange, now I think of it. He's usually around here sooner or later, but it's been quite some time now."

The bag felt very heavy suddenly. She put it down. "Oh."

"I'm sorry," Mel said.

"It's not your fault."

Mel was still frowning. "What did you say your name was? I didn't quite catch it over the noise."

"Catrina Ashdale. Most people call me Cat."

"Cat!" His brow cleared. "Of course! Now I know who you are. I've heard quite a lot about you. *And* met you, though I must say you look quite different now." He chuckled. Cat couldn't help smiling.

The man beside Mel, who'd also swung his legs over the bench, had been an absorbed spectator to all this. "I hate to intrude, and do so only because there seems to be some problem. Are you searching for someone? Could I possibly be of some assistance? I would be more than delighted to help so charming a lady." The flash of teeth again, the flare of charm. If he had been standing, Cat was sure he would have given her an elaborate bow.

Mel glanced at him. "She's looking for Garth Spellman. Have you seen him around lately, Andreas?"

"Garth?" Andreas asked slowly.

"Yes, you know. Slight, dark-haired fellow. Plays the lute, sings, composes. He was one of the winning musicians in the competition last Midsummer."

"I know who you mean, of course, though I don't really know him. But I'm afraid I haven't seen him lately. Or if I have, I don't remember. As I said, I don't really know him. I'm sorry." Andreas's eyes moved to the front of the room. "Look, Master Thornhill is about to share one of his new drinking songs with us."

"So he is." Mel smiled at Cat. "Sit down. We can squeeze over enough to make room for you. This is sure to be a good song, and we can all join in the chorus."

Cat looked at the man who stood, harp in hand, waiting to begin. For a moment, she was tempted. It would be good to forget her worries, let herself be absorbed by the music.

But no. She had come to Freyfall to find Garth, not to listen to music. She would go where she should have gone in the first place.

"No, thank you," she murmured. "Some other time." She picked up her bag and walked to the door. It was still open, letting in a cool breeze. She could see the sun, resting low behind the buildings to the west. At the door, she glanced back over her shoulder. Mel was facing the harpist, but the man beside him – Andreas – was gazing after her, frowning.

Cat hesitated. She almost went back to the table. But then the harpist started to play. She left.

TALISA

TALISA STARED AT THE CLOSED DOOR FOR A long time before she turned and headed back down Gotham Street.

She would pay a messenger to deliver her letters. If she got them there tonight, wizards in Freyfall would be reading them tomorrow. And surely those to Freybourg would arrive the day after. She strode faster.

But by the time she reached the streets that had been so noisy with carts and shoppers earlier, they were almost deserted. Only a few vendors could be heard, shouting the virtues of their hot potatoes or eel pies. She hurried on, hunting for a stall bearing the sign of a pigeon. There! She stopped in front of it. It was closed. So was the next one. And the next.

She stood by the third, staring at its wooden shutters, its decorated sides and front. Whoever had painted the birds that flew this way and that on the blue background had a strange sense of proportion. Cory would have laughed.

Down the road, someone else was laughing.

She should have brought her letters to the messengers earlier, not depended on Konrad Spellman. She couldn't do *anything* right. Who was she to think she could save Cory?

The sun flared, making the wings of the nearest pigeon look as though they were stained by blood.

Something hard, and heavy, and lumpish, settled in her throat. A fist. A huge fist.

Talisa took a deep breath. She would *not* give in to despair. She would visit the Coynes. If Master Coyne were to mobilize the Musicians' Guild on Cory's behalf, the sooner he started the better. And they would know where Garth was. The sooner she found him, the better too.

The afterglow faded, leaving grey dusk, then dark. She made her way slowly and uncertainly at first. Once she'd crossed the bridge onto the central island, though, her pace quickened. She had walked these streets with Cory so many times last autumn. It was the only way they could be alone together, to talk, to laugh, to be silent under the stars. And she'd lived in this neighbourhood with the Coynes for five months before...

Before breaking her apprenticeship contract and running away to Uglessia.

Her feet faltered. Stopped.

Perhaps she should go to her inn now. Return in the morning.

No. Time was vital. Whenever Cory's trial came, it would be too soon. And she had to face Master and Mistress Coyne sometime.

Candlelight glimmered through the Coynes' windows. Talisa knocked. The door opened and Mistress Coyne peered out. Behind her, Talisa saw lighted candles on low tables beside two comfortable chairs. Master Coyne sat in one, spectacles balanced halfway down his nose, a sheaf of papers in his hand. Neither Lem nor Shep were in sight. They must be out, as they often were in the evening. Good. She didn't want to have to deal with the apprentices tonight.

"Yes?"

She was in the shadows, Talisa realized. Mistress Coyne couldn't see her face. "Mistress Coyne, it's me. Talisa. May I come in? I need to talk to you."

The papers in Master Coyne's hand jerked down. He stared at the door.

"Come in," Mistress Coyne said after a moment.

It was so familiar, the hall, the sitting room, the plum-coloured chair that Cory had always perched on, even the smell of beeswax candles and bread, baked earlier in the day. Talisa could almost see herself sitting there, reading, talking quietly with the Coynes, waiting for Cory to come so they could go walking.

"Well, don't just stand there, child. Sit down," Mistress Coyne said.

Talisa sat on the plum chair, Cory's old chair. It was, after all, the one visitors used. And it was the closest. Her knees felt shaky. Mistress Coyne reseated herself. There was silence.

Master Coyne broke it at last. "So, Talisa. You want to talk to us, you said."

"Yes. But first, before I say anything else..."

"Yes?"

"I'm sorry. I'm so sorry."

They were both silent.

"I shouldn't have left like that. I shouldn't have broken my contract. It was wrong. Especially after you had been so kind to me." Her voice was shaking. She stopped, then continued. "I wouldn't have done it if it had not been urgent. But that's no excuse, I know. I'm sorry."

Tears were trembling behind her eyes. She blinked hard. She would *not* cry like some naughty child, who thinks all will be forgiven if she sheds a few tears.

"It was because of that boy, wasn't it? That Cory?" Mistress Coyne asked. Her eyes, sharp and bright as a magpie's, were fixed on Talisa's face.

Talisa nodded.

"I knew he was trouble from the day he appeared. Oh, don't take me wrong. I liked him well enough, once he'd got to the point where he'd say more than 'Yes, Mistress' or 'No, Mistress.' But he was too angry."

"We've blamed ourselves, Lizbet and I, for allowing you to see him," Master Coyne said heavily.

"It was my decision."

"It was indeed, and so you made it plain. Nevertheless, your grandfather had placed you in our keeping when he signed the apprenticeship papers."

"Grandfather would never blame you. None of my family would."

He shook his head. "We didn't know at the time, when

you left so abruptly. We believed what you said in the note, that you were homesick. I must admit I was angry. Angry and hurt, after the time I'd taken with your teaching. And to have you leave a note rather than tell us yourself..." He shook his head again.

Talisa looked at his kind face, his round, comfortable body, then away. *I mustn't cry.*

"It wasn't until this week, when we heard the news that the army had arrested Cory Updale, who'd set fire to the barracks last autumn, and that he'd been hiding out in Uglessia, that we knew the real reason you left in such a hurry."

"The soldiers came to arrest him. We had to flee," Talisa whispered. "But I was so sorry to leave you like that."

Neither of the Coynes said anything. Talisa cleared her throat. "Do you know where he is?"

"In prison here, though I understand they might take him to Freybourg for trial."

She looked down at her hands. They were shaking. A twig snapped in the fire in the hearth.

"You said you wanted to talk to us," Master Coyne said.

She raised her eyes. "Yes. I do."

"Well, if it's to ask whether you may resume your apprenticeship, the answer is yes. That is..." He glanced at his wife. She nodded. "As I said, I was angry when you left. But part of the anger was disappointment at losing such a promising student. You learn quickly, and your voice...Well, I will take you back, though many would not. And I will need a promise first that you will stay your full term."

Talisa stared at him, then at Mistress Coyne. Both were watching her expectantly. The fire murmured. The candles glowed. Warm. Welcoming.

To be accepted so readily, after she had abandoned them...

"Thank you. I never thought...You're very kind. I would so much like to be your apprentice again. But I can't. At least not now."

"You can't?" A frown gathered on Master Coyne's face.

"Why did you come, if not to ask William to take you back?" Mistress Coyne demanded.

Talisa took a deep breath. "I came to ask you to help Cory."

"Help Cory?" Mistress Coyne echoed blankly.

Master Coyne's frown had deepened into a thundercloud. Talisa had never seen him look so black. "So you came not to beg forgiveness, not to say you want to study music again, but to ask us to help this firebrand. Even if we could do so – and I see no way we could – even if we could, I say, why should we? Oh, I was willing enough to assist him when I thought he wanted to be an artist. The boy has talent when it comes to carving. But it's obvious his ambitions lie elsewhere. Rather than devote himself to his craft, he turned his back on the opportunity I'd won for him to become apprenticed to the best carver in Freyfall, and committed a wanton act of violence that killed two men. And you expect me to help him?"

"But he didn't! He didn't kill the soldiers! He didn't set the fire!" The hard edge of the chair dug into her thighs as she leaned forward.

"He didn't? That's why the army arrested him, I suppose." Master Coyne's face was flushed with anger, his hands clenched tightly around the arms of his chair.

"It's a mistake. Cory —"

"Mistake! Ha!"

"Now wait, William. There's no need to get so upset with Talisa. Don't you remember, you yourself said she must have thought the boy was innocent if she helped him escape? If she thinks so, it's natural enough for her to come seeking our aid." Mistress Coyne's voice was calm, but she too was frowning when she turned to face Talisa.

"I *do* understand your wanting to save him, child. But you must also understand that we have little reason to believe him innocent. And to offer aid to someone who has caused the death of two men, and they with families too...Well, it's not something William or I could see ourselves doing."

Talisa gripped her hands together so tightly they ached. "Yes, I do understand that. And there is evidence against him. Someone saw him coming away from the barracks that night, and he is known to be bitter about how his family, and others like them, were thrown off their land and left to starve. But he didn't set the fire."

"He told you that, I imagine." Scorn lashed Master Coyne's voice.

Talisa raised her chin. "Yes."

"I suppose it's natural for you to trust him, though I would think better of your judgement if you displayed some scepticism. But why should you expect *us* to?"

"You've met him."

"Yes, but all I really know about him is that he carves well. That I admire. What I do *not* admire, aside from this despicable act, is his willingness to throw away his chance to do something with his talent, yes, and your chance too, by dragging you off to Uglessia with him."

"He didn't want me to go, but I told him I would no matter what he did."

Master Coyne shook his head reprovingly.

"Why was he close to the barracks that night?" Mistress Coyne asked.

"Someone told him that there was going to be trouble. He went to try to stop it but was too late. On his way back, a man recognized him."

Master and Mistress Coyne exchanged glances. Then their heads swung back to Talisa.

"Are you saying that this boy of yours knows who set the fire, though he didn't do it himself?" Master Coyne demanded.

She paused. There was danger in this question. But how could she hide the truth? She nodded.

Mistress and Master Coyne looked at each other again.

"If he knows who did it, all he has to do is inform the authorities."

"He won't."

"Why not?" Mistress Coyne asked. "Are they friends of his?"

"I don't know whether they're friends exactly. But he knows them and he feels...He has said he will not betray them." Better not tell the Coynes that Cory understood and sympathized with the anger that fuelled the action, if not the action itself.

"What happens if they aren't apprehended? If they commit another such act?" Master Coyne asked.

"Cory doesn't think they will. He doesn't think they intended to kill the soldiers. He thinks –"

"*Thinks*. And what if he thinks wrong?"

She was silent.

"No, Talisa. Even if I could help, and I don't see how –"

"The Musicians' Guild. It has influence."

"It can't stop the course of justice. Nor would it. No, the only person who can save Cory is Cory himself."

The room was silent. The fire burned low in the hearth. One of the candles flickered. The world beyond the window was very black.

"When did you last eat?" Mistress Coyne asked suddenly. When Talisa looked at her blankly, she clucked. "You must take care of yourself, child. And that includes eating. Come to the kitchen. I'll get you a bite, then William will escort you to wherever you're staying. Or you may sleep here, if you want."

Tears pricked Talisa's eyes again. "You're very kind, but I must return to my inn. And thank you, but I'm not hungry, and I really don't need an escort."

"Of course you do," Mistress Coyne said firmly. "And you need to eat whether you're hungry or not. Have you had supper? Or lunch?"

Talisa shook her head.

Mistress Coyne clucked again. "Then stop arguing and come with me."

As Talisa rose, she glanced over at Master Coyne. His hands – those hands that could create music to make winds dance and birds go quiet – were still clenched around the arms of his chair.

The kitchen was as familiar as the sitting room. How many hours had she spent here, helping Mistress Coyne? Now she sat on a wooden chair and watched the woman cut a slice of cold pork and a hunk of bread. Her mouth watered. Five months in Uglessia hadn't erased her memory of Freyan bread. She found she was hungry after all. When she was finished, she raised her head and smiled.

"You really care for this boy, don't you?" Mistress Coyne asked.

Talisa nodded.

Mistress Coyne sighed. "William is right, you know. The only way Cory can free himself is to tell the authorities who *did* set the fire. You must tell him so."

"I have. He won't."

Mistress Coyne shook her head. "Daft."

"Maybe." Talisa glanced down and traced a line in the table, then looked up again. "But I'm proud of his loyalty." At least, part of her was. Another part wept at his folly.

Mistress Coyne shook her head again.

"I must go. Thank you for the food. It was very good."

"Plain enough fare it was, but you're welcome, child." Mistress Coyne took the plate and started to rise, then stopped. "You mustn't worry too much about what William said. He was angry because he was disappointed. When you came tonight, he was sure you were here to ask to be his apprentice again. It's been a hard year for him. First you left, then the Spellman boy."

Talisa stared at her. "Garth left? I don't understand. He wanted nothing more than to study music."

"So we thought, until a messenger came with a note a month or more ago. All it said was that he could no longer fulfill his apprenticeship, and that he was sorry. The next day, Master Spellman came. Offered his apologies and money to compensate us for our pains. William wouldn't take it, of course. He was very upset. So was Master Spellman, though he said little enough, only that his grandson's behaviour was reprehensible. Very stiff, he was, and very angry, all the more so for bottling it up inside. Truth to tell, I was sorry for the man." She sighed. "It hurt William badly, losing two such pupils in one year. He would have been so happy to have you return."

"I'm sorry." Talisa was silent a moment, then said, "I would love to be Master Coyne's pupil again. If he will have me when all this is over..." She looked at Mistress Coyne's face, then away, unable to bear the pity she saw there.

"Yes. Well, I'm sure he will take you, and gladly, though he may have a harsh word or two to say." Mistress Coyne was silent a moment, frowning. Then she said, "In a day or so, when he's had time to get over his disappointment, I'll talk to William about helping Cory." She held up a hand as Talisa opened her mouth. "No, Talisa. I don't know whether

I can persuade William or not. Even if I can, and even if the Guild listens to him... Don't hope for too much, child. Don't break your heart."

GALIA

IF ONLY SHE HAD A HORSE. TRUE, THE FREYAN beasts were so big they made her a bit nervous. But if she had one, she'd be at the college by now.

Well, she didn't. She half-walked, half-ran through the streets of Freybourg and down the lane, and arrived panting at the gate just after the bell had finished its call to dinner.

"Afraid you'll miss your supper, are you?" Fergus asked as he let her in. She gave him a distracted smile and headed for the refectory.

It sounded as raucous as a beach full of squabbling gulls, Galia thought as she scanned the long lines of tables. She couldn't see Raven.

No. There he was, in a far corner. Even without the silver streak in his hair, he would have been unmistakable. No one else had hair as black as the bird he was named after.

As she hurried forward, she realized there were several teachers – Master Clark, Master Bows, even the head of the college, Master Wisher – at Raven's table. Sitting with them were the two men she'd seen Fergus greet that afternoon, and a dark-haired, hawk-nosed older man. Branwen was among them, listening intently.

"Yes, there was enough snow this winter to make for good planting, or so I've been told," one of the younger strangers was saying. "Although if my advice had been followed, your people wouldn't need to worry so much about moisture."

"What advice was that?" someone asked.

Raven sat quietly, his eyes on the speaker. Galia touched his arm. "Raven."

He turned his head and smiled at her. "Galia. Come join us."

She ignored the invitation. "There is a man in town who needs you. His head..." She touched the back of her skull.

He rose instantly, as she had known he would. Raven responded to the call for healing as mothers answered their newborn infants' cries.

"What happened?"

"There was a fight. I wanted them to send for you, but the captain said a Freyan healer would do."

"Can you lead me to him?"

Galia nodded.

"Wait." Master Wisher was frowning. "What's this about a fight and a captain?"

"I...We were walking, Thannis and I, and...Well, there was a fight. One man hit his head on the stones. Then the soldiers came and took Thannis off to prison."

"Prison!" Branwen exclaimed. She was staring at Galia. They all were.

The frown on Master Wisher's face cut like a knife. "Why was there a fight?"

"I will tell you later. The man who is hurt –"

"I can find him if you'll tell me where he is," Raven interrupted. "Then you can explain what happened and what needs to be done for Thannis."

"It was in the centre of the city, where all the shops are. I'm sorry. I do not think I can explain how to get there."

"Any recognizable landmarks?"

Galia screwed up her face in thought. "The shop in front of us had a sign with a picture of a...I do not know the name. You play music on it." She demonstrated.

"A harp. That would be Master Shore's music shop," murmured the hawk-nosed man.

Master Clark smiled. "I'm not surprised you know it, Master Spellman. I imagine it's one of your grandson's favourite spots in Freybourg."

The other man's lips tightened. "Quite." He turned to Raven. "I can lead you there." He rose.

Raven nodded. Galia watched the two men stride away.

"Well?" Master Wisher demanded.

"Perhaps explanations can wait until Galia has had her supper," Master Clark suggested. The smile he gave her lightened his long, serious, horse face.

Galia returned his smile and sat down. Master Clark might not understand her magic, so unlike his own, but he always meant well.

"And introductions are in order, I think. Galia, please meet Master Leonard Ford and Master Melton Granton. They are teachers at the college, but have been away this year in Uglessia. And this is Mistress Galia Soradotter, one of our two Islandian guests."

Galia and the two new wizards exchanged greetings. Master Ford was the older, taller man. Master Granton was the one with the intense blue eyes. It was he who'd been talking as she arrived.

A servant placed a plate of stew in front of her. She was as hungry as a baby bird, but she chewed each mouthful slowly, trying to give herself time to gather her thoughts and her words. It would be so much easier if she could have used her own language, not this foreign tongue.

"Well?" Master Wisher demanded again as she ate her last forkful.

Galia chose her words as carefully as she would have picked her way along a beach covered with sharp rocks and entangling kelp. "Thannis and I went walking in Freybourg. Classes were over," she added, in case anyone thought they had forsaken their studies. "As we started back, a man behind us said something that was not nice. It was..." She hunted for the right word.

"Insulting?" Master Bows suggested.

She nodded. "Insulting. Yes. Thannis turned and ran at the man and his friends. There was a fight, then the soldiers rode up and stopped it. One man did not get up, the one who had hit his head on the stones. The captain of the soldiers took Thannis away to prison. He said it was Thannis who started the fight, but it was not. It was the man who insulted us."

"Was he the one who was hurt?" Master Bows asked.

"No. He only had a bloody nose. A *very* bloody nose." She couldn't keep satisfaction out of her voice.

Master Wisher's frown was only slightly less sharp. "What precisely did he say?"

Galia tried to recall the exact words. "He said, 'Have you ever seen such an'" – she paused, trying to remember – "'outlandish pair? That little brown-skinned girl from the Islands and that great lout of a long-haired Uglik.'"

The men exchanged glances. Branwen was looking down at her empty plate. Her long straw-coloured hair hid her face.

"Not the most tactful thing to say, certainly. And the speaker should not have used the word Uglik. That *is* reprehensible. But scarcely a statement that justifies a brawl, especially one that leaves one man seriously injured," Master Wisher said.

"It was the way he said it. The way he laughed. They all laughed."

"Still, I am disappointed in Thannis. I was worried about accepting him here, after his shocking display of temper at the council last year, but he promised he would leash it in. Until today, he has."

"Was he the one who tried to attack the musician who sang that offensive song about Uglessians?" Master Ford asked.

"Despite the fact that they had all been warned that such a song would be sung as part of the conspiracy to wreck the council. Yes. Although, actually, it wasn't the musician he went for but a courtier near Queen Elira who laughed at the song."

Laughter hurt more than the most insulting words, Galia thought.

"So the soldiers took Thannis to prison?" Master Wisher's attention returned to Galia.

"Yes. I told them what had happened, but the man in the blue coat pretended that what he had said had not been insulting, and the captain believed him." She looked at Master Wisher earnestly. "You *will* get Thannis out?"

"I certainly will not."

She flinched as though she'd been slapped. "But –"

"Thannis struck the first blow, and caused serious damage, from the sound of it."

"That was an accident. And there were five of them to one of him."

"That just goes to show how dangerous he is. And I really cannot see that there was adequate provocation for him to lose his temper in that most deplorable way. No, Galia. It will do Thannis no harm to cool his heels – and his temper – in prison for a while. If the injured man recovers, then Thannis will be let out shortly, I'm sure. If not...Well, we'll have to see what's to be done then."

"But he came here to learn! If he is in prison, he cannot do that."

"Then he should have thought of that before he caused this most regrettable incident," Master Wisher snapped.

"We can make sure he has books to study," Master Clark said quietly.

"I'm sure even Branwen agrees with me. Don't you, my dear?" Master Wisher turned to the Uglessian girl.

She looked up, her face whiter than usual, her pale blue eyes strained. "Yes," she said after a moment.

It was rude to glare, Galia reminded herself. She stared at the table instead. She had left a piece of suet on her plate. It looked the way Master Wisher sounded. Fat. White. Smug.

"Don't worry. He'll come to no harm," Master Clark said. Master Bows nodded.

There was a moment of silence, then the blue-eyed wizard resumed talking about his plans for Uglessian prosperity. When a temporary lull occurred, Galia muttered her excuses and left.

SHE WAITED FOR RAVEN by the dormitory door. Students lingered outside, enjoying the softness of the spring evening. No one spoke to Galia.

The sun disappeared. The last loiterers left the common to head indoors. Still Raven didn't return. Was that good? Bad? If the man died, what would that mean for Thannis? She thought of his face as he rode away. He had looked so...so lost.

Raven and Master Spellman returned in the dusky purple twilight, walking slowly and in silence. Galia's heart thumped as they approached.

"Raven."

They hadn't seen her standing in the shadows by the door. They jerked to a stop. She stepped forward.

"Is he all right?"

Raven nodded. The lines on his face, even in the dim light, looked more deeply etched than usual. It was hard, sometimes, to remember that he was almost sixty. It was not hard tonight.

"He'll live, and without any permanent damage either, which I feared at first."

"It was a great healing," Master Spellman said quietly. "I am glad I was there to witness it."

Raven smiled. "And *I* am glad you were there to persuade the Freyan healer to allow me to help his patient."

His companion snorted. "A self-important little man. He should have grasped his good luck with both hands, grateful to have an Islandian healer there, not only to do what he could not, but to learn from him. All too many of our wizards are like that, afraid of new ways and ideas. Or maybe just afraid that their own inadequacies will be shown up."

"Many local healers have come to talk to me," Raven said mildly.

"I'll wager that one tonight hasn't."

"No."

The other man snorted again. Raven turned to Galia. "Galia, I don't think you've been introduced to Master Spellman. He's a wizard from Freyfall who's staying at the college for a week. Konrad, this is Galia Soradotter, who is gifted with weather magic."

Master Spellman bowed. "A privilege to meet you, Mistress Soradotter. You must be talented indeed to be here, and you so young."

Galia mumbled something polite, then turned back to Raven. "Can you help Thannis? He is in prison because of the fight. Master Wisher said it would not hurt him to stay there for a while, but it *will*. He will not be able to learn, and he will hate being locked up." Thannis was used to the freedom of his mountain home, as she was to the freedom of her sea-washed island. She shivered, just thinking of the imprisoning walls.

"Who is Thannis?" Master Spellman asked.

She explained.

"A very big young man, as I remember from the council. And capable of doing a great deal of damage when aroused, I'm sure. It might be difficult to persuade the army to release him immediately."

She swallowed.

Master Spellman smiled at her. "Don't worry. He might stay in prison longer than he'd like, but he *is* a guest of the college and, in a way, of the queen. He'll be treated well, and I don't imagine his incarceration will last too long."

Some of her fear eased.

A cool wind had sprung up. The twilight was deepening towards true night.

"I'd better head off to Martin Bows's. I'm staying with him for the duration of my visit. I look forward to seeing both of you again." Master Spellman bowed, then strode towards the far end of the common and the candlelit windows of the teachers' homes.

"Raven..."

He looked down at her. "I'm sorry. I was lost in memories of another head wound, when Rilka was struck by a stone. It made the Wise Women see that I was a true Healer, though it was thought then that no man had one of the Mother's gifts."

She nodded. She knew the story.

"I'll try to convince Master Wisher to help Thannis." Raven yawned. "But that will be in the morning. Time for bed now."

She could ask no more of Raven. He had done all he could tonight. He would do all he could tomorrow. She trudged up to her room. She would have to be patient.

CAT

A SMALL INN STOOD ON THE CORNER. IT looked clean, with white clapboards and a freshly swept yard. Respectable. Not too expensive. Cat paused in front of it. Perhaps she should rent a room for the night. The sun had set. She would cause trouble, arriving at the Spellmans' so late. They would have to make up a bed for her.

They always had a bed or two ready for guests.

Mistress Fairway would sniff and look down her long nose at her for arriving at such an hour.

The housekeeper would sniff and look down her long nose no matter what hour Cat arrived.

Still...

No. She wanted answers. She *did*. She walked on.

How intimidated she had been by the tall, restrained grandeur of the houses on these streets, the first time she had seen them. Later, viewing them through cat's eyes, they had seemed even larger but less imposing, somehow.

She could use cat's eyes now. The moon had not yet risen, and the candlelit rooms she passed were discreetly curtained. She walked more slowly, trying not to trip on the cobblestones. Her bag dragged at her shoulders, delaying her further. She shifted it from hand to hand.

Even so, she was in front of 6 Gotham Street before she was ready. She set her bag down and stood looking at the tall stone house which bore, she knew, a modest brass plaque marking it as the home of Konrad Spellman, Wizard.

She had gone up to that door before and knocked on it. And then she had been a ragged, dirty street singer, not a respectably dressed young woman already known to the household.

Yes. But what would she see on Garth's face at his first glimpse of her?

You came all the way from Frey-under-Hill to find out, Catrina Ashdale. Don't shy away like a skittish colt afraid of a shadow.

She squared her shoulders, grabbed the bag, marched up to the door, and banged.

After a moment, the door was opened by the tall, unbending figure of the housekeeper. "Yes?"

"I'm here to see Garth."

"As I told that other girl, Master Garth is not here."

Other girl? What other girl?

Mistress Fairway started to close the door.

"Mistress Fairway! Don't you recognize me? It's Cat. Catrina Ashdale."

The door paused in its swing. Mistress Fairway peered into the darkness.

"Catrina? So it is." The woman hesitated, then said grudgingly, "You'd best come in. Mistress Spellman will wish to see you, I'm sure." She inched the door open just enough for Cat to edge herself and the bag inside. The housekeeper looked at the bag suspiciously.

"This way." She led Cat down the tapestried hall and up the broad staircase with its ornately carved wooden banister. Cat followed, glancing around. She had forgotten how the Spellman house gleamed with polish, how her feet sank into its carpets.

They stopped in front of Mistress Spellman's private sitting room. After knocking lightly, Mistress Fairway opened the door. Over her shoulder, Cat saw tables, a tall window, chairs drawn up around the fireplace. Annette Spellman sat in one of those chairs, staring down at dying embers, her usually busy hands idle on her lap.

"A visitor, Mistress Spellman."

Annette raised her head. Her eyes looked tired. Then she saw Cat. "Cat!" She sprang to her feet, warmth and surprised joy lighting her face. "What an unexpected pleasure. Why didn't you let me know you were coming? Come in. Sit down and tell me what brings you to Freyfall. Mistress Fairway, would you take Cat's bag to a guest room and make sure it's ready for her?"

Cat felt her fears crumbling away as she allowed herself to be led to a chair facing Annette's. Nevertheless, she protested, "I don't want to be a nuisance. I can stay somewhere else –"

"Nonsense. Of course you'll stay here. Where else, when you're in Freyfall? You're practically one of the family, after last year."

Lips folded in a dour line, Mistress Fairway picked up Cat's bag and left.

"Would you like something to eat? Or drink?"

"I'm fine, thank you." She hadn't had anything to eat since her noon meal on the boat, but her stomach was much too nervous to accept food.

"All right. Now, tell me what brings you here."

"Well, I..." Cat hesitated.

"Yes?"

"I've come to see Garth," Cat blurted. "I...I need to talk to him."

"I see." Annette looked down at her hands.

Cat waited. And waited. The silence stretched on. It seemed to pulse with unspoken words. Cat wrapped her arms around herself, though the room was not cold.

"Cat..." Annette was looking at her again, her forehead furrowed. Cat's fingernails dug into the flesh of her upper arms.

"When you see him, could you tell him that it's important that he tell us where we can reach him if we need to?"

Cat stared at her, speechless.

"I know he and his grandfather don't agree on many issues. I understand...Tell him I *do* understand why he felt he must leave, even though I wish he hadn't. He's too young, just sixteen, and...Well, it hurts that he didn't trust me enough to at least tell me he was leaving. Don't say that, though. Just tell him... Even if he doesn't want to let us know where he's living because he's afraid we'll hound him to come home, he *must* send us word, now and then, of how he is. I know my father-in-law is as worried as I am, though he'll never admit it, of course, or even talk about Garth. Will you tell him that when you see him, Cat? Please?" Annette was leaning forward, her brown eyes pleading.

Once, when Cat was ten, she had fallen out of a tree and landed on her back. She felt like that now, as though all the breath had been knocked out of her. At last she managed to croak out a question.

"You mean you don't know where Garth is?"

"No. That's why it's so important that you give him my message."

Cat swallowed. Swallowed again. "I can't. I don't know where he is either. I thought I'd find him here."

It was Annette's turn to stare at her. Now the silence hummed with unspoken questions. Cat tried to clear her head. "You said Garth and his grandfather didn't agree. Is that why Garth left?"

'I don't know." Annette looked down at her hands, which were clenching and unclenching on her skirt.

"I thought things were better between them, ever since Master Spellman agreed that Garth could be a musician rather than a wizard."

"I thought so too. Things *were* better, especially at first. But later they argued so much, about the queen, and the courtiers, and tenants who'd been evicted from their land, and on and on. But I never dreamed it *meant* anything. Not that Garth didn't take the arguments seriously. But the two of them didn't seem to be angry with each other. At least, that's what I believed at the time. I never even tried to make peace between them, the way I always used to when Garth just *wouldn't* pay attention to his studies and Konrad got so annoyed. Ever since Garth left, I've wished that I had."

"He didn't say goodbye or tell you where he was going?"

"No. He left one morning, about six weeks ago, to go to the Coynes' as usual. He'd told me he'd be late, so I didn't worry when he wasn't home for dinner, or even as the evening wore on. But by morning, when he still wasn't here, I became frightened. Konrad said he'd go to the Coynes and find out what they knew. But before he left, Garth's message arrived."

Annette's breath was ragged, on the edge of tears. Cat waited a moment, then asked, "What did it say?"

"Just that he had decided it would be best if he didn't live with us anymore. Nothing about being sorry. Nothing about *why*."

"That doesn't sound like Garth," Cat said slowly. "Are you sure the message was from him?" Her skin prickled. If the message wasn't from Garth but from someone pretending to be him, who? Why?

"The note was in his handwriting, and Konrad cast an identification spell to make sure." Annette bowed her head, but Cat could see the tears sliding down her cheeks. Cat's hands curled into fists. Garth had no right to hurt his mother like this. It was wrong. Intolerably wrong. When she saw him – *if* she saw him – she would tell him so.

She cleared her throat. "Can't Master Spellman use a spell to find where he is?"

"I asked him to, but he said he wasn't going to waste his time looking for someone who didn't want to be found."

"What about the Coynes? Won't they tell you?"

Annette raised her head. "In the note, Garth said he wouldn't be studying with Master Coyne any longer."

It was as though the tree she'd fallen from had leaned down to wallop her and keep her breathless. "But Garth's always wanted to play, to sing, to compose. He wouldn't –"

"That's what I thought. But Konrad said that Garth may have found someone else to teach him. He said Garth had once mentioned someone who was a fine musician but had walked out of the Musicians' Guild. Garth was impressed by him."

Was he the musician Garth had met the night he and Talisa had fled with the boy accused of setting fire to the barracks? Cat's eyes left Annette's face and stared at the dense blackness of the night beyond the window.

"I think Garth's breaking his apprenticeship upset my father-in-law more even than his leaving home so abruptly. He hated having to apologize to Master Coyne ."

"Yes."

There was silence again. The wind must have picked up. Cat could hear it moaning around the house.

"We haven't heard from him since."

Cat closed her eyes, pictured Garth at Midwinter, dark hair dusted with snow, voice hushed with secrets. Did those secrets have anything to do with his disappearance?

It was very quiet, except for the wind.

Annette's voice broke the stillness. "Garth hasn't said anything about this in his letters? About leaving home? About studying with another musician?"

Cat looked down at the rug beneath her feet. Clusters of violets were woven into the cream background. "He hasn't written in over a month. That's why I came to Freyfall. To ask him why."

Annette gasped.

Cat's head jerked up. Annette was on her feet.

"Something's wrong. I could believe that Garth had left home without a word to me, because of quarrels with his grandfather. I could believe that he had abandoned his apprenticeship with Master Coyne and started studying with another master. Both actions are unlike him, but what else could I think? I saw his note. But to leave you without a word... No. He wouldn't do that."

Cat swallowed. "He may have lost interest in me."

Annette shook her head.

"If there's someone else... Mistress Fairway said a girl came to the house asking for him."

Annette frowned. "I wish she'd asked her in so I could talk to her."

"So you see..."

"No. If he hasn't written, there must be something preventing him from doing so. Maybe...maybe there's something preventing him from coming home."

Was it the wind, moaning softly in the night, that made the room so cold?

"Don't look like that, Cat." New colour was in Annette's face. "When Konrad hears about this, he'll cast a spell. He'll find Garth."

"Yes," Cat whispered. She rose. "Is Master Spellman here? Can I talk to him?"

Annette shook her head. "He left a day ago for Freybourg. He was planning to stay at the college for a week or so. But I'll send a messenger first thing tomorrow. I'm sure he'll be here very soon."

The wind still moaned, but Cat didn't feel as cold now. Not quite.

TALISA

TALISA WOKE EARLY AFTER A FITFUL SLEEP. She lay staring into the darkness, trying to think.

Alain Swanson. In Uglessia, she had planned to go to him. The musician might not have any influence, but he had his songs. Powerful songs. Added to hers, they might sway the queen and her court. Win Cory's freedom. And Master Swanson would want to help Cory. She was sure of it.

But how could she find him? It was no use asking people where he lived. She had discovered, last fall, that no one seemed to know. True, she'd been to his place once, guided by Garth's spell. But that had been at night, through a maze of twisting streets. Even Garth had lost his way. She chewed her lip, trying to remember the route they'd taken, while the sky gradually lightened into a pre-dawn pallor, but it was no use. The streets jumbled in her mind like threads hopelessly entangled.

She didn't know where Garth was. She didn't know how to find Alain Swanson. If she could use magic, like her sister, like her father, like all her family…

No. She'd spent most of her life brooding over her lack of ability. Talisa kicked off her blankets and rose. Once she'd given her letters to a messenger, she would ride to Freybourg and ask to see the queen. Use the gift she did have. Her gift of song.

She found a messenger stall not far from her inn. The owner was just raising the shutters as she walked up. She handed him her letters and watched him stow them in a bag, then turned away.

Other stall owners and shopkeepers were opening up. The sun touched the waterfall with golden drops of mist. Cory had once said the waterfall almost made up for his family having to leave their farm in the hills and come here.

Before she left Freyfall, she must see Cory's sister. Offer Rina hope, if she could.

Like Master Swanson's house, the Berrymore apartment was surrounded by a rat's nest of winding streets and cul-de-sacs. But she knew how to find Bart's stall on Weavers Street. Angry as Cory's brother-in-law might be with him – and Talisa shivered, thinking how angry he would probably be – Bart would not refuse to lead her to Rina. Maybe she could make Bart see that Cory was innocent, too. If so, it would help Rina, who had always felt torn between her husband and her brother in their arguments.

Weavers Street was more than a mile away, but Talisa covered the distance quickly. It was still too early for many

shoppers, though carts were busily unloading their
Talisa saw fish, still wet from the river, slide onto one
smelled daffodils, newly picked, on another.

Weavers Street, as its name implied, was lined with s
displaying woven goods, but the bright pictures and drama
designs that Rina used to decorate the clothes she made we
unmistakable. Talisa recognized the stall even before she saw
the tall, lean figure standing with his back to her in front of
it. As she moved closer, she saw that Bart's long fingers were
caressing something. It was... Her breath caught.

She had never seen it before, but she knew it. Made of
grey stone, it was as much a part of Uglessia as were its
granite mountains. The young ursell stood, sturdy hooves
planted firmly on the stall's plank, small pointed head raised,
viewing the world with bright surmise.

Cory must have carved it while he was hiding on the
mountainside, keeping out of sight of Freyan soldiers.

She didn't think she made any sound, but Bart must
have sensed her presence. He turned. His eyes widened.
"Mistress Thatcher."

She swallowed. "I'm glad to see you, Master Berrymore."

He nodded, but didn't smile. "And I you, though it
would have been better perhaps if you had stayed in
Uglessia."

"I couldn't."

He nodded again.

"You've seen him? He gave you that carving? When..?"

"Two days ago."

"How is he?"

...like an ursell trying to identify a dis-
...at then I gather he'd been hiding for
... walked into the soldiers' camp."

... captors treated him well on the way here."
... to smile.
...eemed..." Bart searched for words. "Peaceful.
..., almost."
...es."

A plump, pretty woman with smooth brown hair
stopped in front of the stall. She picked up a blue skirt,
embroidered with yellow flowers. "How much is this?"

Bart told her.

"Too much. I'm not made of money."

"A skirt like that takes a long time to make, and you'll be
the envy of your neighbours when you wear it," Bart said,
but Talisa could tell his heart wasn't in it. She half listened to
them bargain while she waited. More shoppers were strolling
down the street now. A cart lumbered off.

The woman handed some coins to Bart and walked
away, looking as smug as a bird that's captured a fat worm.
Bart looked at the money, then shrugged and put it in his
pocket.

"How is Rina?"

"About as you'd expect, with Cory in trouble."

"The baby..."

"Will come in six or seven weeks' time, she thinks." He
paused, then added, "We're hoping we'll have enough saved
by then to move. We're doing better than we've done since

we came to Freyfall. We have some regular customers, even ones who've begun to commission work. What Rina would really like is to go home to the hills."

Talissa nodded. Cory's voice had always ached with longing when he spoke of the hill farm where he and Rina had lived until the Count of Eastlands had evicted their family, along with countless others, including Bart's, from the land they rented from him. The ache in Cory's voice had turned to black bile when he talked about the eviction.

"That's impossible, of course. Still, we should be able to find a decent place in Freyfall to raise a child."

"I'm glad," Talisa said softly.

Bart smiled. "So am I." His eyes followed a man who paused in front of the stall, fingered several items, then walked on. "But I'm worried about Rina. She's so thin. So pale. Cory's disappearance, and now his imprisonment... It's eating into her."

Did anger edge his voice? Talisa searched his face, saw the tightness of his lips, the smudges under his eyes.

"He didn't burn the barracks, Bart."

"I know."

She blinked. "You do?"

"Oh yes. He says he didn't, and I don't think he'd lie to us. Anyway, setting torches to buildings, especially ones that have people in them, isn't the type of thing Cory would do. Expressing his opinions and getting into trouble *is*. But being innocent doesn't help much, does it?" Bart's voice was tired. He looked down at his boots, which were scuffed at the toes. "Rina begged him, over and over, to tell them who did set fire to the barracks. I didn't even try. I knew he wouldn't."

Talisa swallowed. "He told you what happened that night? How someone warned him about what was going on? How he tried to stop it?"

"Yes."

"If enough people believe him..."

"It wouldn't help."

She stared at him.

Still gazing at his boots, Bart said, "I think they'll be just as enraged and suspicious if they think he didn't do it but is deliberately hiding the identity of those who did." He looked up at her, his dark eyes heavy. "I'm sorry."

He's wrong. He must be wrong.

"I'm sorry," he repeated.

She nodded jerkily.

Someone brushed by. The street was busy now, and noisy. The sun was beginning to get warm. Why were her hands icy? Another woman stopped by the stall.

She couldn't give up. When she had left Uglessia, she had known her chance of winning Cory's life was small. But it *was* a chance. Bart's words changed nothing.

"Do you or Rina know any of the people who might have been involved?"

He glanced at her, frowning.

"If you could talk to them... If they confessed..."

Bart shook his head. "We thought of that. The trouble is, we don't know. Cory never mentioned names, and we...Well, I guess I never wanted to know."

The shopper, a wiry woman with yellow hair fading to grey, must have overheard. She gave them a startled look and hurried away.

Talisa clutched her lifeline of hope. "I've sent letters from my grandparents to wizards they know, including Kerstin and Jem Brooks and Konrad Spellman. There are others who might help too." Master Coyne. But would he? Alain Swanson. If she could find him.

Bart smiled. "That's good." He sounded like an adult praising a child's efforts to hold up a tottering ledge. She looked away.

"If you want to see him, I can take you to the prison."

Her heart jumped, then started racing. To see Cory...

But they'd said their goodbyes in Uglessia. What did she have to offer now? She wanted, how she wanted, to let him know there was hope. But how could she do that, when her lifeline was fraying?

She had accomplished so little. She hadn't even found Garth, or Master Spellman, or –

Or Alain Swanson. Few people knew where he lived. But Cory did.

"Yes. Thank you. I would like to see him."

Bart nodded and reached up to close the shutters. A round-bellied man who had paused by the stall said indignantly, "You're not closing?"

"Yes."

"But it's early. Everything's just opened."

"I have an errand to do. Come back later."

"If you'll give me directions, I can go by myself," Talisa said.

Bart shook his head. "It's best I go with you. Anyway, I don't feel like haggling over prices today. Come on."

The prison was smaller than she'd expected, but even grimmer. Behind a wall stood a windowless brick building. Two heavily armed soldiers guarded the gate. Despite her height, Talisa had to look up to see their faces.

"We're here to see Cory Updale," Bart said.

"Thrasher!" the taller guard called without removing his gaze from them. "Escort these two to the Captain. They want to see Updale."

The new soldier was shorter but as solid – and as expressionless – as the granite rocks that made up the mountains of Uglessia. Without a word, he led them through the courtyard, then opened the prison door and ushered them in. There were torches in wall sconces and a lantern on a table, but they gave little light after the bright sun outside.

"These two are here to see Updale, Captain," their escort told the man behind the table.

The captain made Talisa think of a bald eagle. He studied Bart.

"You've been here before."

"Two days ago. I'm Cory's brother-in-law."

The captain nodded and switched his attention to Talisa. "And who are you?"

"Talisa Thatcher." She was ashamed of how small her voice sounded.

His eyebrows lifted. "Ah. The Uglessian girl who helped Updale escape."

A sneer lay behind the words. She raised her chin. "We travelled to Uglessia together."

"Well, you won't be able to help him escape from here. Very well. You can see him. Just don't take long. We're moving him later today."

"Moving him?" Talisa echoed.

"Where to?" Bart asked at the same time.

"Freybourg. They're going to try him there, it seems."

Talisa moistened her lips. It didn't help. She moistened them again. "When will the trial be held?"

"Soon." The captain waved a hand towards the guard. "Thrasher, show them to Updale's cell."

Soon. The word thudded through Talisa's head just as their boots thudded on the stone floor as they walked along a hall, down a flight of stairs, and along another corridor lined with iron bars. The guard stopped.

"People to see you."

The cell was a small grey box that contained nothing except a bucket and a wooden plank with some blankets on it. Cory sat on the plank, head against the wall, eyes closed. They opened, blinked, closed. Cory rubbed them, then opened them again.

"Talisa?"

He spoke her name as though in a dream. Then he shook his head, rose, and walked towards the bars. "You shouldn't be here."

She felt as though cold water had been dumped on her.

He must have seen the look on her face. "I'm sorry. I didn't mean...You know I'm happy to see you. But *why*,

Talisa? We've said...You would be better at home, with your family."

She took hold of one of the iron bars. It was cold, but then it would be, here, beyond the reach of the sun. "I came to help."

"Help? But, Talisa, there's nothing you can do. You know that."

Bart had said Cory seemed peaceful, almost content. He did not seem peaceful now. His voice was strained, his forehead wrinkled in worry. A smudge darkened one cheek. She wished she had a damp handkerchief to wipe it away.

"I have letters. My grandparents wrote them to wizards they know, who they think may be able to help."

"That was kind of them," Cory said. "But Talisa –"

"I must try. I *must*."

"Yes," he said after a moment. "Just...don't get your hopes too high."

If he knew how low her hopes were right then, he would not have said that.

"It's good to see you," Cory said softly. He reached out his hand to touch her face, then withdrew it. She wished he hadn't.

"Cory –" She looked over her shoulder at the guard, who stood within easy earshot. At her glance, he moved back a few paces, taking the light with him. The only other light came from dim torches in two wall sconces at either end of the corridor. What was it like for Cory, living in near darkness? Were other prisoners here? She had heard no sound of them. Perhaps they were as silent and blind as moles in an underground tunnel. Talisa shivered, then took a firmer grip on the bar and leaned forward. "Cory, there are other people who may be able to help you. Could you tell me how to find Master Swanson?"

"Alain?" He stared at her, brown eyes wide.

"Yes."

"But why him? He's poor. He has no influence."

"He has his songs."

Cory gave a short laugh. "His songs have about as much power as my carvings do. None."

"Songs *do* have power." She had to believe that. "Remember how mine made my people vote against Master Granton's proposal?"

"Yes," he said slowly. "I do. But... Anyway, Alain is busy with his plan."

"What plan is that?" Bart asked.

Cory hesitated, glanced at the guard, then lowered his voice even though the man was standing beyond earshot now. "Alain is going to gather all those who are poor, all those who are homeless, to march to Freybourg and show Queen Elira the plight of so many of her subjects, people who've been kicked off their land by landlords like the Count of Eastlands. I was helping him spread the word."

"Oh," Bart said slowly. "I thought whatever you were involved in was more...drastic. This sounds harmless enough."

"Harmless but important. Alain shouldn't be diverted."

"If he's too busy, he can tell me so," Talisa said. "Cory, *please.*"

"All right," he said after a moment. "But it's not that easy to find. And the area's not a safe place for girls on their own."

"I'll go with her," Bart said.

Cory nodded and gave directions. Talisa listened carefully. So did Bart, who interrupted twice to make sure he had it right.

When he'd finished, Cory said, "Talisa, you must be careful. All you're doing... I'm so grateful. But you mustn't get involved further. You could get into trouble."

"I won't," she said, then added, "and I won't jeopardize what you've done to make sure Freya doesn't react against Uglessia and withdraw rain. That I swear."

There was silence. Then Cory asked, "When this is over, will you return to Uglessia?"

When this is over. When Cory has been tried and – what? Freed? Hanged? No! "I...don't know. Master Coyne wants me to return to my apprenticeship with him."

"He does?" Cory sounded as if she'd given him an unexpected gift.

She smiled. "Yes."

"I'm so glad."

The guard moved forward, his candle making his shadow twist in grotesque shapes. "The captain said you could only talk a short time."

"We'll go in a minute," Bart said. He turned back to Cory. "You're all right? You don't need anything?"

"No." Cory laughed suddenly. "I wish they'd let me have a knife so I could carve, but I suppose that's asking too much."

Talisa winced. Cory might laugh, but she knew how empty he felt when he couldn't create his dogs and urchins and beggar women and ursells.

"Cory," Bart said, then stopped.

They stood gazing at each other. Talisa's throat ached, watching them. "*Bart cares for Cory,*" Rina had told her once. "*He grew up on the farm next to ours. He was like an older brother to Cory. He gets so angry because he cares.*"

Cory broke the silence. "Tell Rina to take care of herself."

Bart smiled faintly. "You told her that yourself two days ago. But I will."

"Thank you." Cory paused. "I hope everything goes well with the baby."

"It will."

Cory nodded. He glanced down, then back up. "I'm sorry."

"I know."

Silence again. Then Bart said quietly, "Freyn be with you, Cory," and turned away.

Talisa felt Cory's eyes on her. "Talisa..." His face was very solemn. Was it paler then before? Perhaps it was just her imagination. But the smudge seemed darker, so maybe it wasn't. She shouldn't have come.

"I'm glad you came," he said softly.

If only there weren't bars between them. If only Bart and the guard weren't there. But they were.

"I'm glad I did too," she said. "I'll see you in Freybourg."

And that was all, though there should have been more. There should have been words that meant something, words that meant everything. But there weren't. All she could do was smile at Cory, then follow the light down the corridor, up the stairs, and out of the prison. She thought of Cory, and tried not to welcome the warmth of the sun, the light of the day.

GALIA

HAD ANYONE TOLD THANNIS THAT THE injured man had recovered? If not, was Thannis lying awake right now, thinking himself responsible for a man's death, thinking himself doomed to a life in prison?

The thought kept Galia awake. Hours passed. The night wind whispered to the trees. At some point, she must have fallen asleep.

She woke with worry heavy on her mind, and it went with her all morning. By midday, she could stand it no longer. She hovered by the refectory door after lunch. When Branwen came hurrying out, she touched her arm. "Branwen, I need to talk to you."

"We'll be late for class." But Branwen halted obediently.

"I am not going to class. I am going to see Thannis."

Branwen raised startled eyebrows. "Has he been freed, then? I hadn't heard."

"No, he is still in prison. I am going there, to let him know that Raven healed the injured man."

"But surely someone's already told him."

"Perhaps. But perhaps not. I want to be sure he knows."

Branwen frowned. "Did you ask permission to miss classes?"

"No."

"No? You'll get in trouble." Branwen paused. "Or maybe you won't. The teachers never seem to criticize you."

This was true. They never criticized her, they never even questioned her. Sometimes Galia wished they would. She might feel more at home here then. More as though she belonged.

Branwen looked over at the hall, where the tag end of the students was disappearing. "Well, it's up to you. I'd better go."

"Wait." Galia grabbed hold of her sleeve. "Will you come with me?"

There was a fractional pause. "No."

"But... Don't you want to see him?"

"Why would I want to do that?" Branwen asked coldly.

Anger bubbled up inside Galia. "You are both Uglessians. You should care about him."

"Did Thannis care about me or his country when he lost his temper yesterday, as he did at the council last Midsummer and almost lost us both the chance to study here? Did he care about anything except his own rage?" The blue eyes looking down at Galia were bright. Hectic colour flushed Branwen's usually pale cheeks. "This is my opportunity, probably my only opportunity, to study magic. All my life I've dreamed about coming here. Not just for myself. For all of us. Our lives can be so much better if only we know more. When I see everything there is here, how much everyone has, and then think about our bare mountainsides, our bare huts... It's all very well for you. You don't need Freyan magic. Everyone knows that. But for me... I'm not going to let Thannis throw away my chance as well as his own." She glared at Galia for a moment, then almost fled down the path.

Galia watched her go, the anger draining out of her, then turned and walked towards the gate.

As she made her way down the lane, a carriage passed her. Glancing inside, she saw the hawk-nosed face of Master Spellman. A bag was beside him. Was he leaving? That was strange. Hadn't he said he'd be here a while?

She had no idea where the prison was. The first person she asked, a matronly woman with a kind face, looked shocked. "The prison? I don't know, I'm sure." She walked on, shaking her head. A middle-aged man with a dapper moustache was more informative. It was further away than she had expected. She hurried past imposing homes, bow-windowed shops, the Royal Gardens, and the palace. It was hot for spring. She wiped her forehead. More shops, more houses, more gardens.

If the palace was a symmetrical white swan, the prison was a one-winged gull. Like the houses of Freybourg, it was constructed out of grey stone. Unlike them, there were no trees or bushes surrounding it, only walls. And soldiers.

Large soldiers. Galia felt very small as she approached the two stationed at the gate.

"Excuse me."

The soldiers seemed to look down from a very great distance.

"I would like to see a prisoner."

"Rather young to be visiting prisoners, aren't you?" rumbled one with a sagging hound's face.

Galia ignored the question. "His name is Thannis. He was brought in yesterday."

"The Uglessian," supplied the other, younger soldier.

The first one nodded. Mournful hound's eyes regarded Galia. "Do your parents know you're here?"

She thought of her parents, back home on Rork. A small smile tugged at her mouth. "No, but they would not mind if they knew. They are not here. I am at the college."

"That's where the Uglessian was staying," said the younger man.

"Friend of yours, is he?" asked the hound man. "Well, I suppose there's no harm in your seeing him. Come in."

Galia started towards the door in the central block. "Not there," he called after her. "That's where the bad ones are kept. You don't want to go there. Over that way." He pointed towards a door in the wing. She veered in that direction.

There was another guard stationed at that door, a round-cheeked young man who regarded Galia with interest.

"I would like to see Thannis, please."

"Thannis?"

"He is a prisoner."

"Most of the people in here are," the soldier retorted. "What's his last name?"

"I do not think he has one." If he did, she had never heard it. "He was brought in yesterday afternoon. He is Uglessian."

"Oh, right. The one who was in a fight and cracked open someone's skull. Five to one, I heard. And he won." There was admiration, even awe, in the young man's voice.

Galia smiled at him. "Yes."

"Well, he's big enough for it, I suppose. Go in. You'll have to ask the warden for permission, though." He stepped aside and opened the door for her.

Stone walls kept the interior cool. Galia shivered. She spoke to a soldier with hair the colour of flames. He turned and called to yet another guard who left, presumably in search of the warden. Galia waited. When the warden appeared at last, he listened to her request absent-mindedly, then nodded to the guard who had fetched him. "Escort her to the Uglessian's cell, then return here." As Galia walked off, she heard him say something to the flame-haired man about getting ready for a revolutionary.

Though sparsely furnished, the cell that held Thannis was large, and clean, and had a window high in the wall. Thannis sat on the cot, shoulders hunched, head in hands.

"Visitor to see you," announced the guard before departing.

Thannis raised his head slowly, like a man dragging himself out of a deep bog. Then he jumped to his feet. "Galia!"

"The Mother's blessings on you, Thannis." She regarded him. "How are you?"

"All right."

He didn't look all right. His face was ash grey, except for the mauve shadows beneath his eyes and the dark bruise on one cheek. His arms were wrapped around himself as though he were trying to still inner tremors.

Galia came right to the point. "The man who hit his head is well. Raven healed him."

For a moment, Thannis just stared at her. Then, slowly, his face brightened. Galia had seen the sun breaking through fog in the same way. She felt a smile touch her own face.

"He's really healed?"

"Yes."

Thannis heaved a sigh that seemed to come from the soles of his boots. His arms unfolded.

"I was so frightened."

Galia nodded.

"I was worried about what would happen to me, but that was only a small part of it. To think I'd killed a man..."

She nodded again.

"All night, I kept seeing him lying on the ground."

"They should have told you."

Thannis shrugged. His face was still pale, but his eyes looked like the sky when dark clouds have passed. "I know now. Thank you. Thank you very much."

"You are very welcome."

Their formality made them both laugh, but Galia sobered quickly. "I talked to Master Wisher. He will do nothing to help you be free. At least not now."

"I'm not surprised."

Galia cocked her head, surprised at his tone. "Nor angry?"

"I'm not happy about being here," he admitted. "And I hate the idea of missing classes. But I know I have only myself to blame. All my life, I've been told to stamp down on my anger, and all my life I've let it flame up anyway. I almost wrecked the council last year. Yesterday I almost killed someone."

"You didn't mean to."

"No. Still, he might have died. Last night, I was glad I was here. I *wanted* to be punished. Now...Well, I don't want to stay here *too* long." Thannis smiled. Then his smile faded. "I suppose Branwen is angry with me."

Galia hesitated.

He sighed. "I guess I can't blame her."

"I have to go now, but I will be back soon. And I will bring books, and notes so you will not miss anything the teachers say." She would have to pay more attention in class, she realized. Oh well.

"Thank you. You *are* a true friend, Galia."

Warmth flowed through her. "May the Mother keep you in her care."

Once outside, Galia took a deep breath. The air tasted better out here. She started across the yard, then stopped as the gate swung open, letting in a column of horsemen. The warden, flanked by four guards, hurried out to meet it.

There seemed to be a great number of big, snorting horses and tall, green-uniformed soldiers. Galia watched them come to a halt in the centre of the courtyard. The leader dismounted and saluted the warden. The two men exchanged a few words, then the warden looked towards the middle of the company. Galia followed his gaze to where a man with a shock of brown hair falling into his eyes sat on a roan horse. What she noticed first was that he was the only one not in uniform. Then she saw that his hands were bound before him.

A prisoner. Like Thannis.

The man's eyes scanned the walls, the prison, the courtyard. For a moment, they rested on Galia. They were large eyes, too big for the thin face. So were the long nose, the protruding ears, the wide mouth. The mouth stretched into a smile as his eyes met Galia's.

Galia reddened. She must have been staring. She had been rude. But his smile had not been unfriendly.

He looked young, only a few years older than Galia. Again, like Thannis.

She continued to watch as soldiers surrounded the roan horse. The prisoner dismounted. He was marched towards the heavily guarded doors of the central block. Not like Thannis.

The bad ones are kept there, the guard had said.

Galia resumed her walk to the gate. As she passed the soldiers who had just ridden in, she heard one of them say, "That one's slated for hanging."

Galia shuddered.

"Good," another grunted. He spat. "Emmett Lake, one of the men killed in the fire that rebel set, was a friend of mine. I'll thank Freyn the day I see him dangle."

Galia hastened her steps. She was almost running by the time she reached the gate and passed through.

CAT

"I'VE SENT A MESSENGER WITH A NOTE TO MY father-in-law. He should be home by this evening or tomorrow at the latest," Annette said.

Cat nodded. The act of sending the message seemed to have soothed Mistress Spellman. The sun gliding in through the dining room window betrayed few of the lines that had eaten into her skin the night before. Cat raised her cup of kala to hide her own face. If she had slept better last night, she might be less tense now.

After a cheerful maid had cleared away the breakfast dishes, Annette asked, "Would you like to do some shopping while we wait?"

About to refuse, Cat stopped. She needed to do *something* to occupy herself. And she should buy a birth gift for the baby who'd be born come harvest.

"Thank you. Yes."

"Good. I'll fetch my cloak." Annette sprang to her feet.

Perhaps the shopping expedition would help her too.

They emerged into a morning bright with sunlight and fresh with dew. Somewhere, a lark was singing. The fear clutching Cat eased its grip a little.

Annette Spellman knew all the best shops to find items for babies, and she surprised Cat with her skill at bargaining. Even so, Cat couldn't afford the hand-carved wooden toys and lacy clothes they examined. She looked with regret at a brightly painted clown, a soft blanket that was the colour of newborn chicks, and – best of all in Cat's eyes – a tinkling chime that could be set in motion by a baby's hand. But it didn't matter. She enjoyed wandering from shop to shop, looking at all these possible gifts. She liked Annette's company and found it gratifying that Annette seemed to like hers. Best of all, she was doing something other than brood.

After leaving yet one more too expensive shop, Annette exclaimed, "The weaver's stall!"

Cat glanced at her enquiringly.

"There are lovely clothes there. Usually I wouldn't recommend making a serious purchase from a stall – the items tend to be cheaply made, as well as cheaper in price. But I've gone to this one several times. Not only are the clothes exquisitely sewn, the weaver has a true artist's eye. And there were a number of things for babies there the last time I visited it."

They flagged down a carriage, that jostled through crowded streets and across a bridge to the central island. Cat felt sure they could have walked to their destination more quickly.

Weavers Street was filled with shops and stalls displaying clothes, blankets, cushions, and hangings. Cat paused several times to inspect various stalls.

"There are better clothes at the one I mentioned. You'll see," Annette said. But when they reached it, the shutters were down.

"What a shame." Annette sounded like a child who had wanted to show a favourite toy to a friend and been disappointed.

"Berrymore closed early this morning," said a man standing beside the adjacent stall. "Started talking to a young woman – a Uglessian from the looks of her, quite a beauty too – then he pulled the shutters down and left with her." He smirked. He was a sandy-haired man with a flamboyant moustache.

"Do you know when he'll be back?" Annette asked.

The man shrugged. "He didn't say. He might never come back, if he gets in trouble like his brother did – or maybe it's his brother-in-law. You must have heard about *him*," he added, when both women looked at him blankly. "Up something. Updale, that's it. Set fire to the barracks and killed some soldiers last fall, then fled to Uglessia, where they sheltered him till the army found out where he was and fetched him. Rode in about a week ago now. Berrymore's been looking pretty grim lately. Not that he doesn't most of the time, if you ask me."

"Poor man," Annette said.

The vendor shrugged again. "He's probably as much of a firebrand as his brother-in-law, if the truth be told. A lot of these folk from the hills are. But you needn't bother about him. I've got just as fine clothes on my stall, yes, and cheaper too. Take a look. You won't find better wares in the whole of Freyfall."

"No, thank you. We must go," Annette said politely, and turned away.

But Cat lingered for a moment. "What's happened to Master Berrymore's brother-in-law? Where is he now?"

"In prison waiting for his trial. Then he'll be hanged."

Annette was waiting for her, but Cat still lingered. "This Uglessian girl you saw. Did she have red hair?"

The man's eyes narrowed. "That's right. How did you know?"

"Cat," Annette called, and Cat escaped before she had to fumble for an answer.

They took a carriage back to 6 Gotham Street. Annette was quiet. Cat was glad. She had to think.

So the boy Garth had helped had been caught, and Talisa Thatcher had returned to Freyfall. Did that have anything to do with Garth's disappearance?

Surely not. Garth had been gone for six weeks, after all.

Nevertheless, it raised a question. When they reached the Spellman home, Cat slipped away and went in search of the housekeeper. She found her in an upper room, supervising the work of the cheerful maid, who was now busy polishing furniture and, from Mistress Fairway's grim expression, making poor work of it.

"Mistress Fairway..."

The housekeeper wheeled. Her expression didn't change when she saw Cat. "Yes?"

"You mentioned that a girl had been here asking for Garth. Did she have red hair? Was she Uglessian?"

"Yes," Mistress Fairway said shortly, and returned her attention to the maid.

So it was Talisa Thatcher who had come calling. Why? Had she been seeking Garth's help for a second time? Cat's fingers curled. Garth had already risked getting into trouble by helping her.

Did it matter? Garth hadn't been here for Talisa to find.

No. But her presence was one more strand in the web that linked Garth to a musician named Master Swanson, and to danger.

This evening – or tomorrow – Konrad Spellman would return. He would use a finding spell to locate his grandson. There was nothing she could do that he couldn't do more quickly, more effectively. She should wait patiently, like Annette. She had her whistle in her bag. She should go to her room, or to the garden out back, and practise the new tune that she was learning. Garth would like it.

No. She couldn't. She was too restless.

Annette didn't seem surprised when Cat told her she was going for a walk. "Don't get lost," was all she said. Perhaps she too wanted to pace, to roam, to *do* something.

But Cat was interested in more than just walking. She had some finding of her own to do.

Mel wasn't in The Laughing Lute. Cat nursed a cup of kala and sat quietly, watching the door. She knew there were other musicians she could question, ones who were just as likely to know where Master Swanson lived. If Mel didn't arrive within an hour, she would make the rounds. But she would rather ask someone she knew. Someone who knew her. Someone who knew Garth.

She was finishing her second cup when Mel wandered in, lute slung over his shoulder. Cat jumped to her feet and hurried over to him before he could sit down. "Mel."

He smiled at her. "Mistress Ashdale! What a pleasant surprise, to meet you twice in two days. Will you join me for a drink?"

She ignored his invitation. "I'm looking for someone."

"Someone else?" He raised his eyebrows, head cocked.

She flushed at the amused interest in his eyes. "Yes. Master Swanson. Alain Swanson, I think. He's a musician."

"Yes," Mel agreed slowly. "He's even played here once or twice, though not recently."

"Do you know where he lives?"

"No. He keeps to himself, I hear, ever since he walked out of the Musicians' Guild, or was thrown out, one or the other."

"Do you know anywhere else he might go? Another tavern like The Laughing Lute?"

"No. I'm sorry." Mel paused. "Why do you want to find him?"

Cat hesitated. Dare she tell him that she hoped Master Swanson might lead her to Garth? Mel and Garth were friends, after all.

No. She couldn't risk it. Garth had broken the law when he helped Talisa's friend escape.

"I heard how good his songs are. I'd like to hear them."
It wasn't a complete lie.

"He is a good songsmith," Mel agreed. "Let's ask the others, shall we?"

It took a long time to go around the tavern. Everyone had a few words they wanted to say to Mel, or a new song to share with him. And that, of course, led Mel to strike up his lute and sing at least a few bars. But at last they had completed their circuit. Everyone had the same answer. No. They had no idea where Alain Swanson lived, or where he might be found. Most, though not all, had heard of him. Some said he was a fine singer. Others dismissed him as a troublemaker and a crackpot.

"Too gloomy," said a fair-haired young man. "You'd be better off with me." He grinned at Cat and patted the bench beside him. She reddened and shook her head.

"No luck. Sorry," Mel said when they were done.

"It's not your fault. Thank you for trying." But she couldn't keep the discouragement out of her voice.

Mel eyed her, a small frown puckering his forehead. "What about your other quest?"

"My other quest?"

"Have you found Garth?"

"No."

His frown deepened. "Is anything wrong? With Garth, I mean?"

For the second time, she hesitated. Then she shook her head. "No." Again, it wasn't a lie. There was nothing wrong. Or, rather, there wouldn't be once Konrad Spellman found Garth.

"All right," Mel said slowly. "When you do find Garth, tell him…" He stopped.

"What?"

He grinned suddenly and shrugged, unable to maintain the strain of being serious any longer. "Tell him to return to The Lute soon. I have a new and very funny song that he'll love."

"I'll tell him."

"Good." His attention was drawn by a burst of laughter from a nearby table. "Best of Freyn's luck with both your searches," he said over his shoulder. He took two steps towards the table, then stopped and turned back to Cat. "Andreas."

She blinked.

"Andreas Wells. I should have thought of him before. He's Alain Swanson's apprentice."

Hope leapt in her heart. "Do you know where he lives?"

"With his master, I presume. Most apprentices do."

Hope subsided. "Oh."

"But he comes here quite often. In fact, he was here yesterday. You met him, the young man with the dark hair sitting beside me. The next time I see him, I'll ask him where he and Master Swanson live," Mel promised before heading towards the merriment.

Andreas Wells. The dark-haired man with the flashing white-toothed smile. He had said he didn't really know Garth, but that couldn't be true. Garth had visited Master Swanson several times. And Andreas's eyes had followed her as she left the tavern.

She should have gone back then and confronted him.

Well, she hadn't, and she couldn't turn back time. Mel had promised to ask Andreas where he lived, the next time he saw him. Not that it mattered. Konrad Spellman would soon be home. In the meantime, she had better hurry back to Gotham Street. It must be approaching dinnertime, and she didn't want to keep Annette waiting.

Dinner was a delicately spiced fish stew inside a pastry shell. Cat consumed it quickly. Then she waited.

Master Spellman might not be back tonight, she reminded herself several times. Nevertheless, she jumped every time she heard a carriage drive by. So did Annette.

Beyond Annette's sitting room window, the sun went down. The sky darkened. The moon rose. Still no Konrad.

"Will you sing for me, Cat?"

Cat did, first the new piece she was learning, then some old favourites. It helped, though she still jumped at every sound.

Finally, close to midnight, she heard a clop of hooves and clatter of wheels that didn't go by, but stopped. She and Annette almost jostled each other as they hurried out the door and to the top of the stairs.

A tall man with dark hair only slightly streaked with white stood in the hall, removing a black cloak. He looked up when he heard them.

Konrad Spellman was home.

TALISA

BART SPOKE ONLY TWICE AS THEY MADE THEIR way to Master Swanson's house. Once was to curse the driver of a cart, who whipped his horse into motion just as they started to cross in front of it. The second time he said, as they got further and further into an area of dingy streets, deserted houses, and derelict warehouses, "I'm glad I came with you."

"So am I." Talisa didn't feel in any real danger here, not in the sunlight. But his company, silent as it was, kept her from falling over the cliff edge into despair.

The murmur of water grew stronger. Master Swanson's house bordered the river. Last fall, it had covered the noise of their escape as they crept through the wild grass and thistles that grew beside it.

They stopped in front of a narrow house that looked as crumbling and empty as its neighbours. Talisa walked up to the door, with its peeling white paint.

"Are you sure this is the right place?" Bart asked.

She nodded. She had only seen it by the light of the moon before, but she couldn't mistake it. She knocked firmly. Waited. Knocked again.

"I think I see a face at the window," Bart said.

She knocked once more.

The door opened to reveal, not Master Swanson's tall, lean form, but a young man with dark hair. She inclined her head. "Master Wells, I am glad to meet you."

"Mistress Thatcher! What an unexpected pleasure. It has been all too long since Freyn has blessed me with a sight of your lovely face. To what do we owe the honour of your visit here?" Andreas's smile was as charming, his teeth as white, his words as flattering as Talisa remembered. But was there a hint of wariness in his eyes? Perhaps it was Bart's presence: she'd seen Andreas's gaze flicker over her shoulder.

"We want to see Master Swanson."

"I'm sure Master Swanson would be as delighted to see you as I am. But alas, he isn't here."

For a moment, Andreas's figure wavered in front of her. Garth. Master Spellman. Now Alain Swanson. All the people she'd counted on for help. Gone.

"When will he be back?" Bart asked.

Andreas shrugged. "In an hour or two, perhaps."

The relief that swept over Talisa was so strong she had to lean against the door frame for support. The wood was rough, full of slivers. "May we come in and wait?"

Andreas paused just a second too long. "It would fill me with joy to have your company, but I'm afraid this house, though frequently awash with songs that nightingales would envy, is sadly humble."

"I'm not accustomed to palatial surroundings," Bart said dryly. "It will do."

"But –"

"Andreas, this is Bart Berrymore, Cory's brother-in-law," Talisa interrupted.

"Oh." For once, Andreas seemed bereft of words. He stared at Bart for a moment, then said simply, "I'm sorry."

Bart's mouth flinched into a thin line. He took a deep breath. "Thank you."

"Have you seen him?" Andreas asked.

"Yes," Talisa said.

"How is he?"

"He's…" Alone. Locked in a dark hole. At peace, or was until she visited. "He's being taken to Freybourg today for trial."

"Oh."

Talisa's hands clenched into fists. "I will not let him be convicted. I will not let…" Let him be hanged. She could not say it. "I need help. That's why I came here."

"Yes, of course. Please come in." Andreas glanced at Bart again. "I should have recognized you. I've been to your place."

"Delivering messages for Cory. Yes, I know."

The long narrow hall was oddly familiar, as though she had walked down it often, not just once. So was the windowless room at the back, with its uneven stone floor, sagging ceiling, and the table and chairs that stood in the middle. Even the mugs and squat candle on the table were as she remembered.

But the two men sitting at the table were not familiar at all. They turned in their chairs and stared as the newcomers entered.

"This is Talisa Thatcher and Bart Berrymore," Andreas said. "Talisa is a friend of Cory Updale's, and Bart is his brother-in-law."

The two men exchanged a glance, then stood up and bowed. "Freyn's Day," one muttered.

"We were talking about Updale just now," said the other.

"You know him?" Talisa asked.

"We've met," he said guardedly. He was a short, thin man. Talisa found it hard to judge his age. There were lines around his eyes, and his face, though pale, was weathered, but his brown hair had no trace of grey, and his voice was younger than his face. Perhaps he was one of Cory's hill farmers, used to hard outdoor work before eviction from his land forced him into an indoor life in Freyfall. The other man was bigger all over, and younger. His nose looked as though it had been broken once and mended crookedly.

There was an awkward silence.

"Perhaps you could introduce your companions," Bart suggested.

Andreas started. "Yes, of course. This is Ennis," waving to the smaller man. "And this is Wendell." No last names, Talisa noted. In Freya, that was strange. "Please be seated."

There were only four chairs, which left Andreas hovering on his feet near the table.

"You said you've met Cory," Talisa said. She took a deep breath. "I'm trying to find people who will speak on his behalf. People who will convince the queen and her judges to set him free."

Wendell snorted. "As much chance of that as there is of the Freyn-cursed Count of Eastlands giving us back the land he stole from us." His voice rumbled like angry thunder. Andreas swept the room with his eyes, then placed a finger to his lips, despite the fact that there was no one within earshot. Play-acting, Cory would say.

"But he didn't do it. He didn't set the fire."

Wendell and Ennis exchanged another glance. "Did he tell you that?" Ennis asked.

"Yes."

"Did he tell you anything more, such as who *did* set it?"

"No. And he won't. But –"

"Then they won't let him go," Ennis said flatly.

Talisa shook her head. "If enough people – influential people – will only speak for him –"

"Influential people? Like who?"

"There are some wizards my grandparents know."

"Wizards!" Ennis spat. "Little enough they'll do for Updale, or for any of us, for that matter. None of them stirred a finger when we got evicted, did they?"

"No. But –"

"And they won't now. They know who can pay them their fat fees. The only ones who'll help us is us."

"By doing what?" Bart asked coldly.

Wendell leaned forward. "By *showing* them they can't do that to us."

"You think that will get you your land back?" Bart demanded. "Talk like that only gets you into trouble. Look what it did to Cory."

"So what do we do? Nothing?" Ennis challenged.

"Make a new life for yourselves here in Freyfall. Forget the past."

"There are folk from the hills who are *starving* here. What do you think they should do?" Ennis asked.

"Go out and earn a living. I did," Bart snapped.

Ennis's eyes narrowed. "We don't all have wives who have a gift for making beautiful clothes."

Colour surged into Bart's cheeks. "So what else can you do? Whine about how badly you were treated? Set fires?"

Wendell's fist slammed on the table. Ennis stared at Bart, his eyes hot with anger.

"Bart," Talisa said quickly. "There are other alternatives. Cory told you about Master Swanson's plan, remember? He was helping with it. So is Andreas, and I'm sure Ennis and Wendell are too. There *are* ways to change things."

"Yes," Andreas said emphatically. The other two said nothing.

"It won't work."

"You can't know that," Talisa protested.

Bart just shook his head. No one spoke. The silence was heavy with hostility. And hopelessness? No! Talisa gripped the table so tightly that the edge dug into her fingers.

Ennis got to his feet. "We'd better go."

"I'll show you out," Andreas said. The three men left.

"I'm sorry," Bart said after a couple of minutes.

Talisa glanced at him, then away. She said nothing.

Andreas returned. "Well," he said brightly, then stopped. "Well," he tried again. "I imagine Master Swanson will be home soon. While we wait, would you like me to play for you?"

"Please," Talisa murmured.

His touch on the lute was sure, his voice deep and true. His songs were of street beggars and homeless children. Cory would have approved.

Andreas was in the middle of his fourth song when the door opened and quick footsteps came down the hall. A moment later, a tall, spare man with dark hair and eyes and prominent cheekbones appeared in the doorway.

Talisa rose. "Master Swanson, I don't know whether you remember me. My name is Talisa Thatcher, and I'm a friend of Cory's."

"Of course I remember you." He bowed.

"And this is Bart Berrymore, Cory's brother-in-law. Bart, this is Master Alain Swanson."

Master Swanson moved into the room and shook Bart's hand. "Freyn's Day, Master Berrymore. Cory spoke of you often."

Bart's mouth twisted. "Not too favourably, I'm sure."

"On the contrary, though he did say you often disagreed."

Bart's eyes dropped. "Yes."

"You are here, I imagine, because of Cory."

"Yes." Talisa took a breath, tried to speak clearly, concisely. "They're taking him to Freybourg today. I don't know when his trial will be, but I think soon. He didn't set the fire, but he won't say who did."

Alain Swanson nodded. He knew.

"I'm hoping enough people will speak on his behalf that he'll be set free." Talisa took another breath. "Will you go to Freybourg? Will you – well, not speak, but sing? Sing one of your songs that shows what it's like for those who lost their land. Will you help Cory?" Despite her best efforts, her voice trembled on the final words.

He frowned. "I would love to help him. But even before I turned my back on the Guild, I was not exactly influential. And now..." He shook his head.

"But your songs have power. I've heard them."

He smiled faintly. "I am happy that you found them so. Unfortunately, few people do."

She remembered Lem's and Shep's reactions to his performance at The Laughing Lute, remembered Master Coyne's scathing words about Alain Swanson and his songs. But she would not give up.

"Won't you *try*?"

He was silent for a moment, then sighed. "I don't think it will work, but yes. I will try, as long as the trial isn't held within the next two weeks. But they may not allow me to speak, much less sing, at the trial."

She ignored his last comment. "Why won't you speak if it's held in the next two weeks?"

He glanced at Bart and said nothing.

"Don't worry," Bart said. "I gather your march on Freybourg will happen within that time. I don't agree with your plan, but I won't inform on you."

A small smile touched the other man's lips. "Thank you. I don't think the army will try to stop us once we are all gathered and on our way to Freybourg. We are, after all, peaceful people. None of us will have arms. But it is possible, if they hear about it beforehand, that they may decide the best course is to stop us before we start."

"And you really think you'll gain something by this?"

Alain Swanson regarded Bart soberly. "You don't?"

Bart shook his head. "I'm not that naive. The Count of Eastlands is not going to give us back our land and nobody, including Queen Elira, is going to make him."

"Probably not," Alain Swanson agreed. "But conditions can be improved. Even before so many hill farmers arrived, this city – and other towns and cities in Freya – had homeless and destitute people. The evictions made folk swarm to the cities, looking for work – and finding none. Now everywhere I look I see people in need. All too often, they die, from hunger, from cold, from disease. The queen and her court must *see* that they exist, and that something must be done to help them."

"There'll always be those who are poor. It's inevitable," Bart objected.

"No, it's not," Talisa said.

Both men turned to look at her.

"We don't allow people to suffer like that in Uglessia."

Bart raised his eyebrows. "I thought everyone in Uglessia was poor."

She met his eyes. "No one at home has much – certainly not the riches I've seen in Freya. If it's a year of little rain, everyone goes hungry. But if one person has food or shelter and another is lacking, then the food and shelter are shared."

"It is a fine land you come from," Alain said softly.

Talisa felt a glow of pride. "Yes." But she could not let herself be diverted. "I hope it won't, but if Cory's trial takes place in the next two weeks, couldn't you come anyway?"

He was silent for a long time. "If I can, I will," he said at last. "But I cannot let anything interfere with this march. I'm sorry."

Talisa looked down. There was a crack in the floor by her feet. "I understand." And she did. She *did*. But oh, it hurt.

"What about you?" Alain asked. "You spoke of my singing. But you also are a singer, and a fine one. You were chosen as one of the five best musicians in three lands. Have you thought of your ability to sway the judges by your songs?"

"Yes." But she'd hoped there'd be others there to help.

"Cory told me your grandparents are Alaric and Redelle Thatcher, well known both for their past deeds and their present role as wizards and spokespeople for your land. You might do well to ask for an audience with Queen Elira, even before the trial."

"I'm going to ride to Freybourg this afternoon and ask for one."

He smiled. "Good."

"*Will* she see me?" It had never occurred to Talisa, making her plans in Uglessia, that the queen would refuse. But so many things had failed already.

"I don't know," he answered truthfully. "You can try."

"Yes. Thank you," Talisa said, though she wished he'd been less honest and more hopeful.

"How is Cory?" Alain asked.

"Well enough, except for being locked up in a small dark cell," Bart said. "He hasn't been badly treated."

"And how is he feeling? Inside himself?"

"He's...peaceful," Bart answered.

Alain raised surprised eyebrows. "Peaceful? Why is that?"

"He gave himself up. The Freyan soldiers were on the point of leaving Uglessia without him." Talisa stopped. Swallowed. "If they had, they would have returned to Freya with reports of Uglessians who refused to cooperate. Freyan wizards might have shifted the winds to their old pattern. Refused to send us rain. Cory knew that, so..." She stopped again. Swallowed again. "He told me he turned himself in to prevent that." She didn't speak of the other things Cory had said the night he was arrested: how he had found peace, returning to the hills, how he had found joy loving her. Those words belonged to Cory and her.

The room was silent. The candle on the table spluttered.

"We should go," Bart said.

"Yes," Talisa agreed. But she had one more question to ask. "I was wondering whether you might know anything about where Garth Spellman is. He's the boy who came with me to your house the night Cory fled. I thought perhaps he might have come back. He was very interested in your songs."

"He did come back. Many times. In fact, he had begun to help me in spreading the word about the march. But I haven't seen him for over a month now. I suppose he decided the work wasn't really for him." Alain shrugged, but it didn't hide the bitter edge that had been in his voice. He glanced over at Andreas, who was leaning against a wall. "You haven't seen him lately, have you?"

"No," Andreas said promptly. It was the first time he had spoken since Master Swanson entered. Talisa had almost forgotten he was there.

The musician escorted them to the door. "May Freyn be with you in your endeavours. I'll help if I can."

Neither Bart nor Talisa spoke till they had left the river and the dingy, decrepit buildings behind them. Then Bart said, "I think he means well, but his plan has as much chance of succeeding as a sheep has of laying eggs."

Talisa said nothing. They walked on.

A few blocks later, he tried again. "At least his plan is peaceful. Even so, people might get hurt." Still she said nothing.

Bart glanced at her. "Look, I'm sorry if what I said upsets you. I know it goes against everything Cory believes. But I have to say it as I see it."

Talisa stopped. "You say Master Swanson's plan won't work. Ennis says mine to save Cory won't work. What do you want to *do?* Nothing? Well, I won't. I won't give up without even trying. Nor will Alain Swanson. If no one even *tries,* how can anything be changed?" Her voice rose higher and higher, finally cracking, like a singer trying for a top note and failing. A woman passing by gave them a startled glance and hurried on.

Bart stared at Talisa for a moment, then looked away. "Sorry," he muttered. After another moment, he said, "Maybe you're right. It's just... Sometimes I think I don't dare hope."

They stood there. A tired looking horse dragged a heavy cart down the road. A man passed by on the other side. Finally Bart asked, "Will you come for lunch? A late lunch it will be," he added, glancing at the sky. "Rina would love to see you."

Talisa hesitated, then shook her head. "And I'd love to see her. But I want to reach Freybourg today. If I'm to have an audience with Queen Elira, the sooner I ask for one, the better."

GALIA

THE REFECTORY WAS NOISY AS USUAL. GALIA paused in the doorway, then selected a chair as far away from any of the other students as possible. Today was one of those days when she felt that coming up with the right Freyan words would be as exhausting as rowing home after being becalmed far out at sea.

She was concentrating on her porridge when a voice said, "May I sit here?" Looking up, she saw the blue-eyed wizard she had met two days ago, one of the men who had returned from Uglessia. What was his name? She couldn't remember.

"Yes, certainly."

He smiled and sat down opposite her. She bent her head back over her bowl.

"I understand you are blessed with the gift of weather magic."

She looked up and nodded.

"Master Clark says you have tried to explain your gift to him, but he has difficulty understanding."

"It is a different kind of magic. I find it hard to learn Freyan spells."

His eyebrows rose. "You do? I would have thought our magic would seem almost ridiculously simple to someone who has so much more power than we do."

"No," she muttered.

"Hmm." He studied her for a moment, his eyes intent on her face. She took his silence as a sign that she could resume eating without being rude.

"It's possible that I could understand what Master Clark could not," he said. She glanced up again. He was leaning towards her. "Will you teach me?"

She hesitated.

His voice hardened. "That *is* why you came to Freya, is it not? To share your knowledge with Freyan wizards?"

She supposed it was. But this man made her skin prick, the way it did when a storm was brooding.

His eyes were blue wells you could disappear into if you weren't careful. "Will you do it?"

To pause any longer would be an insult. "Yes."

He smiled. "Good girl." She wondered if he would have patted her head approvingly if she'd been closer. "Perhaps I can help you understand Freyan magic in return."

"Perhaps." She was doubtful.

"Shall we start today?"

"I have classes," she said quickly.

"Of course you do. I meant after that."

She couldn't think of a reason to say no. She opened her mouth to give a reluctant assent.

"Melton! There you are." The other Freyan who had been in Uglessia plumped himself down beside Galia.

Annoyance crossed the blue-eyed wizard's face. "I was in the middle of a conversation, Leonard." His voice was as cold as ocean water.

The other man ignored his tone. He gave Galia a quick, apologetic smile. "Updale was brought to Freybourg yesterday. We're both called on to testify against him at his trial."

"Well, well," the younger wizard said softly. A small smile tugged at his lips.

"Captain Meadows, who's in charge of gathering evidence, wants to talk to us. He sent a messenger asking us to meet him at the Officers' Mess this morning."

"Of course." The wizard rose. "My apologies, Mistress Soradotter, but this is important. I shall seek you out later." He bowed, then strode away. The older man gave Galia another quick smile before hurrying after him.

Galia watched them leave. Did their conversation have anything to do with the young prisoner she had seen yesterday? She frowned, then finished her porridge.

"Galia." A hand touched her arm. She turned to find Raven standing beside her. "After classes today, I plan to visit the man whose head Thannis cracked open. Would you care to come with me?"

"Yes," Galia said promptly.

"Good. Meet me at the gate after your last class."

Galia was smiling as she walked out of the refectory. Not only would she get a chance to be alone with one of her own kind for a while, she would also have a good excuse to be out of the way when the blue-eyed wizard came looking for her.

Galia's eyes widened as Raven stopped in front of a house five stories high and a block long. "The injured man lives here?"

"So I was told." Raven walked up to the door as confidently as though he were approaching the circle house on Atua. Galia trailed a couple of paces behind.

The grey stones around the door were carved with intricate designs. The door looked thicker than many tree trunks, and Galia was sure someone must spend an hour a day polishing the knocker to make it so bright.

The door was opened by a man who looked as puffed up as a sail billowing in the wind. Perhaps owning such a house would make anyone swell up.

"Yes?"

"I am here to see the injured man," Raven said.

The owner's eyes narrowed. "Who?"

"The man whose head was hurt two days ago. I'm sorry, I don't know his name."

The man puffed up even more. "And who are you to ask to see him?"

"I healed him," Raven said simply.

The other's voice was frosty. "Yet you do not even know his name? Master Casper has no need for the likes of you. The count's healer has tended to him most devotedly."

"I'm happy to hear that. However, I would still like to see him, if only for a minute, to assure myself his wound is healing properly."

The man confronting them was tall. Now he drew himself up even higher so that he could look down on Raven. "If your intention is to ingratiate yourself with the Count of Eastlands, your efforts will be fruitless. Be off with you before I summon the footmen to escort you forcibly from these premises."

Galia didn't know what all his words meant, but she understood his tone all too well. "If it had not been for Raven, that man would have died. You have no right to speak to him like that!" Her voice rang out, loud with outrage.

He stared at her as though she were a beetle that had just crawled out from under a log. Then his attention returned to Raven. "I will count to three. Then I will call the footmen. One –"

"Wait, Hall," someone called. A moment later, a young man – or a boy, for he only looked a couple of years older than Galia – appeared in the doorway. Galia recognized him immediately. It was the youth who had come to stand beside her as she gazed down at the bleeding head wound.

He recognized her too. "I thought I knew that voice." Then he saw Raven. A broad smile burst into bloom on his face. "The healer! Have you come to see my brother? Come in."

The puffed-up man stiffened. "But, Master Mallory –"

"It's all right, Hall. This is the Islandian healer who came to our rescue. Without him, Casper might have died. Even

Master Wellman acknowledges that. Come with me," he told Raven and Galia. "I'll take you to Casper's room."

He led them down a long hall, then up a broad flight of marble stairs. Galia glanced over her shoulder once to see Master Hall staring after them, as surprised as if a strong undertow had tugged him off his feet. Galia was almost as surprised. She had assumed that the man owned this house, yet the boy – Mallory – had talked to him the way the masters at the college talked to the servants. And this house...The stairs were so polished she kept looking down to see if she could see her face in them. She glanced up, way up, and gasped in wonder. The ceiling displayed a painting of men and women dressed in foamy, cascading lace, seated on impossibly green grass underneath arching willows, eating, drinking, and laughing. Galia climbed the rest of that flight, then another, with her head tilted upwards.

At the second landing, they left the polished marble and walked on golden carpet so soft that Galia felt as though she were walking on goosedown pillows. She kept looking at her feet to make sure she wasn't. Halfway down the hall, Mallory put his hand on a gleaming doorknob and ushered them inside.

As she entered, Galia heard a cross male voice. "I see no reason why I can't get up. I'm perfectly well."

"Master Wellman –"

"Hang Master Wellman! I don't even have a headache, for Freyn's sake."

The bedchamber – for it was obviously that, even though it was almost as large as Galia's whole house on Rork – held a massive curtained bed. The cross voice came from a young man a few years older than Mallory who lay there, his bandaged head resting on a pillow. Beside the bed was a chair with pale blue satin lining. Galia gaped at the woman sitting in it until she remembered that it wasn't good manners to stare. But it was hard not to, for the woman's hair – could hair really be that bright a yellow? – was piled in such elaborate waves on top of her head that Galia wondered they didn't come cascading down.

"Mother, this is the Islandian healer who saved Casper's life, and the girl who sent him to our aid," Mallory said.

The woman's head turned. She rose in a flutter of skirts, and Galia gawked again at the richness of lavender silk and creamy lace.

"Ah, Master..."

"Katirason. Raven Katirason."

"Master Katirason, I am glad indeed to meet you. Mallory told me how you saved my older son's life with your skill, and Master Wellman has confirmed that Casper's wound was indeed of a serious nature. I was sorry that you left before I had a chance to meet you and thank you properly." The woman's voice was a low contralto, her smile a gleam of sunlight. Galia found it hard to believe she was old enough to be Mallory's mother, much less Casper's.

"You are most welcome," Raven said. "I am happy that I was able to help."

"My husband the count is not at home, but if you will wait, I am sure he will return presently. He will be as pleased to meet you as I am, I am sure, and as eager to reward you as you deserve."

"No reward is needed."

"Nonsense." There was a ripple of laughter. "Of course there must be a reward."

"That is kind, Mistress Eastlands, but –"

The slender body in the lavender gown stiffened. The mouth hardened. For the first time, Galia saw lines in the creamy skin. Perhaps this woman *was* old enough to be Casper's mother after all. "Not *Mistress* Eastlands. The *Countess* of Eastlands."

Raven gave a slight bow. "My apologies. In Islandia, there are no such titles. We are used to a simpler life."

"Indeed."

"I came to assure myself that your son is fully recovered. May I do so?"

The countess hesitated. Was she uncertain whether she could trust someone who did not know how to address her properly? Then she inclined her head. "Of course."

"After you assure yourself that I am recovered, perhaps you could assure my mother that I'm perfectly able to get up," the patient said. He still sounded cross. Raven glanced at him but made no reply. His face went blank, his body still. Galia knew he was extending gentle fingers of thought and inner perception to examine the injury. The woman opened her mouth, then looked at Raven's face and closed it again.

After a couple of minutes, Raven relaxed. "You are indeed doing very well."

Casper sent his mother a triumphant glance. "Then I *can* get up."

She frowned. "Master Wellman said you must stay in bed until you're perfectly healed."

"But I *am* healed." Casper sounded as frustrated as a small child denied a treat.

"You are," Raven agreed. "But it was a grievous wound. For today – and perhaps tomorrow – you might be better off in bed. If that becomes too irksome, you could walk around this room a few times, or sit in a chair."

Both mother and son looked satisfied at this.

"I am *so* grateful," the countess said, looking up at Raven through long-lashed eyes that were the colour of rain-washed skies. Her gaze brushed over Galia, then returned to Raven. *As though I'm a dog tagging along at its master's heels,* Galia thought. "Have you heard what will be done with the ruffian who attacked my son?"

Galia stiffened. Raven shot her a warning glance before answering the countess. "He's in prison at the moment."

"I know that. I trust he will stay there for a long, long time. My husband and I will try to ensure that he does. He's far too dangerous to be let loose."

"He is not dangerous! If people were not rude, he would not fight them."

The countess looked at Galia as if she really saw her this time. "I'm sorry if this young man is a friend of yours. But I'm afraid I am right. He is dangerous. He nearly killed my son, who had done nothing to injure him."

"Denys *was* being deliberately nasty, Mama," Mallory said. Galia looked at him gratefully.

"I have heard the story, thank you, Mallory. Even if

Denys inadvertently said something to ruffle the Uglessian's feathers, there was no reason for him to hurt anyone. Not Denys. Certainly not my son." The woman's eyes were now the colour of frozen water.

"There were five of them and only one of him." Galia ignored Raven's frown. "They were fighting him too."

"Naturally they had to defend themselves. That —"

"And they all laughed when the blue-coat said what he did."

Mallory's face went tomato red. The countess looked as though an ugly — and possibly poisonous — spider had crawled onto the cream-coloured rug. Casper was frowning. Raven glanced at him thoughtfully. "Do you remember what happened before and during the fight?"

There was a moment's hesitation before Casper said, "No."

"Is there anything else you have trouble remembering?"

"No." There was no hesitation this time.

Raven nodded. "Don't worry. It frequently happens that people forget what happened immediately before they suffer a head injury. As long as you remember everything else, it doesn't matter."

The young man's face eased. He's been fretting about this, Galia thought. How did Raven know? It was one of the things that made him such a good healer.

The countess had seen her son's face change too. She smiled at Raven. "Again, my thanks, healer. Mallory, please escort our guests to the door."

Galia was too angry — and worried — to gaze upwards as she followed Mallory down the polished stairs. When they reached the bottom, Mallory stopped and turned to her.

"I'm sorry I laughed. I didn't mean...I don't even *like* Denys, but when he sneers like that and expects you to laugh with him...Well, I usually do, even if I don't feel good about it afterwards." His face was still tinged with red and he was having trouble meeting Galia's eyes. He did, though. His were the same colour as his mother's.

Galia smiled. Mallory was nice. Then her smile faded. "Will your mother really try to keep Thannis in prison for a long time?"

"She might. She's very angry."

"Will she..." Galia hunted for the right word. "Success? No. Succeed?"

He hesitated, then shrugged. "Possibly."

Possibly – or probably? The Countess of Eastlands did not look like someone who was used to being opposed. Something hard and lumpish lodged in Galia's stomach.

Mallory smiled at her. "Don't look so bleak. I'll work on her – or, rather, I'll work on Casper to persuade her and Father. She's so happy Casper's still alive that she'll do as he wants, I'm sure."

"And can you persuade your brother?" Raven asked.

"Oh yes. Casper goes along with Denys, but I don't think he's always comfortable with what Denys says and does either. Anyway, he owes me a favour. After all, I let you in and you persuaded Mama it was all right for him to get up." He grinned. "Don't worry."

The hard lump had dissolved. "Thank you."

Mallory opened the massive door. Behind him, Galia caught a glimpse of the man who had so reluctantly let them in. He was hovering in the background. Making sure they left, Galia thought.

When they reached the street, Galia looked back. Mallory still stood in the doorway, watching them go. She waved. He waved back.

CAT

"You're still up. I thought you would have retired." Konrad Spellman placed his cloak on the stand in the hall.

Annette descended the stairs. Cat remained on the shadowy landing above. "No. I hoped you'd return tonight. Thank you for doing so." Her voice trembled ever so slightly.

"You said it was important. Nothing wrong, I trust."

Annette hesitated. "I'm not sure," she said finally. "I... But before I tell you, have you had any dinner?"

"I have, thank you. But a cup of kala would be welcome. The days may be warm, but the nights retain their winter chill."

Annette nodded. Cat climbed down the stairs. Konrad's eyes widened.

"Catrina!"

"Freyn's Evening, sir," she murmured, and bobbed a quick curtsy. Her initial fear of this sharp-eyed, sharp-tongued wizard had vanished, but she still felt like a young and awkward calf in his presence.

"I am delighted to see you again, Catrina. Welcome to my house." He stood back to let her precede him. In silence, the three walked down the long hall to the kitchen at the back.

Annette lit two candles, stirred the embers in the fireplace, and placed a kettle over them. Konrad seated himself at the wooden table. Cat sat opposite him. She watched Annette, conscious all the time of Konrad's eyes on her face.

Annette placed mugs in front of Cat and her father-in-law, then sat beside Cat, holding her own mug. "Cat came here yesterday, looking for Garth."

The lines around the man's mouth deepened. "She won't find him here."

"No. But the fact that she came – and that she hasn't heard from him for over a month now – made me wonder. *Why* hasn't he written?"

"Much as it shames me to say it, I'm afraid my grandson lacks courtesy. My apologies on his behalf, Catrina."

"*No!* No," Annette repeated more gently. "I know you were angry when Garth left home without a word. But *think*. To leave home that way was not like him. To abandon his studies with Master Coyne was even more unlike him. But to abandon Cat without a word... He would not do that. Not if he had a choice."

Konrad glanced at Cat, frowning, then back at his daughter-in-law. "What are you suggesting, Annette?" His kala sat in front of him, untasted.

"I think..." Annette took a deep breath. "I think it is time you used a finding spell."

There was a long silence. Unspoken words, unvoiced fears, trembled in the air. Finally, the wizard nodded. "Yes."

Cat had thought he would go to his study, but he didn't. He didn't do anything, in fact, except speak the words of the spell in a low voice, then gaze into the empty air before him. Gradually, his face went blank.

Cat waited. And waited. She should drink her kala. But the noise of raising her mug, putting it down, swallowing, would intrude on the silence. Her hand hurt. She looked down and saw that it was clenched so tightly around the handle of the mug that it was a wonder the handle didn't break.

It shouldn't take this long for Konrad to find Garth. Not when he knew him so well. Not when he was one of the most powerful wizards in Freya.

His face no longer looked blank. His brows were drawn in a fierce frown.

Why was it taking so long?

She closed her eyes tightly, saw Garth's face at Midwinter, a fat snowflake dabbed on his nose. Heard his voice, singing his song of an old street woman.

Find him. Find him.

The wizard's fist banged on the table. Cat's eyes flew open. At sight of Konrad's face, something cold and hard blocked her throat.

"What...?" Annette whispered.

"No, no. Don't look like that. He's not dead. The impression I got of him was very faint. At first I thought that might be because he was asleep, and when I finally caught a brief glimpse of him, I realized I was right."

"Then you *did* see him. You know where he is," Cat breathed.

The wizard shook his head. "No. All I could catch was a smudged image of Garth lying on a mat in a small room. Nothing else."

Annette cleared her throat. "You'll see more in the morning, when he's awake."

Konrad hesitated. "I'll try. I will certainly try. But... Annette, I'm sorry. I should have listened to you and used a finding spell earlier. I should have had more faith in my grandson." His voice was heavy, his forehead deeply lined. "I don't know whether I'll be able to discover Garth's whereabouts when he wakes. I should have been able to find out more, you see, even when he was sleeping. But his mind was too..." Konrad stopped, his mouth tightening into a thin line, then concluded harshly. "His mind was too hazy. Too confused. Either he is under some spell, or he is drugged. Heavily drugged."

AT HOME, wild crocuses and daisies would be dotting the fields. There were no flowers in the garden at the back of the Spellmans' house, but the apple tree in the corner still had some blossoms, and there was grass. Cat sat down on it and rubbed her face. Her eyes felt hot. Her head ached. If she had slept at all last night, she wasn't aware of it.

She didn't think either of the Spellmans had slept either.

Annette's face had been drawn with fatigue this morning, and Konrad had looked so grim that even the cheerful maid had lost her smile and tiptoed around the room as she served breakfast. At the conclusion of the meal, the wizard had retreated to his study, leaving Cat and Annette in the dining room staring at the half-eaten food on their plates.

When he'd returned, Konrad had looked even grimmer. "Nothing more, I'm afraid. He's awake, but his mind is very unclear."

Cat had swallowed, but the hard lump in her throat hadn't dissolved.

"What now?" Annette's cup had rattled when she'd put it on its saucer.

"I'm going to the authorities. I want every soldier in Freyfall out looking for him."

"Garth would hate that." Cat had scarcely recognised her own voice as she spoke.

"Probably. But I can't think of anything else to do. Can you?"

After a moment, she'd shaken her head.

Now, Cat scowled down at the grass. She should have told the Spellmans about Master Swanson. About how Garth had helped Cory Updale escape, and later returned to the musician's house.

Garth's disappearance might have nothing to do with Master Swanson. Garth would hate it if the man got into trouble because of him.

But what if Master Swanson *did* know something?

Mel had said he would ask Andreas Wells where he lived

147

the next time he saw him. Once he did that, she could go to the musician, ask him what he knew.

But Andreas Wells might not return to The Laughing Lute for days. Weeks.

Garth might hate it, but she had no choice. As soon as Konrad returned, she would tell him about Alain Swanson. She rose and walked towards the house.

With her hand on the doorknob, she stopped.

Talisa Thatcher. The Uglessian was in Freyfall. And she had been at Master Swanson's house, like Garth, the night Cory fled. She would know where it was. And Talisa had also been at the weaver's stall, talking with its owner, who was Cory Updale's brother-in-law.

She would go to the stall and ask for Talisa. If she had no luck...Well, then she *would* tell Konrad Spellman all she knew.

THE STALL WAS UNSHUTTERED. Cat breathed a sigh of relief. She had worried, all the long walk from Gotham Street, that she would arrive only to find it closed.

Two plump, middle-aged women who bore a strong resemblance to each other stood in front of the stall. Cat waited for them to go. They took their time, fingering each item, holding blouses and skirts and dresses against themselves to see whether they fit, asking the price of everything and shaking their heads at the answers.

The street was filled with smells of meat pies, cooking sausage, frying onions. Despite the fear gnawing at her stomach, Cat sniffed hungrily. It was well past noon.

Finally the women wandered off, having examined all the clothes and bought none. The stall owner, a tall man in his early twenties with dark eyes and hair, glared after them, then turned to straighten the goods on the counter. Cat waited till he finished before approaching him.

"Excuse me."

"Freyn's Day, Mistress. What can I do for you?"

"Could you tell me where to find Talisa Thatcher?"

The man's eyebrows rose. "Talisa?"

"Yes. She's a friend of mine." That wasn't quite true. Not true at all, in fact. Talisa wouldn't even recognize her if they met, having only seen her as a cat. But they *were* both friends of Garth's.

His face was wary. "What makes you think I know her?"

"He told me." She jerked her head towards the stall to his right. "I came here yesterday, looking for something for a baby, and he said you'd left with a red-haired Uglessian girl. That sounded like Talisa." And, of course, there was the connection with Cory Updale. But she didn't mention that.

'Yes," he said slowly. "I did leave with her."

"Do you know where she is now?"

"In Freybourg."

"Oh."

He must have heard the dismay in her voice. "I'm sorry."

"Thank you." She started to leave.

"You said you came yesterday looking for baby clothes. There's plenty here."

She was not in the mood for shopping. Still, she *should* go home with a gift for her sister or brother to be.

There was a wealth of items to choose from, not only beautifully woven clothes but also small wooden carvings that told stories in every line and curve. They wouldn't do for a baby, though. She left them reluctantly to inspect the clothes. A woman, then a man, came up to the stall. The woman left, carrying a skirt. Cat finally settled on a baby's gown the colour of new spring leaves. It was soft, and held a picture of a lamb that looked just like the ones that grazed in the meadows at home.

"How much is this, please?"

"Eighty-five coppers."

She should bargain, Cat knew, but she lacked the skill. She took a silver coin from the purse at her belt. As she was pocketing the change she asked, on impulse, "Would you happen to know where a musician named Master Swanson lives?"

The dark brows rose again. "I do, as a matter of fact. Why do you want to know?"

"I... I'm looking for a friend, and I think Master Swanson might know where he is."

"Another friend?"

Was there a trace of mockery in his voice? Of disbelief? Cat lifted her chin. "Yes. His name is Garth Spellman. He's a friend of Talisa's too."

"Yes," he agreed. "Talisa asked about him yesterday, but I'm afraid Master Swanson said he hadn't seen him for some time."

As a child, Cat had sometimes chased after bubbles, only to have them burst before she could reach them. It was like that now.

The man who had been inspecting the objects on the counter coughed. The stall owner – what had his neighbour called him? Berrymore, wasn't it? – turned to him.

"How much are you asking for this?" The man held up a carving of a small dog, its head cocked to one side.

"One silver coin."

"Too much."

The bargaining began, but Cat didn't hear it. When the customer walked away, carving in hand, she asked, "Would you tell me where Master Swanson lives? I know you told me... It's not that I don't believe you. But I want to ask him myself. Maybe he knows something that will lead me to Garth."

Master Berrymore shook his head. "Another person who refuses to give up hope," he muttered. But he gave her the directions. She listened intently, then thanked him and left.

It was midafternoon by the time Cat stood facing a narrow house that leaned against its neighbour, as though years of neglect had left it too weary to stand erect.

She was tired, and hot, and hungry. She should have stopped to buy a meat pie before starting her journey. She had seen few food vendors on her way, and the taverns she had passed had made her want to hurry by, not go in for something to eat.

The house looked deserted. Even if Master Swanson were home, what help could he give her? Master Berrymore had already told her the musician didn't know where Garth was.

Well, she was here now. She knocked.

After a moment, the door was opened by a tall, dark-haired man with winged eyebrows and jutting cheekbones.

"Master Swanson?"

"Yes. What can I do for you?"

"It's about Garth."

He frowned. "I'm afraid I can't help you. I haven't seen him for a month now. More."

Cat swallowed. "No one has."

His eyebrows shot up. "No one?"

"No. May I come in? I know you said you can't help, but...but *please*." Her voice wobbled.

"Yes, of course." He stepped aside.

With the door closed, the only light came from a candle at the back of the building. Cat followed the man down a dark hall and into a sparsely furnished room.

"Please sit down Mistress..."

"Ashdale. Catrina Ashdale. Everyone calls me Cat."

He smiled. "Yes. Garth's spoken of you. Would you care for a cup of kala, Mistress Ashdale?"

"Yes, please." Even more than kala, Cat wanted food. Her eyes were drawn to a loaf of bread and chunk of cheese on the table. Master Swanson must have followed her gaze, for he cut some of both and placed them on a plate in front of her.

"Thank you." Cat ate greedily. The musician sipped his kala and waited. Hunger satisfied, Cat leaned back and sighed. "Thank you," she said again.

"You are most welcome. Now, what is this about Garth? No one has seen him for over a month?"

"No. His mother and grandfather would have looked for him, but he sent a note — at least, it *looks* like his note — saying he was leaving home and abandoning his apprenticeship. It wasn't until two days ago that his mother was convinced something must have happened to him. Last night Master Spellman cast a finding spell."

"And he still can't be found? Konrad Spellman is reputed to be one of the best wizards in Freya."

"He is. And he did see Garth. At least we know that Garth is alive." Cat stopped and took a breath, trying to keep her voice steady. "But Master Spellman saw so little. Not enough to know where Garth *is*. He thinks Garth is either under a spell or drugged."

The musician was silent.

"So I came here because Garth told me that he and Talisa Thatcher found Cory Updale here and helped him escape, and that he came back later and was helping you. He told me in secret," she added.

"And you haven't told anyone? Not even now?"

"No."

He smiled faintly. "Good." His smile faded. "I am angry at myself for misjudging him so. When he failed to show up, I thought he had merely lost interest."

She couldn't blame him. She, too, had thought Garth had lost interest. "Is there anything you know that will help find him?"

He regarded her, frowning.

"From what Master Spellman saw, it sounds as though someone must be keeping Garth captive," she said. "I can't think *why* – unless it has something to do with what he was doing for you."

"I see," he said slowly. "Have you thought... But no. If his captors had wanted money, they would have contacted the Spellman family immediately. But I cannot see how his involvement with me could lead to his disappearance." He was silent, then asked, "Did Garth tell you what we are trying to do?"

"A little. Not much."

"Then I think you should know more, though I must ask you to keep it quiet."

She nodded.

As Master Swanson talked, Cat remembered last spring, when she had wandered the streets of Freyfall, looking for her father, looking for work. Hunger had gnawed and growled in her belly. Doorways had offered the only refuge from the wind and rain that dug cold fingers into her bones. To help others whose constant companions were hunger and cold...

But she couldn't dwell on that now. She leaned forward.

"It *must* be because of this that Garth was taken and held. There's no other reason. No other enemies."

"The only enemies of our cause are the army and the court. Garth, as the grandson of a wealthy and respected wizard, would not be their first target. And if he were, they would have put him in prison, not hidden him away."

He was right. Cat closed her eyes, then opened them again. Cobwebs hung from the ceiling. Dustballs lurked in corners. Her grandmother would be horrified.

"What about the man who evicted all his tenants? He might want to stop you."

Master Swanson smiled. "I think the Count of Eastlands would use other methods. All he would have to do, I'm afraid, is go to the authorities."

Cat was silent.

The musician rubbed his forehead. "I will do anything I can to help Garth. But I don't see how my activities could have endangered him."

Bread crumbs had fallen off her plate onto the table. Cat picked them up, one by one, and put them back.

"I'm sorry."

She didn't look up. "It's not your fault."

"I'll ask my apprentice if he knows anything. He and Garth frequently went together to speak to individuals and groups about the march, especially when Garth first started helping. Andreas doesn't know where Garth is either, but maybe he noticed something while they were together."

"Thank you." Even the tiniest whisper of hope helped. "I should go." She rose.

Master Swanson escorted her back down the dark hall and opened the door. Bright afternoon sunlight made Cat squint.

"May Freyn smile upon your search. If I hear anything at all, I will send you word. You're staying with the Spellmans?"

"Yes." She started to go, then turned back. "And may Freyn smile upon your plan. It deserves to work. I pray that it will."

He bowed. "I pray that too."

TALISA

SHE'D BEEN HERE FOUR DAYS. IT FELT LIKE forever.

Talisa sighed and shifted her weight on the hard, elegant chair. Her buttocks hurt from sitting so long. Oh, to pace the room, or stand staring out the long windows. But that would make the others stare at her even more than they already did. There was only one other woman in the antechamber, and certainly no other Uglessian. She stood out like a white crow in a flock of black feathers. Nor did the room, with its deep soft rugs, embroidered chairs, and polished, three-legged tables, invite pacing.

She shifted again and went over, for the thousandth time, what she would say when she saw Queen Elira.

If she saw Queen Elira. There was no guarantee of that. She had told the chamberlain who her grandparents were, hoping their names would win her an audience. He had asked if she was here on official business for Uglessia.

Perhaps it was not too late to change her mind and tell him she was.

No. If she brought Uglessia into her fight for Cory's life, she might endanger her country's relationship with Freya. She would not throw away Cory's sacrifice as though it were a meaningless gift.

Four days of waiting, while Cory's trial drew ever closer. Four days of watching courtiers come and go. Some bustled into the antechamber, drunk on their own importance, then bustled out again. Others wandered in casually, as though the room and its occupants were only one more flower on which to rest their butterfly wings. Talisa wasn't deceived. They were there because they wished to see Queen Elira badly. But not as badly as she did, she was sure. Nobody's need could be as great.

When would her name be called?

The door to the corridor opened and let in a man dressed in amber satin.

"Eastlands!" called a man two seats from Talisa. He raised a plump hand, laden with rings, to draw the other's attention.

Talisa stared at the newcomer. Eastlands. The landowner who had come, riding a tall black stallion and surrounded by soldiers, to tell his tenants they had one day to take themselves and their possessions off his property. He didn't look evil. He was a sandy-haired, middle-aged man with no outstanding features. Someone who might have melted into the crowd had it not been for the air he wore as easily as he wore his clothes, that said he owned the world and everything in it.

"What are you doing here?" the seated man asked.

"Queen Elira requested my presence."

"Oh. Well, when you see her, put in a word for me, won't you? I've been waiting to see her for days now."

The Count of Eastlands said nothing.

The other man squinted up at him. "How's your son? Recovered, I hope."

"He's been up and about for a couple of days now. Valeria frets, but he seems well enough to me."

"I'm happy to hear it. From what I've been told, he received a very nasty crack on the head. Might not have lived if it hadn't been for that Islandian healer who's staying at the college."

The count frowned. "Possibly not. The man *is* a good healer. Arrogant, though. I sent him a purse most men would grovel for, and what does he do but send it back with his thanks, as though money meant nothing to him."

Talisa bent her head to hide a smile.

"Is the Uglessian who injured Casper still in prison?"

Talisa's head jerked up. Uglessian?

"Yes, and will stay there for as long as I can manage. He's a dangerous young man. My sons – even Valeria, for some reason – may argue that he's been punished enough, but I intend to make sure he either remains in prison or is returned to Uglessia, where he belongs."

A servant dressed in blue-and-silver livery approached him and bowed. "Queen Elira is ready to see you, My Lord."

"Very well. Freyn's Day, Rivers."

A roomful of eyes watched the Count of Eastlands follow the servant through the end door. Then one man shrugged and stood up. Others rose as well. Talisa glanced at the late afternoon light slanting in through the windows and trailed them from the room. Queen Elira would see no one else today.

There might be a number of Uglessians living in Freybourg. But there were two she knew for certain were here, studying at the college. And one was big, and hot-tempered, and could be considered dangerous. Thannis.

He was in prison, the count had said. She could go there and talk to him. And after she visited him...

What could she tell Cory if she saw him? That Alain Swanson would help him if the trial didn't interfere with the march? That she had sat in an antechamber at the palace for four days waiting for an audience with the queen?

No. She was too close to the edge of despair. A visit would only hurt Cory.

But she *would* see Thannis. A face from home might cheer him up. And the visit would delay her return to her cramped, windowless room in the inn, where her only companion was fear. She stopped to ask a palace guard where the prison was, then walked through the courtyard and down the hill to the street below. It was a relief to breathe fresh air and feel the warmth of the sun on her face.

You couldn't mistake a prison for any other building, Talisa thought when she reached it. The one in Freyfall was made of red bricks, the one here of grey stone, yet they looked the same.

The young, freckle-faced guard at the gate pointed to the right wing of the prison. "Thannis? The Uglessian? He's over there, along with the others who've committed minor offences."

And those who'd committed major crimes? Was Cory in the centre block? It looked...grim.

A guard led her down a wide, well-lit hallway. Perhaps this prison was different than the one in Freyfall after all. Or perhaps not. What were the halls and cells in the central block like?

Thannis was seated on the cot in his cell, his bead bent over a book.

"Thannis."

He looked up, then rose. "Talisa? What are you doing here? I thought you'd returned to Uglessia."

"I'll explain in a minute. But first, how are you?"

"I'm well enough. Better if I were out, of course –" he glanced at the bars on his cell –"but I guess I deserve to be here. Did you hear what happened?"

"Only that you injured the Count of Eastlands' son."

"The brown-haired man. Yes. The trouble is, I lost my temper."

Talisa laughed. "I'm sorry," she said quickly, seeing his face. "But you said that as though you were making a great confession. Thannis, you *always* lose your temper."

"I know." He looked as miserable as a mother ursell whose baby is missing. "I promised your grandmother, after the trouble I caused at Midsummer, that I would never do so again, at least not while I was in Freya. But then a man insulted us, and...Well, I didn't think. I didn't mean to hurt anyone, but I did."

"I hear he's recovered."

"Thanks to Raven. If he hadn't been at the college, the man might have died. I'm so happy I didn't kill him that I don't mind being locked up. At least, I wouldn't mind if I weren't missing so much. They're all angry at me – Branwen, the teachers at the college, everyone. I might not be freed until college is over for the year and it's time to go home."

"Oh." Knowing that he had cut himself off from the chance to learn must be a blister on Thannis's heart. "At least you have books," Talisa said, trying to offer comfort. He was still holding the one he'd been reading. She could see the words *Spells of Air and Water* engraved on the cover.

"Yes, Galia brings them."

Talisa was about to ask who Galia was when the guard reappeared, escorting a girl. A child, Talisa thought at first, seeing the short, slight frame topped by a mass of dark curls that tumbled around her face. When she got closer, though, Talisa realized that the girl was only a couple of years younger than she was. She studied the triangular face, the eyes that were the colour of kala, the brown skin, darker than that of any Freyan Talisa had met. The newcomer was examining her too, her head cocked to one side like a curious sparrow.

"Talisa, this is my friend Galia Soradotter. Galia, meet Talisa Thatcher, a Uglessian like me. Galia comes from Islandia," he informed Talisa. "She's staying at the college for a year, along with Raven."

Talisa smiled. "I'm happy to meet you, Galia."

Galia smiled back, a little shyly, Talisa thought. "And I you." She turned to Thannis. "I brought another book." She held it out.

He took it. "I don't know what I'd do without you. I'd almost finished this one."

"I meant to pay attention so I could tell you what the teachers said, but their words slipped out of my mind like wet fish through my hands."

"It's all right." Thannis turned to Talisa. "Galia has a great gift for working with weather. But she does it the Islandian way, not by spells."

"Are you here to teach Islandian magic to Freyan wizards?" Talisa asked the girl.

Galia sighed. "I think that is what I am *meant* to do, but I cannot. I have tried, really I have –" she frowned fiercely, as though daring anyone to doubt her words –"but I cannot explain my magic to Freyans any more than I can learn their spells."

"Magic can be very difficult to explain and to understand," Talisa murmured. She should know. All of her father's patient teaching, all of her grandparents' explanations, had been as much use to her as language lessons would be to an ursell.

Galia nodded, then said reluctantly, "The new wizard – Master Granton – understands what I say better than anyone else has done."

Talisa stiffened. "Master Granton?"

Galia cocked her head again. "You do not like him?"

"No." She hadn't liked him from the moment she'd met him, when he'd made her feel like an insignificant worm for having no gift for magic. "Be careful. He can be dangerous if his pride is hurt." She thought of the cold fury in his eyes when she and Cory had defeated his proposal to turn kala roots into a crop that would bring Uglessians – or some Uglessians – many Freyan coins. He had hunted out information about Cory and reported it when he returned to Freya.

Galia nodded. "That is easy to think. To believe, I mean." Her voice was glum. "I cannot *not* teach him, though. I am here to teach Freyan wizards."

"Did you meet this Granton in Uglessia, Talisa?" Thannis asked.

"Yes."

"Why did you leave Freya? And why are you back?"

Talisa hesitated. Then, as clearly and concisely as possible, she told them. When she finished, the bare bones of her tale lay like a broken bird on the floor. The others were silent. She looked away from them, down the long corridor. There were other prisoners in some of the cells further down.

Galia touched her arm. "I am sorry."

Talisa looked at the girl's hand. It was small but strong, the hand of someone used to hard work. "Thank you."

Thannis cleared his throat. "What are you doing now?"

"I'm waiting for an audience with the queen." And waiting. And waiting. "I'm renting a room in an inn on Freymont Street. It's small, but I spend most of my time at the palace anyway."

"You can stay with me at the college," Galia said.

Talisa glanced at her, surprised. "Can I do that? I'm not a student."

Galia tilted her head. "I do not see why anyone will mind. The other bed in my room is not used."

"Very well," Talisa said slowly. "I'd like that. Thank you." Being at the college would save money. And companionship might push her panic back, for a while at least.

Galia beamed.

The door at the end of the hall opened to let in a guard pushing a cart. Smells of kala and mutton filled the air.

"Supper," Thannis announced, then looked at Galia with a worried frown. "You'll miss dinner again."

"With the money I'll save on my room, I can afford a good meal for both of us," Talisa said. She smiled at Galia. "Shall we go?"

Galia hesitated, then asked, "Do you want to see him before we leave? Cory?"

Talisa shook her head. "No. Not until I have news to give him." Not until she had hope to give him, she added silently. And she would. She *would*. Soon.

GALIA

"**I** WONDER WHETHER THERE'S A WAY TO COMBINE Islandian magic with Freyan spells."

Galia glanced at the wizard seated opposite her. Master Granton's eyes were brighter than ever, his face intent. If he were a dog, he'd have his nose down, sniffing the trail, Galia thought.

"Has it ever been tried?"

"I do not think so."

"Mmm. If it worked, the magic produced would be very powerful indeed."

Galia said nothing. She looked towards the window, but only darkness met her gaze. She and Master Granton had been cooped up in this small classroom for close to three hours.

"My apologies, Mistress Soradotter. I have kept you for some time, and I am sure you have other things you would like to do tonight." The wizard rose and bowed. "You are very kind, giving me so much of your time." He picked up the candle and escorted her to the door.

He was certainly more pleased with her today than last night, Galia thought as she escaped down the stairs and out the massive oak door of the hall. He had been upset that she returned so late yesterday. Nor had he been happy to see her companion. Galia smiled faintly, remembering.

SHE AND TALISA HAD STOPPED at a small, well-lit kala shop. Away from Thannis, shyness had risen to cover Galia like mist enshrouding the islands at home. The older girl was so beautiful, with her red hair and fine features. And so capable. Think of coming all the way from Uglessia by herself! Galia gave brief replies to Talisa's attempts at conversation and kept her head down.

Then Talisa asked her about Islandia, and the words came, slowly at first. Galia described her life in the Circle, the island of Atua, the sea that surrounded it. And then, her shyness evaporating in the warmth of Talisa's interest, she talked about Rork, the westernmost isle, and of her parents, her sisters and brothers, little Mala. She even told Talisa about Arlan and his death. It was not something she spoke of often, though it was always there, an emptiness in her heart.

"You must miss your home and family very much," Talisa said when she was done. Her voice was low and full of sympathy.

Galia nodded. "You have a beautiful voice," she said

after a minute. "Both in speaking and singing. I heard you at the council last year."

Talisa smiled. "Thank you. I like to sing. Perhaps I shall return to my apprenticeship when...when this is all over." She looked away.

Galia was silent. She wished she knew what to say. She cleared her throat. "Why is it that you have a last name and Thannis and Branwen do not?"

Talisa looked back at her. "My grandfather came from Freya originally. I use his name when I'm here, but at home, if anyone needs to distinguish me from someone with the same name, they say 'Talisa of the red hair,' or 'Talisa, daughter of Davvid.'"

"Oh." Galia digested this. "Was it hard for your grandfather to be accepted in Uglessia?"

"A little, at first, though even then his devotion to Uglessia was well-known. Now most people have forgotten he wasn't born there, and no one even seems to notice he doesn't have six fingers." Talisa hesitated, then said softly, "I think they'd accept Cory the same way, knowing how he sacrificed himself for Uglessia." She fell silent. The candle flickered, casting shadows on her face. They were alone in the room now except for the serving woman.

"And your name?" Talisa asked. "Thannis introduced you as Galia Soradotter, but you said your mother's name is Mala."

"It is a clan name, tracing our descent from the women who first held one of the Mother's nine gifts," Galia explained.

"Does everyone in your clan have a gift for weather magic?"

Galia shook her head. "Few have gifts, and the first daughters of the Mother lived so long ago that the gifts are mixed up now. I do not know why I have one. It just happened." An accident, she thought, remembering her father's words when Arlan died. Accidents just...happened. Sometimes.

"I see." Talisa rose. "We should go. It's getting late, and I still have to collect my ursell and bag from the inn."

The door opened, letting in a group of laughing young men. "I'm glad you've been let out of your sick bed, Casper," one said. "I thought you'd be confined to it forever."

Galia's head swung in their direction. She saw the man Raven had healed along with three others, including Casper's younger brother.

Mallory saw her too and came over. "It's good to see you again."

Galia smiled, then glanced at the men seating themselves at a corner table. "I am happy that your brother is well."

Mallory grinned. "He's been well enough to go out for the last few days, but Mama kept fretting. He was as much a captive as some poor prisoner locked in a cell."

Galia stiffened. "No."

His smile disappeared. "I suppose not. I'm sorry. I did talk to Father about the Uglessian. So did Casper. But Father said the man was dangerous and should be kept behind bars."

Beside her, Talisa stirred. "You are the Count of Eastlands' son?"

"I'm sorry," Mallory said. "I should have introduced myself. My name is Mallory Ravenford and yes, I am the Count of Eastlands' younger son."

Galia flushed. "It is I who should have introduced you to each other. I am sorry. Talisa...Well, Mallory has already told you who he is. It is his brother who Thannis hurt in the fight. Mallory, this is Talisa Thatcher. She is from Uglessia and is a friend of Thannis."

One of the men at the table called, "Mallory, are you going to join us or not?"

"I'll be there in a minute," Mallory called back. "Order me some kala, will you?" He turned back to Talisa. "I'm glad to meet you, Mistress Thatcher, and sorry that your friend is imprisoned."

"I have other friends, ones who are imprisoned by poverty. Families who live in dark and crumbling buildings because your father evicted them from the land they had farmed for generations." Talisa's voice was quiet, but it lashed like an ice-edged whip. Mallory jerked as though struck.

Talisa strode away. Galia wavered, then followed her. At the door, she glanced back. Mallory stood staring after them, looking like a child who's been punished and doesn't really know why.

The sun was gone, leaving mauve fingers in the sky. Talisa walked briskly, saying nothing. Galia had to scurry to keep up.

"I'm sorry," Talisa said suddenly. "I shouldn't have said that. I lost my temper, like Thannis."

Galia was quiet for a moment. They had left the main

roads now and were on a street with tall houses on both sides. Candles glowed in the windows.

"Is it the Count of Eastlands you were talking about when you told Thannis and me about Cory?" she asked. "The one who threw people off their farms?"

"It is," Talisa said grimly.

Galia sighed. "You were right to be angry. Though," she added scrupulously, "I do not *think* Mallory would act as his father did."

"Perhaps not." Talisa sounded tired. They continued on their way in silence. At the inn, Talisa packed her clothes and told the thin, defeated looking landlord that she was leaving. He nodded as if it was only to be expected.

"This is Terrin," Talisa said as a groom saddled the ursell in the inn stable. Galia examined the shaggy grey coat and pointed head with interest. When Talisa invited her to mount behind her, she was delighted.

By the time they plodded down the road leading to the college, the last light had left the sky. The moon had not yet risen, but Terrin seemed to have no trouble keeping to the dirt path. At the gate, Galia introduced Talisa to Fergus, who gave the Uglessian a curious glance but only said, "Welcome to the college, Mistress Thatcher."

There was no one in the stable at that time of night. Talisa unsaddled Terrin, then left him in an empty stall with some oats to munch. Galia patted the ursell. He didn't seem to mind.

As they approached the dormitory, they almost ran into a shadowy figure on the path. If Talisa hadn't swerved onto the grass, there would have been a collision. Galia gasped.

The shadow spoke. "Is that Mistress Soradotter?"

"Yes."

"I was just returning from the dormitory, where I'd gone in search of you. You promised to continue your lessons tonight." His voice was tight with anger.

She hadn't *promised*. True, she hadn't told him she wouldn't either. But that was not the same.

"There is still some time tonight, though not as much as I had hoped."

"No! I mean... I am sorry. I have a guest."

Master Granton turned to peer at Talisa. Just then, the moon rose above the horizon. He started. "Mistress Thatcher?"

"Indeed." The icy edge was back in Talisa's voice.

"What are you doing here?"

"As Galia said, I am her guest. She very kindly invited me to stay with her while I am in Freybourg."

"I didn't think you were here to study wizardry." His voice dripped with sarcasm.

"No."

"I'm not sure it's in accordance with college rules to have non-students here."

"There have been others," Galia protested. "Master Spellman was just here."

"That is different. He is a wizard and was staying with a teacher."

Galia's chin rose. "I am a teacher too. I am here to teach Islandian weather magic."

"So you are. I trust you will not neglect your duties in

the future." He stalked off. Galia glared after him.

Talisa touched her arm. "If having me here gets you into trouble…"

"It will not. Master Granton was just angry."

"He always is when things don't go his way," Talisa said.

WELL, THINGS HAD GONE HIS WAY TONIGHT, Galia thought as she sped down the path and up the stairs to her room. She had tried to show him how she *felt* the air around her, how she and the air became one. Raven had already taught him how to mind-speak, and that had helped. The wizard had done surprisingly well.

When she opened the door to her room, she saw Talisa on one of the narrow beds, facing someone whose back was to Galia. Someone large, and male, and –

"Thannis!"

He spun around and hugged her exuberantly.

"When did you get out of prison? You *are* out? You do not have to go back?"

"Early this evening, and yes, I'm out for good," he assured her.

"But how? Did Master Wisher ask to have you freed?"

Thannis made a face. "I doubt it. I reported to him when I arrived, and he didn't seem very pleased to see me. Made sure I knew just how badly my behaviour reflected on the college. I assured him I never intend to fight again. And I don't."

"Intentions and actions aren't always the same thing," Talisa said dryly.

Thannis threw her an annoyed glance but said nothing.

"But *how* then?" Galia persisted.

Thannis shrugged. "I don't know. I was told today that no one would be laying any charges and that I was free to go."

Perhaps Mallory had been able to convince his father after all.

"However it happened, I'm just happy to be out. It feels so good to be able to walk more than four steps in any direction, and to smell fresh air rather than prison dust."

Galia glanced quickly at Talisa, then away. Talisa had spent another weary day at the palace, waiting for an interview that didn't come.

Galia was sorry – so sorry – about Cory. But she couldn't be sad. Life in Freya was growing brighter and warmer, just like the spring days. Now she had three people here – Raven, Talisa, and Thannis – with whom she could feel at home.

CAT

IF ONLY THERE WAS SOMETHING SHE COULD *do.*

Cat got out of her chair, walked over to the window, and stood looking out. She felt Annette's eyes on her back. Annette might sit quietly with her endless embroidery, but her eyes were smudged with sleeplessness. It must be hard on her, watching Cat pace the room or jump up unexpectedly. But Cat couldn't help it. She *couldn't* sit still.

Five days now. Five days of intense search, resulting in nothing.

She had written to Lianna and Kenton, assuring them that she was well, telling them she was staying with the Spellmans. But nothing more. Nothing about Garth. There was no sense worrying them too.

The houses opposite her stood quietly, shadowless in the early afternoon sun. Down the street, a carriage waited. A man in a grey cloak emerged from a house and entered it.

The carriage drove away. There was no other sign of life, not even a stray dog or cat wandering by.

She shouldn't have waited so long. When Garth first failed to write, she should have come to Freyfall *immediately*. She should have known.

She blinked back tears. Behind her, she heard Annette shift in her chair.

A man appeared at the far end of the street. He walked slowly, glancing from side to side as he came. Not someone who belonged here, Cat decided, not with the patched and faded brown homespun he wore. He paused in front of the Spellman house, then walked up to the door and raised his hand to the brass knocker. Cat pressed her nose to the window.

"What is it?" Annette asked.

"I don't know. A stranger."

"Someone seeking my father-in-law's services, perhaps."

"I don't think so." She doubted that this man could afford to pay a well-known wizard like Konrad Spellman. "Maybe someone looking for work." If he was, Mistress Fairway would dismiss him or send him to the back door, as she had tried to do when Cat first came calling.

The man reached into a pocket and drew out an envelope. Cat couldn't see what happened next, but he must have handed it to the housekeeper, for he turned and left. He walked briskly now, his mission accomplished.

"Someone with a message."

Annette drew a sharp breath. Cat turned and looked at her. The woman was staring at her, eyes wide, embroidery dropped to her lap.

A message. Her own words echoed in Cat's head. She was a step ahead of Annette as they sped out the door and down the stairs.

Mistress Fairway was just turning away from the door, the envelope in her hand.

"Who is it from?" Annette asked.

"I don't know, I'm sure. It's for Master Spellman. I'll place it on his desk in the study."

Annette hesitated, her eyes as hungry on the envelope as those of a starving child's on a piece of bread.

"The man who delivered it wasn't an ordinary messenger," Cat said. "I think we should open it."

Mistress Fairway looked at her coldly. "The message is addressed to Master Spellman. If he chooses to share its contents, then he will do so after he returns."

Cat glared at her, but the woman ignored her and started to walk towards the study.

"No." Annette stepped forward, her hand outstretched. "I will open the letter."

The housekeeper couldn't have looked more startled if the flowers in the tall vase on the hall table had spoken. "The letter is for Master Spellman."

"I realize that." Colour burned in Annette's cheeks. "I will apologize to my father-in-law later. But if the message concerns my son, I must open it. Now."

The other woman drew herself up to her full height. "I cannot hand over Master Spellman's private correspondence."

"Mistress Fairway." For a moment, Annette's voice trembled on the edge of rage. She steadied it. "I appreciate your sense of duty and your loyalty to my father-in-law. But this is more important than either. You do not have the right to deny me a message that might concern Garth. Give me the letter."

The two women stared at each other. Cat held her breath. Then, slowly, reluctantly, Mistress Fairway handed over the envelope.

"Thank you."

The housekeeper stalked away.

Cat wanted to throw her arms around Annette and hug her. She knew how much this tug of wills had cost Garth's mother. But that could come later. She watched, nails digging into her palms, as Annette tore open the envelope, extracted a single sheet of paper, and read it. Her body went very still.

"Is it...?"

Annette looked at Cat as though she didn't really see her. Then, wordlessly, she handed her the sheet.

The message was printed in uneven capital letters. It was short.

WE HAVE GARTH SPELLMAN. WE WILL RETURN HIM UNHARMED WHEN CORY UPDALE IS FREED FROM PRISON. IF UPDALE IS NOT FREED, YOU WILL NEVER SEE YOUR GRANDSON AGAIN.

Konrad put the paper down on his desk as though holding it soiled his hands. "Do either of you know who in Freyn's name this Cory Updale is?"

"He's the man accused of setting fire to the barracks last year," Cat said.

Konrad nodded. "I heard about the arrest. I'd forgotten the man's name."

"Do you think you'll be able to do it?" Cat asked. "Get Cory Updale released?"

Konrad looked at her. The creases on his face were very deep. "I don't even know if I'll try. Certainly it's not the first thing I'll do."

"But..." Cat stopped. Something cold twisted in her stomach. The wall she was leaning against was hard, as hard as Konrad Spellman's voice.

"They said...They said if you didn't..." Annette whispered. They were the first words she'd spoken since she read the note. Her face was waxen.

"It's all right, Annette. I'm not abandoning Garth. But there are other, better ways to help him than by letting an arsonist and murderer go free."

Garth didn't believe Cory was an arsonist and murderer, Cat thought. But she couldn't break her promise to Garth by saying that. Instead, she asked, "What ways?"

"Find the person or people who are holding him."

"How?" Cat demanded.

"Question Updale's friends and acquaintances."

Like Master Swanson? Cat wondered. Another secret she must keep.

"I'll ask the army to make enquiries. Once we know who wants Updale out of prison, we'll know who would have reason to take Garth in exchange."

Something was wrong with this statement. Cat chewed on it for a moment. Then she knew. "But Garth disappeared over six weeks ago. Nobody in Freya even knew Cory was taken prisoner until the last two weeks."

"True," Konrad said after a brief pause. "Still, those who have him must know Updale or they wouldn't be bargaining for his freedom." Lines deepened in Konrad's face. "I want everyone who knows this man questioned. If they aren't involved themselves, they might be able to throw light on who's holding Garth."

"The stall owner," Annette said.

"What stall owner?" Konrad asked.

"There's a man in Weavers Street who sells beautifully woven clothes. We went there the other day, didn't we, Cat? He wasn't there, but his neighbour told us he was the brother-in-law of the man who'd set the fire."

"What's his name?" The wizard grabbed a pen.

Annette thought for a moment, her brow wrinkling. "I can't remember."

"Catrina?"

"Master Berrymore."

The wizard wrote down the name.

Would Master Berrymore know anything? Be willing to share his information? She didn't know. But she did know someone else they should ask. Must ask.

She had promised Garth. Promises were sacred. But sometimes that just didn't matter. Couldn't matter. Cat took a deep breath. "You should ask Cory himself."

The wizard shook his head. "He's the last person who'd help."

"No." She took another deep breath. "Cory knows

Garth, and is in his debt. Garth helped him escape from Freya last fall."

"He did *what*?" There was incredulity in Konrad's voice. Both Spellmans were staring at her as though she'd said the sky was green.

She swallowed. "Garth helped Cory escape," she repeated. "He told me at Midwinter. I'm sorry I didn't tell you before, but he asked me not to."

"I don't understand," Annette said faintly. "What —"

"*Why*?" Konrad demanded.

"Because of Talisa Thatcher. She was apprenticed with Master Coyne too."

"I know that. What —"

"She and Cory had become friends. Then Cory disappeared. She asked Garth to use a finding spell, and he did. But after they found Cory, soldiers came to arrest him. Garth and Talisa helped him escape."

They were still staring at her.

"Garth doesn't think Cory did it," she added. "Set the fire, I mean."

Konrad frowned. "Nevertheless, it was a very foolish thing to do. And wrong."

"That doesn't matter." Annette rose. Colour had returned to her face. "Cat is right. If this man has reason to be grateful to Garth, then surely he'll want to help him."

Her father-in-law looked at her. "Yes," he said slowly. "Yes, he might. Very well. I shall ride to Freybourg and talk to the man myself."

"May I go with you?" Annette asked.

The wizard hesitated, then nodded. "Your persuasions may be more effective than mine in the circumstances. Can you be ready in fifteen minutes?"

"Less than that." Annette almost ran from the room.

A faint smile flickered over Konrad's lips. It was, Cat thought, the first time she had seen him smile in over five days. He glanced at her. "Catrina, will you stay here? I don't expect further messages, but if there are, it would be best if someone is here to receive them immediately."

No! She must go too! She opened her mouth to protest, then closed it. He was right. She would be more useful here. It might be the hardest thing she'd ever had to do, but she would stay here.

TALISA

"**M**ISTRESS THATCHER?"

Talisa looked up. Blinked. She could scarcely believe the man in blue-and-silver livery had stopped by her chair, spoken her name. Her heart began to race. "Yes."

"Her Majesty will see you now."

Talisa rose and followed the servant down the long room. Eyes trailed after her. Eyes that wondered why she had been chosen.

The audience chamber was smaller than she had expected. It held only five people besides Talisa: a man-at-arms by the door, two ladies-in-waiting sitting on low stools behind the queen, a secretary seated at a table laden with papers, pens, and an ink bottle, and, of course, Queen Elira.

Talisa had seen the queen once before, at Midsummer. She was less regally dressed now, in a simply cut blue gown. No tiara crowned her braided auburn hair. But she was just as elegant, and gave just as great an impression of authority. Talisa sank into the deepest curtsy she could manage and hoped she did it properly. In Uglessia, no one bowed or curtsied.

"You may rise."

She did so. "Thank you for seeing me, Your Majesty."

"I am happy to do so. I only wish I had been able to make time for you sooner. I am always glad to meet people from Uglessia, especially members of your family. Also, I have vivid memories of your lovely voice from the opening of the council."

"Thank you, Your Majesty."

"But I understand that it is not about Uglessia that you are here, but about one of my subjects."

"Yes, Your Majesty."

Queen Elira waited. So did the man at the table, pen poised.

"I came to see you about Cory Updale," Talisa said, then stopped. There was more silence. One of the ladies-in-waiting shifted, making her taffeta skirt rustle.

Talisa took a deep breath. "Cory is accused of setting fire to the barracks in Freyfall last autumn, but he didn't do it."

The words were as naked as a newborn baby. Where had her carefully rehearsed sentences gone?

"If he did not do it, then he should be able to prove that at his trial."

"I am afraid..." The truth of those words stopped her. She struggled to continue. "There are many who will think Cory guilty because he made no secret of how he felt."

"And how did he feel?"

Careful, Talisa, careful. Tread as cautiously as you would along a slippery ledge that threatens to crumble.

"He was unhappy about the many people who have no homes and too little food."

"I do not think many people rejoice about that," the queen said dryly. "I doubt that expressing his unhappiness would be enough to make him a suspect. Perhaps he expressed more than mere unhappiness."

"He felt something should be done to help those people."

"Such as?"

Careful. "There are many things that could be done. Shelters could be built. Food distributed."

"Or landlords like the Count of Eastlands could be forced to accept tenants back?"

Was the queen guessing, or did she know? Either way, Talisa realized she had made a mistake. She should have been more open. More honest. Now Queen Elira would doubt her words. Talisa felt sick.

She abandoned caution. "Yes. That too. He thought it was unfair that tenants were thrown off the land their families had farmed for generations."

"And do you share that opinion?"

Talisa looked directly at Queen Elira. "Yes."

There was silence, except for the scratching of a pen as the secretary recorded her response. The ladies-in-waiting were staring at her. They were middle-aged women, one with a round face and plump body, the other sharper, thinner.

Talisa forced air into her lungs, the way she did before starting a demanding song. "There are many people who hold similar views. His opinions do not mean that Cory started the fire."

"Not in themselves. But I gather he was seen near the barracks that night."

Talisa's mouth dropped open.

"Come, Mistress Thatcher. Surely you must have realized I would look into this matter before I talked with you, knowing why you wished to see me."

She hadn't realized. She should have.

"And then to flee when soldiers came to arrest him. A mistake, if he *is* innocent. His flight implies guilt."

The rocks on the ledge began to tumble.

The queen sighed. "I am afraid there is nothing I can do for you, Mistress Thatcher. My judges will determine your friend's guilt or innocence and, I can assure you, will do so honestly."

Talisa felt the ledge slipping out from under her feet. She reached frantically for a rope.

"Your Majesty was kind enough to remember the night I sang before you. May I sing a song now?"

Talisa didn't wait for the queen's assent. What could she do if it didn't come? She sang Cory's song, the song that had come to her in snatches last fall as she and Cory walked the streets of Freyfall, the song that had only emerged fully when she returned home, the song she had sung to show her people how wrong it would be to allow the hope of prosperity to trick them into becoming like

Freyans, with some owning most of the land and others owning nothing.

The song told how Cory and his family had been forced from the hill farm they loved, how they and others like them – many others – had gone to Freyfall, seeking work and finding none, how his parents, like others, had died of fever and despair. And it told of a young man's efforts to prevent destruction, for she had added new verses since the winter day when she first sang it on the plateau behind her grandparents' hut.

> *Word comes.*
> *A fire will be set this night*
> *To right a wrong, or else at least*
> *To ease the rage that blazes bright*
> *Within men's hearts.*

> *No!*
> *The whispered words raise alarm*
> *In Cory's soul. He vows to stop*
> *The burning, and the needless harm*
> *That it would bring.*

> *He runs*
> *Through Freyfall's twisting rough-stoned streets*
> *Feet pounding, heart and lungs aflame.*
> *As he draws near, fire meets*
> *His anxious eyes.*

Too late.
Screams pierce the night, the building burns
Soldiers spill into the street.
Heartsick, Cory stops, then turns
And hurries home.

As Talisa sang, the ladies-in-waiting leaned forward on their stools. The secretary put his pen down. Queen Elira's face was intent. Not that Talisa needed those signs. She knew she had never sung better.

There was a moment of silence when she finished. Then the queen said, "Thank you. Your voice is beautiful, and your song is moving. But surely you must know that it cannot make a difference."

The sick feeling in Talisa's stomach grew. "But –"

"Can you produce proof that your friend did not set the fire, that he tried, in fact, to prevent it?"

"No, but –"

"You said in your song that word came of the intention to set the fire. Do you know who brought that word?"

Talisa shook her head.

"Then I'm afraid there is nothing I can do."

"But you have power! You can tell them to let him go!"

"Yes, I have power. But even if I were convinced of Master Updale's innocence – and I am convinced of nothing except your belief in him – a ruler cannot be above her own laws, whether those laws refer to courts of justice or landlords' rights to do what they wish on their property."

"You could change the laws."

Queen Elira smiled. "It's not quite as simple as that. Nor would changing certain laws be wise. You were present last Midsummer when conspirators, including my own cousin, tried to kill me because they thought me too friendly to your land. No, if there is to be change, it must be gradual – very gradual – and not offend those who have most power and influence." She was quiet. Talisa studied her face and thought, for the first time, that she looked tired. Tired and old.

"I trust that Freyn will smile on your attempts to prove your friend's innocence."

She was dismissed. She curtsied. As she rose, the queen smiled. "Give my regards to your grandparents. I remember your grandfather, when he was about your age, fighting for Uglessia as valiantly as you are fighting for Master Updale."

Talisa didn't feel valiant. She felt very weak and very frightened as she turned and walked out of the audience chamber.

TALISA STOOD ON THE STREET below the palace for a long time. Then she started walking towards the prison.

There was no reason not to visit Cory. She had wanted to bring him good news, hopeful news. But Cory wasn't expecting it. He wouldn't be disappointed. She was the one who had insisted on clinging to hope.

The guard at the gate was the same young, freckle-faced man she'd met before.

"No need your coming today," he said cheerfully. "Your friend's been released."

Talisa's heart leaped in sudden, incredulous joy.

Then it fell. She forced herself to smile. "Thank you. Yes, I know Thannis is free. I am here to see another friend. Cory Updale."

"Oh. That one. He's in the central block." No smile now. Disapproval thick in his voice.

She followed a taciturn guard down a corridor lined with bars to the very end. Cory was sitting, head bowed, on the narrow cot at the back of his cell. He looked up as light from the guard's candle splashed onto his face. Then he sprang to his feet.

"Talisa!"

She swallowed. "Hello, Cory."

They stared at each other. The guard turned and started to walk away, taking the light with him..

"Could you please leave the candle here?" Talisa called.

"No."

"But I can scarcely see!" The only other light came from a torch in a wall sconce at the other end of the hall.

"Call when you're ready to leave. I'll escort you out."

"But —"

He was gone. They were left in dim twilight.

"I'm sorry, Talisa."

"It's not your fault. Do they never allow you any light?" She could see the outline of Cory's body, but that was all. His face was a pale blur.

"Only when someone comes with food. They probably think I'd set fire to the prison if they gave me a candle."

She should be angry, Talisa thought. Cory should not be

treated so. But anger required energy, and she had none. Depression pressed down on her, as heavy as a gravestone.

"It doesn't matter. It won't be for long."

Were his words meant to comfort? They didn't.

"It's good to see you," Cory said softly. Then he laughed. "It *was* good to see you for a few seconds," he amended. "It's good to know you're here."

He was trying so hard to sound cheerful. She should make an equal effort. But she could think of nothing to say that wouldn't deepen the gloom.

"When did you arrive in Freybourg?"

"Six days ago."

"You've been here six days?"

"Yes."

"Then why..." He stopped.

"Why what?"

"Well, I... It's just that I would have thought you'd have been here sooner."

Anger, Talisa found, was possible after all. "So you think I've been neglecting you? Well, I haven't. I've been sitting for six days in an antechamber at the palace, waiting to see Queen Elira to beg her to save your life."

"And you saw her today?"

She was silent.

He sighed. "Talisa, thank you for trying, even if it was a waste of your time. But please stop banging your head against a brick wall. There's no hope."

"*Someone* has to try, since you won't. As for hope, there would be plenty of hope if you would only say who set the fire. Then you'd be free and I wouldn't have to bang my head against *any* wall." She was so angry she was shaking.

"Talisa, I'm sorry. I didn't mean –"

"Didn't mean what? That I was wasting my time? If you didn't mean that, you should have. That's just what I've been doing, ever since I arrived in Freya." Her voice was trembling on the edge of hysteria. She took a couple of deep breaths, but they rasped like sobs.

"I wish we hadn't met." There was such pain in Cory's voice that Talisa cried out.

"Talisa, don't. Please don't. I just... It would have been better if you'd never met me. I've brought you nothing but grief." His voice was shaking too.

This was her fault. She should not have come today. She had taken away his fragile peace. She must try to restore it. If only the bars hadn't been between them. If only she could have held him. "Cory –"

She stopped. The door at the end of the corridor had opened. A light was approaching.

A light, and three people: the guard, a middle-aged woman with smooth brown hair, and an older man with an eagle's nose and dark hair flecked with white. He looked familiar, but Talisa couldn't think where she had seen him before.

"Freyn's smiling on you today, Updale. More visitors." The guard handed the candle to the man, nodded respectfully to him, then retreated.

The candle brought shadows as well as light into the prison. The bars seemed to reach out to enclose them all.

Cory's hands gripped them so tightly that his fingers gleamed bone white.

The man and woman were staring at him. After a moment, the man turned and glanced at Talisa. "You are Talisa Thatcher, are you not?"

"Yes."

"I had the pleasure of hearing you sing last Midsummer." His voice did not sound as though it had been a pleasure. It grated, as though he were speaking through a mouthful of nails. "I also know your grandparents. My name is Konrad Spellman and this is my daughter-in-law, Annette Spellman."

Konrad Spellman! May all the spirits of the mountains be thanked. Perhaps hope was not dead after all.

"You got my letter, then."

"I received a message," Konrad Spellman said slowly. "Yesterday afternoon."

Why so late? She had left her letter eight days ago. Never mind. It didn't matter. "You must have come right away." Her eyes misted with gratitude. With relief.

"We would have been here sooner, but the carriage broke down, making for an unpleasant four hours and a late night. We needed to sleep this morning, despite the urgency of our mission."

No wonder they both looked tired and strained. Talisa raised her eyes to his to express her thanks.

"Talisa." Cory spoke. Warningly. "I don't think they're here to help."

She gaped at him. "Not help? Why else would they have come? Master Spellman said they received a message –"

"A message indeed." Konrad's voice was soft, but there was something in it that raised prickles on her skin. "My grandson has been missing for over six weeks. But perhaps you knew that."

"Yes. At least —"

"Ah." The flame jumped as his hand clenched on the candlestick. Talisa glanced at his face, then at Annette's. The woman was staring at her as though she had fangs.

"The message stated that Garth would be returned safely to us — but only if Cory Updale was freed."

"*What?*" Cory's shout drowned Talisa's gasp.

The guard poked his head around the door. "Anything wrong?"

Konrad had been staring at Cory, then Talisa, then back. "Everything's fine," he said without turning his head.

The guard lingered. "Are you sure? I heard a shout."

Konrad turned then and shooed him away, as he would a bothersome fly. "Nothing's wrong. We'll call if you're needed."

He looked back at Talisa. "Why did you think we had come?" he demanded.

She shook her head, trying to clear it. His words were still beating around in her mind like trapped moths. "I thought you had come to help. I left you a letter over a week ago, asking you to use your influence to convince people that Cory is innocent."

"Something must have happened to the letter. I never received it. But why me?"

"Because you know my grandparents. The letter was from them. And because of Garth."

Annette stiffened. "Garth?"

Talisa glanced at her. "I know Garth. We were apprentices together. We're friends." She didn't think she should tell them Garth had helped Cory escape, but she added, "He knew the soldiers were suspicious of Cory, but he believed him innocent. So I came to your house seeking his aid, and Master Spellman's. But Master Spellman was away, and I was told Garth had been gone for some time. Even when the Coynes told me he had given up his apprenticeship, I didn't think anything was wrong."

"None of us did," Konrad said heavily.

"It doesn't make sense," Cory said. "If Garth disappeared so long ago, what would that have to do with me?"

"Neither of you knew anything about this, did you?" Annette asked. "I'm sorry. I thought you did, when Talisa said she had left a letter. But you didn't."

"No," Talisa said.

"No," Cory echoed. He added, "I like Garth. I wouldn't accept my release on such terms."

Annette smiled at him. Her face still looked desperately tired, but no longer as though the skin had been stretched so tightly it might snap.

Konrad studied Cory. Trying to judge the truth of his statement, Talisa thought. "If you really feel that way, then you'll be willing to help us find my grandson. We need information. We need to know who is likely to be holding him, and where."

Cory said nothing.

The wizard's eyes were fixed on Cory's face. "You know who would want you freed. You know who would be likely to commit such a desperate act."

Still, Cory was silent.

"Can't you use a finding spell?" Talisa ventured.

Konrad didn't remove his gaze from Cory. "I've tried. All I can get is a faint and jumbled impression. It tells me he's alive, but little more. Certainly not his whereabouts. I suspect he's been drugged."

Garth drugged. His mind so unclear it could not form an image of where he was. Talisa looked at Annette, then away. "Cory..."

He glanced at her, frowning, then switched his attention to the wizard. "I'm sorry. I very much hope that you will find Garth soon. But I can't tell you who has him, or where he is."

There was more silence.

"Can't, or won't?" Konrad asked softly.

Cory took a deep breath. Talisa could see it tremble through him. "I do not know who took Garth. Yes, I have my suspicions. But if I name these people, they will be in trouble, even though they may well be innocent."

"If they don't have Garth, they won't be in trouble."

Cory shook his head. The shadow on the wall behind him echoed the motion. No. No. No.

"Please." Annette's plea was more sob than speech.

Cory glanced at her. "I'm sorry," he said again. "If it is the people I think it might be, I don't think they'd hurt Garth. They are not evil men. I think they'll let him go once they realize that holding him serves no useful purpose."

"You *think*." Konrad Spellman's voice hissed. "You can't *know*."

Cory hesitated, then shook his head again.

"Yet you won't do anything to save my grandson, even though I understand he helped *you*."

It was hard to be sure in the feeble light, but Talisa thought Cory went a shade paler. "I will not give you the names of people who may be innocent."

This time the silence dragged on until Talisa wanted to scream. Finally, Konrad turned his back on Cory and looked at her. The flame created cavernous pits beneath his eyes.

"It seems your friend, despite his earlier words, is incapable of showing either compassion or common sense. Therefore I turn to you. You said you were a friend of Garth's. Convince this man to tell us what he knows. If he does, I will use what influence I have on his behalf. If he does not, he will face my enmity. The fate of both Garth and your friend is in your hands, Mistress Thatcher."

He turned to his daughter-in-law. "It's time to go."

Annette's head was bent. Talisa thought she was crying, but when the woman looked up, there were no tears on her face. Her gaze moved from Talisa to Cory, then back again. "Please. For all our sakes, please help."

Talisa couldn't bear to leave her without hope. "I'll try."

A smile almost touched Annette's lips. "Thank you." As they started to walk away, she glanced back at the darkness behind her. "Leave them the candle."

Konrad glanced down at the light he held, then turned back and placed it in Talisa's hand. He and Annette walked down the long dim corridor to the door. A moment later, it opened and they were gone.

Talisa stared at the closed door for a minute, gathering her arguments. She turned. Cory was frowning. "Talisa, I *can't* give him the names."

"I know. The men you think may have Garth are the ones who set the fire, aren't they? You're afraid that if you tell anyone who they are, they'll be arrested even if they have nothing to do with Garth."

His face eased. "Yes."

"But, Cory, Garth can't be left in their hands."

"No," he agreed.

She blinked, feeling as if her arguments had been tugged away by an unexpected gust of wind.

"Talisa, you can't have thought I'd leave Garth in danger. He's your friend. He helped me. He *believed* me, at a time when I needed that belief more than I ever needed a crust of bread."

His voice trembled. His shadow on the wall shook, or was it her hand, holding the candle?

"But I can't save Garth at the expense of people who may not even have him. Especially when I don't think they will hurt him."

"They've drugged him. That's hurting him."

"Yes." Cory frowned.

"So you see —"

"No. There's another way to free Garth, if you'll help."

Talisa stared at him.

"Will you go to these men and tell them...*beg* them, to let Garth go? Tell them I won't accept my freedom on those terms. Tell them that what they're doing can only harm me. Tell them..." He stopped, thought a moment, then said,

"Tell them that I thank them for their efforts, but that if they are really grateful to me, they can show their gratitude by letting Garth go."

Talisa swallowed. "Will they listen to me?"

"I think so. Though... As I told Master Spellman, it doesn't make sense, their taking Garth six weeks ago, if their motive was to use him to bargain for my freedom." He shook his head. "I don't understand."

Talisa didn't either. But it didn't matter. Not now. "Who are these people and where can I find them?"

He hesitated. His shadow wavered on the cell wall. She steadied the candle with her free hand.

"Promise you won't go to them alone. Ask Alain Swanson for help."

"I promise."

Cory gave her the names and directions.

There seemed nothing left to say. Or too much. They stared at each other dumbly. A drop of hot wax scalded Talisa's finger. She switched the candle to her other hand and sucked her finger.

"I'd better go."

Cory nodded.

"I'll be back. I'll get Garth freed, then I'll be back." Talisa drew a deep breath. "May all the spirits of the mountains be with you."

"And with you."

The candle sputtered. It was getting low. Talisa smiled as bravely as she could, then turned and walked down the corridor. Her footsteps rang on the bare stones.

GALIA

BUOYED BY THE FACT THAT THANNIS WAS IN
her classrooms and that Talisa would be with her that
evening, Galia actually listened to her teachers that
morning. True, she spent some time gazing out the window.
But that was understandable, surely. The day danced with
sunlight and was alive with the smell of blossoms and the
chirp of robins. At home, the waves would laugh with
delight on such a morning. Galia sighed and returned her
attention to the lesson just as Master Clark asked a question.
She answered it. The teacher blinked in surprise. So did
Galia. Thannis beamed.

Talisa, dressed in a grey tunic and leggings, was waiting
for them as they left the hall for lunch.

"I'm glad to see you both. I wanted to tell you that I'm
leaving for Freyfall."

The day lost its brightness. "Why?" Galia asked.

Talisa opened her mouth to answer, then looked beyond

them and closed it. Galia glanced over her shoulder and noticed Master Granton standing a short distance away, watching them.

"I have an errand in Freyfall," Talisa explained carefully. "I don't know how long it will take, but I hope to return before..." She stopped, cleared her throat. "Before the trial. When I do, may I stay with you once more?"

"Yes. Of course."

"Thank you. You're very kind." Talisa smiled at them both, then headed for the stable, her tight travelling cap swinging from one hand.

The vegetable soup at lunch was tasteless, Galia decided. She pushed it aside after a few mouthfuls.

"She said she'll be back," Thannis reminded her.

Galia nodded but said nothing.

"May I sit here?" someone asked. Galia glanced up. It was Branwen.

A huge smile spread across Thannis's face. "Of course!"

Branwen fiddled with her spoon for a minute before she said, not looking at Thannis, "I'm sorry I acted the way I did." She glanced up. "I *was* concerned about you, but I was even more worried about whether I'd be allowed to stay here. Whether any Uglessian would be allowed to come in the future."

"I know," Thannis said. "It's my fault. But I've made a solemn vow never to lose my temper again."

Branwen laughed. "That's like one of these Freyan foxes promising never to steal a farmer's chickens." She smiled at him. "Never mind. I know you mean it."

They started talking about the lessons Thannis had missed. Galia stared at the table. How could Thannis be friends with Branwen again? Branwen had ignored him all the time he sat in prison. It wasn't Branwen who had visited him and taken him books.

She sat in glum silence until the bell rang. Thannis and Branwen rose.

"Coming, Galia?" Thannis asked.

She nodded, but waited till they were out the door before leaving herself. She was so intent on not being near them that she didn't realize Thannis was absent till partway through the second lesson. She frowned. Thannis wouldn't miss it voluntarily. At the end of the class, she approached Branwen.

"Where is Thannis?"

"I don't know. A servant came up to him as we left the refectory and said Master Wisher wanted to see him. I thought he'd be back by now."

"Did the servant say why Master Wisher wanted him?"

"No."

They gazed at each other for a moment, then Branwen said, a worried frown puckering her forehead, "I hope he's not in any more trouble."

And if he is, you will not do anything to pull him out of it, Galia thought as she watched Branwen walk to her next class. Galia descended the stairs, left the hall, and crossed the green to Master Wisher's house at the far end.

The door was opened by a plump woman in a navy dress and white apron. "Yes?"

"May I see Master Wisher, please?"

"And who may I tell him wishes to see him?"

"Galia." The woman waited, so Galia added, "Soradotter." Clan names were used so seldom in Islandia that she often forgot how important they seemed to be in Freya.

The woman disappeared, to return a minute later. "Please follow me."

The house smelled of soap, and looked as scrubbed as the woman's apron. It was not grand, like the Count of Eastlands' home, but it was not a place you would come home to after a hard day's fishing, either.

Master Wisher rose from a chair behind his desk when Galia was ushered into his study. "Freyn's Day, Mistress Soradotter. What can I do for you?"

"Where is Thannis?"

She had not meant to ask it so bluntly. She hurried to add, as the man's eyebrows drew together, "Branwen said a servant asked him to come to see you, and he has not been in class since."

"No," Master Wisher agreed. "He wouldn't be."

Galia stared at him.

He sighed. "Do sit down, Mistress Soradotter."

She sat on the closest chair. He reseated himself and made an arch of his fingers, resting his chin on them.

"I'm afraid I had to ask Thannis to leave the college. It is regrettable, since we desire to share our knowledge with our Uglessian neighbours – and with Islandians, of course, though it seems we have more to learn from you than you from us. If Thannis had behaved in a manner befitting a guest and a student of this college, we would have been delighted to teach him as much as he could learn."

"But he was let out of prison. And the charges against him were dropped."

"They were, thanks mainly, I understand, to the intervention of our good queen, who is most concerned that we maintain cordial relations with our neighbours. But to keep him in the college after he has displayed such an unfortunate inability to keep his temper..." Master Wisher shook his head.

Something cold and hard settled in Galia's stomach. "He is gone?"

"So I believe."

The coldness spread, filled her, filled the room. "But he wants so much to learn. And he said he would never lose his temper again. He *promised*."

"I would be happy to believe his promise, had he not already shown that he is unable to keep such a vow. As for his love of learning, I can only regret that his own actions made it impossible for him to remain here. We cannot risk having a student with such a volatile nature. Next time he might actually kill someone. Now, if you'll excuse me, I have work to do. Unless, of course, there is something else I can do for you."

"No."

It was such an effort to stand up, to walk to the door. Everything was an effort.

Her hand was on the knob when she remembered something Thannis had said. She turned.

"Thannis told me you talked to him yesterday. Why did you wait until today to tell him he had to leave?"

"What?" For a moment, Master Wisher looked like a boy caught with his hand on a honey cake his mother had told him not to touch. Then he recovered. "I had thought he could be granted a second chance, given his desire to learn – and ours to help Uglessia, of course. More mature reflection, however, convinced me otherwise."

Something was wrong with his words. Galia was tempted to go inside his mind, see what lay hidden there. But that would never do: one did not invade another's thoughts without permission. She stood still, her eyes fixed on his face. He fidgeted with some papers on his desk. "I am really quite busy."

She remained there, saying nothing.

He glanced down at the desk. A piece of paper caught his eye. He started to shove it under a book, then stopped. Red stained his cheeks. He looked up.

"It's no concern of yours, but I did receive a letter this morning from the Count of Eastlands. He pointed out – quite rightly, I must say – that it was highly imprudent to keep such a dangerous young man at the college. Upon sober consideration, I had to agree with him."

The Count of Eastlands. A man whose house covered an entire block, whose words on a piece of paper could change the mind of the head of the college.

Galia spun around, opened the door, and marched out of the house. Thunder rumbled in the distance.

She was almost at the gate when she heard a voice that was all too familiar.

"You're not in class, Mistress Soradotter?"

Galia wanted to walk on, but such discourtesy would shame the good name of all Islandians. She stopped.

"I am going to Freybourg, Master Granton."

"You will be returning in time for our evening lesson, I hope."

After a moment, she said, "Yes."

"Ah, good."

Again, thunder rumbled. He glanced up. "It looks as though it will rain. You might be wise to rethink your plans."

She said nothing.

"An unusually quick shift in the weather, at least for this part of the country. On the coast, I understand, these changes occur more often –" He stopped, his eyes snapping from the sky to Galia's face. His eyes narrowed. "You wouldn't have anything to do with the transformation, would you?"

She stared at him, then glanced up at the angry sky. She hadn't caused this, had she? The Wise Women on Atua had taught her how to clamp down on her emotions. Never since Arlan's death had she allowed her grief, her rage, to influence the air around her. She had thought she had learned her lessons well.

But never, until today, had she felt so sad, so angry. She had learned nothing.

"Such power," Melton Granton said. His voice was filled with – what? Wonder? Admiration? Galia flinched.

"If only you could show me how to do this."

"I cannot."

"No? I'm not convinced."

"I must go."

She waited until she was well down the lane before she stopped.

"Gather your grief. Gather your rage," the Wise Women of Atua had said. *"Do not toss them into the air, like sparks on dry timber."*

She did not want to smother her anger. She *should* be furious with Master Wisher for throwing Thannis out because a man of wealth and position told him to. She *should* be furious with the Count of Eastlands for using his money to hurt others.

"You have great power," said those voices in her mind. *"Those with power must learn to use it wisely, and never, never, to harm others."*

Thunder crackling in the air would do no one harm.

No. But it might when the lightning came.

She drew a deep breath, as she'd been taught. Another, and another. Bent down, removed her shoes, let her feet feel the earth beneath them, dug her toes into its cool goodness, closed her eyes, raised her face and arms to the flow of air around her. The Mother's earth. The Mother's air.

Gradually, the tension eased out of her. She opened her eyes.

The sky was still grey, but the thunderous clouds had disappeared and there was a promise of blue in the west. She sighed, sat down, and put her shoes back on.

It would have been easier to confront the Count of

Eastlands if she had not bridled her outrage. Galia felt very small as she approached the house, raised the knocker, and faced the imposing servant.

"I want to see the Count of Eastlands, please."

He wavered, if such a self-important person could be said to waver. But he must have remembered her from her last visit, for after a moment he said, "I shall enquire as to whether the count is at home."

She not only felt small, Galia discovered as she stood alone in the vast, shining hall, she felt grubby. Her hands had traces of dirt from brushing earth off her feet. She wiped them on her skirt, but that only smudged it.

The servant was back. "The count will see you. Please follow me."

She did, up one flight of stairs and partway down a hall. Were her shoes leaving dirty prints on the rose rug? Her guide stopped before a door, knocked, then opened it and ushered Galia in.

A man who she presumed was the count was seated on a chair by the window. The countess and Casper sat on a small sofa, and Mallory, dressed in maroon silk and holding a wine glass, stood in front of the fireplace. He smiled at her.

The count stood up and bowed. "I understand our family owes you a debt for your prompt action in fetching your countryman to Casper's aid. I am pleased to see you."

"Thank you," Galia murmured.

The count reseated himself. "What can I do for you? I'd be more than happy to discharge our debt. I was quite disappointed when your compatriot returned the gold I'd sent him."

"Here, come and sit down." Mallory led her to a chair. Galia sat cautiously, hoping the dirt on her skirt wouldn't smear the cream seat with its embroidered flowers.

"Well?" the count prompted.

She had not come to ask anything of this man. She had come to tell him what she thought of him. But now, faced with this civility, this friendliness, at least on Mallory's part, the angry words seemed out of place.

"I don't want to rush you, but we must leave soon or we'll be late for our dinner engagement," the count said.

"Now, Cosmos, you know we don't have to be there right on time," his wife protested.

"If we arrive too early, we'll be cornered by that toady Denzil Fairmount again," Casper added.

The count ignored them. He was neither as tall nor as imposing as the servant at the door, nothing like the man Galia had expected to find. But the gaze he turned on her told her that, no matter what his family said, he expected her to state her request quickly and be gone.

Well, if he expected a request, then she would give him one. She clenched her hands together on her lap. "You sent a letter to Master Wisher telling him to throw Thannis out of the college. I want you to send him another letter, telling him to let Thannis come back."

The words were blunt. They didn't fit the soft rugs, the embroidered cushions, the draped windows. The countess blinked. Mallory's eyes widened. So did the count's, before they narrowed.

"Who's Thannis?" Casper asked.

"The Uglessian who nearly killed you," his father said shortly.

"Oh. Wasn't he released from prison?"

"He was. Queen Elira thought it best, so I acceded to her request that charges be dropped. But the man is obviously a danger, and I sent a letter to the head of the college pointing that out. If Master Wisher agrees with me, I am glad."

"He was going to let Thannis stay until he got your letter." Anger was rising in Galia again. She tried to subdue it but it kept pushing up, like steam from a heated pot.

"Was he?" A small smile curled the count's mouth. Then it disappeared. "My dear young lady, I am sorry to refuse your request. As I said, my family is under an obligation to you. However, my conscience forbids me to pay my debt by allowing this man to remain in Freya. Some other reward, perhaps. I would be happy to renew my offer of gold."

Galia stood up abruptly. She heard Mallory say, "But, Father –" as she walked to the door and opened it. The young man followed her down the stairs.

"I'm sorry," he said. "It's just that Father was so angry when Casper was hurt, and so upset when the queen made him drop the charges."

Galia said nothing.

"I think he honestly believes your friend is a danger."

His comment wasn't worth a response.

"Does it matter that much to your friend?"

Galia stopped. "All his life, Thannis has dreamed of learning magic at the college, magic that he can use to help his country. Yes, it matters that much." And it mattered to her, that she was losing a friend.

"I'm sorry," Mallory said again.

They had reached the front door. Mallory opened it. "The girl you were with the other night...What had I done to upset her?" He wore a troubled frown.

Galia sighed. Anger seeped out of her, leaving weary desolation behind. "It was not you. She was angry because your father made all his tenants leave their land."

"It wasn't their land," he protested. "They only rented it. The land belongs to us."

"It *was* their land. They farmed it."

"But –"

"Anyway, what does it matter whose land it was? When they had to leave, they did not have anywhere to go. Many have no work and no homes."

His frown deepened.

None of this was Mallory's fault, but she couldn't help him. She touched his arm. "I must go now."

As she trudged back up the lane leading to the college, Galia felt a fat drop of rain land on her neck. She glanced up. The promise of blue had vanished.

She should stop again, make her misery ebb out of the air. But her depression left her without energy. She continued to walk. The rain continued to fall.

CAT

WEAVERS STREET WAS BUSY, BUT THAT WAS to be expected. It was just past noon.

Last night, Cat had lain staring into the darkness while the hours ticked by. What if Cory couldn't, or wouldn't, give them the information they needed?

He would.

But if he didn't...

Light was beginning to touch the sky outside her bedroom window when she decided that she would seek out Cory's brother-in-law. Master Spellman had spoken of setting enquiries in motion, but had left before he could do so. Very well. She'd dig up some information. With a plan in mind, she'd been able, finally, to fall asleep.

Cat rubbed a hand across her eyes. She'd slept late this morning, much to Mistress Fairway's tight-lipped disapproval, but weariness dragged her down like heavy stones around her neck. Never mind. She would sleep well when they got Garth back. And they would do that. Soon.

Shoppers were gathered in front of Master Berrymore's stall. She stood back until there was a break, then approached.

"Excuse me. I'm not sure whether you remember me, but I was here the other day."

The stall owner glanced at her. His gaze sharpened. "I remember. You had questions about Talisa Thatcher. And you wanted directions to Alain Swanson's house."

"Yes."

"I told you as much as I knew." His eyes left her to roam the crowd for prospective buyers.

Cat raised her voice. "I have other questions I need to ask."

He glanced back at her. "Other questions?" His tone was wary.

"About your brother-in-law."

"Cory's in prison. Any questions about him will be asked at his trial." He turned his back on her, rearranged the clothes on the counter.

Cat opened her mouth, but closed it as a young woman in a red dress stopped by the stall. After her came a middle-aged couple, a woman with a whining child in tow, then a number of people at once. Cat waited as patiently as she could until they had all moved on. Then she went and stood beside the stall where its owner couldn't ignore her.

"I'm sorry. I wouldn't bother you, but this is important. It's *urgent.*" Despite her best efforts, her voice quivered on the last word.

At least her emotion made him give her his full attention.

She drew a deep breath. "I need to find out who Cory's friends are and where they can be found."

"I know little of Cory's friends. I wasn't interested, and he wouldn't have told me anyway." There was a hard edge in his voice. "I can't help you. Now –"

"Wait." She grabbed his arm before he could turn away again. He jerked it free. "I'm sorry," Cat said again. "But surely you know *some* of them."

Denial was plain in the tight lips, the unyielding jaw.

"You *must* know," she said desperately. "Garth, a friend of mine... He's being held by people who know Cory. They keep Garth drugged, and they sent a note that says they won't let him go unless your brother-in-law is set free."

"*What?*" Master Berrymore stared at her as though she'd just said the waterfall had stopped tumbling over the cliff into the river below.

She nodded. Tears were threatening. "That's why –"

"Excuse me," someone interrupted. "How much are you asking for this?"

Master Berrymore glanced at the thin-faced elderly man who clutched a cane in one hand and a carving in the other. The carving showed a young girl who stood, one hand shading her eyes, gazing into the distance.

"Two silver coins."

The man handed over the money without protest and left, cradling the statue as tenderly as though it were a baby. The other man stared at the coins in his hand. "I didn't think he'd pay that much," he muttered.

"Can you help? Can you give me a name? An address? Please?" Cat begged.

He looked at her, frowning.

"Garth... He helped Cory. When the soldiers came for him, Garth helped Cory escape." She swallowed. "I think your brother-in-law would want Garth found."

"Probably." Master Berrymore's mouth quirked in what was almost, but not quite, a smile. The frown came back. "But I still can't help you. The only one I ever met was the dark-haired young man who used to deliver messages."

"Dark-haired young man?" Hope trembled in Cat's heart.

The stall owner shook his head. "He's Master Swanson's apprentice. Since you asked for directions to his place, I presume you've already talked to the man."

Her shoulders slumped. "Yes."

"I'm sorry."

There was no more to be said. No more to be done. "Thank you. If you think of anything, if you remember any names, would you send word to the Spellman house?"

He hesitated, then said, "If I think of anything, I'll talk it over with my wife, then decide what's best to be done."

She looked at him sharply.

"How much does this cost?" A women held up a yellow blouse.

He ignored her. "Cory might give up his chance for freedom to help this boy, but I'm not sure Rina would be willing to throw away his chance so lightly. If either of us thinks of anything, we'll talk about it," he repeated.

It was a stingy promise, but the best she would get. She nodded, thanked him again, and left. Behind her, she heard a protesting squawk as the woman heard the price of the blouse.

By the time she made her way though the congested streets and across the bridge, the bright sun of the morning and early afternoon had given way to grey gloom. Maybe that was why she shivered as she trudged past the elegant dwellings leading to Gotham Street. As she got closer, she walked slower and slower. She didn't want to enter the Spellman home, to face Mistress Fairway's disapproving eyes, to sit at dinner and in the sitting room with no one to distract her from her thoughts of Garth, drugged, confused, imprisoned.

Head down, she scuffed her way along Gotham Street. She shouldn't scuff. These were her good shoes, not the worn brown ones she used at home. But what did it matter?

"Cat."

She jumped and looked up. "Mel! I didn't see you."

"No wonder, even though I've been standing in front of the house so long my legs are growing roots. What's so interesting about the ground? Do the stones inspire a song?" He cocked his head.

She smiled. "No." She couldn't imagine making a song about stones or anything else. Not now. "You've been here for a while, then? Why didn't you wait inside? Surely Mistress Fairway invited you in."

"She did, but she made it clear that my presence would be as welcome as a muddy boot, so I decided to enjoy the fresh air." Despite Mel's light words, his merry grin and bright yellow shirt, his eyes were unusually sober.

"Won't you come in now?"

He shook his head. "No. I just wanted to give you a message. You asked me to let you know if I saw Andreas Wells, and I have. He was in The Laughing Lute at noon."

A drop of rain hit her head. Then another. "I've already discovered where he and Master Swanson live, but thank you."

"It's good you have, since Andreas was most unforthcoming."

"Oh. Then why... I mean, thank you very much." More rain was falling. It had been kind of Mel to come, but she wished he would leave now, before the rain chilled her more than she already was.

"You were looking for Garth. It seems that the whole city is now. Has anyone found the missing boy yet?" His tone tried for humour, but failed.

She shook her head. If she'd spoken, her voice might have cracked.

"Did your search for Alain Swanson have anything to do with Garth?"

She cleared her throat. "I thought it might. But –"

"So I was right to ask Andreas if he had any idea where Garth was."

Cat's heart jumped. "Did he say he knew?"

"No. Oh no. Not our Andreas. But before he said he didn't, he turned the colour of a hundred ripe tomatoes and looked down at the floor. An intriguing reaction, wouldn't you say?"

TALISA

A CHILD STOOD AT THE SIDE OF THE ROAD, hands over her face, wailing.

Talisa halted. "What is it? Can I help?"

The girl continued to cry.

Talisa dismounted and knelt beside her. "Can you tell me what's wrong? Are you hurt?"

"Lo...lo....los..."

"Lost? Is that it?"

The hands came part way down, revealing a grubby, tear-soaked face. "But...butterfly. Pretty butterfly."

Talisa smiled. "You were following a butterfly and got lost? That happened to me more than once. Don't worry. Terrin and I will get you home. Can you tell me how to find your house?"

The child was three at most, and her directions were extremely confusing. By the time Talisa finally located the right farmhouse, the sun was beginning to descend.

The door was opened by a woman who took one look at Talisa's six-fingered hands and snatched the girl away as though rescuing her from a cougar's claws. There was a bitter taste in Talisa's mouth as she rode away. It started to rain.

Little light was left in the grizzling sky when she reached Freyfall. She hesitated, then left Terrin at the nearest public stable and started walking. It would have been more sensible to find an inn for the night, she knew. She wasn't at all confident of finding Master Swanson's house in the dark. But her fear drove her on. Her fear for Garth. Her fear for Cory.

She'd only gone halfway when she knew she was as lost as the child by the roadside. She felt like putting her hands over her face and wailing too.

If only Garth or Welwyn or her father were here. If only she had inherited enough talent to use a finding spell to locate a house she had visited twice before.

Well, they weren't here, and she had been born with the gift of music, not magic. And if she couldn't use a spell, she could use her mind. Her memory.

The house was by the river. Surely she could find that. Then all she would have to do was follow it.

As she walked, she paused now and then to listen for the sound of rushing water above the steady drip of rain. After she pulled off her travelling cap to hear better, her hair became drenched, and kept falling in wet strands across her face.

The weather kept most people indoors, but not all. A man with a lantern followed her for a few blocks before his light flickered out and she lost him in the darkness. Her heart pounded too quickly for some time after that.

She could hear the river now. She hurried towards it.

She'd forgotten how tall the wild grass was along the riverbank, and how prickly. Several times, she had to stop to free herself from thorns. Her feet squelched through the muddy soil.

Talisa stopped and smeared hair off her face. What a fool she'd been to take this route. She was wet, miserable, and, worst of all, not at all sure she'd know the house from this direction, with rain blurring the view.

Then, quite suddenly, the rain stopped. The clouds drifted apart enough to reveal the moon. Talisa walked faster, but kept her eyes focused on the buildings she passed.

There! That was it, a narrow house leaning against its neighbour. And there was the door Andreas had slipped open so Cory could escape.

With a sigh of relief, Talisa made her way to the house and knocked.

There were no windows at the back to reveal a light inside. But surely, *surely*, someone was home. She knocked again.

The door opened. Alain Swanson stood there, candle held high.

"Master Swanson, I'm sorry to disturb you, but it's important. May I come in? I'm Talisa Thatcher," she added as he continued to gaze at her.

"Talisa! I'm sorry, I didn't recognize you at first. Yes, do come in." He stepped back, allowing her to enter. Water dripped from her hair onto the floor of the small entrance.

"I'm a bit wet," Talisa said apologetically.

"I noticed." There was a hint of laughter in his voice. "Wait here. I'll see if I have anything to help you dry off."

He disappeared up a set of steep stairs, taking the light with him. Talisa stood shivering in the dark.

He reappeared and handed her a blue shirt. Talisa did what she could to mop up her hair and clothes. The shirt was soaked when she returned it.

"Thank you."

"You are very welcome." He regarded her gravely. "You look as though you had a rough journey here. Was there trouble?"

"Only in finding you. I need to talk to you. It's about Garth."

He was quiet a moment, then said, "I have other guests. You'd better meet them. They've come about Garth too."

He opened the door to his kitchen and went in. Talisa followed.

The room was lit by one stubby candle that stood on the table and left the corners in shadow. Two people were seated there, both watching the door as intently as a cat watches a mouse hole. The man, who appeared to be in his early twenties, had curling damp brown hair and a mouth made for laughter. Talisa frowned, trying to think where she'd seen him before. The woman – or girl, rather – was a stranger. Heavy tawny hair, also damp, fell to her shoulders and across her forehead, almost hiding the hazel eyes that were staring at Talisa.

"Please sit down," Alain Swanson said.

Talisa sat. He placed his candle on the table beside the other one and stood regarding the three of them. "Do you know each other?"

Talisa started to say no, but the brown-haired man spoke first. "It's Talisa Thatcher, isn't it? I met you last fall at The Laughing Lute. You honoured us with a song. My name is Mel Beller."

Talisa smiled. "Yes, of course. I knew I'd seen you before, but didn't know where." Though how she could forget the singer of the very ribald song he had honoured them with, she didn't know. She glanced at Mel's companion, who was still staring at her, eyes bright with – what? Hostility? Unshed tears?

"Mistress Thatcher, may I introduce you to Catrina Ashdale," Alain said.

"Cat!" Talisa exclaimed. She added hastily, "Please forgive my familiarity. It's just that I've heard Garth talk about you so much that I feel I know you. And I've met you before too." She smiled, thinking of the tawny cat that had accompanied Garth everywhere. Her smile faded. "Master Swanson said you are here because of Garth."

"Yes."

Talisa glanced from Cat to Master Swanson and back. She wished she'd found the musician alone. How to ask for his help without revealing too much to his company? While she was hesitating, Cat asked, "Do you know about the message that said Garth would be released only when Cory was freed?" Her hands, lying on the table, were tightly clenched.

If it was hostility she'd seen in Cat's eyes, it was no wonder. "Yes."

"Master Spellman left Freyfall to go to the prison and ask Cory who might be holding Garth. Will Cory tell him, do you think?" Cat's hands seemed to clench even tighter, if that was possible. The floor creaked as Alain shifted his weight.

Talisa swallowed. "No."

Cat sucked in her breath. Talisa hurried on. "I was there when Master Spellman asked Cory. Cory refused to name anyone. He has his reasons, ones he feels are good. But he does not want Garth to suffer because of him."

Mel raised his eyebrows. "Noble notes, but no melody. That won't help Garth."

"But it will! He told me who he suspects. He asked me to tell them he wants Garth freed without such conditions."

Cat's eyes closed for a second. When they opened again, Talisa saw something new in them. Hope?

"Why did you come here?" Alain asked. His dark eyes were intent on her face.

Talisa hesitated, glancing at Cat and Mel again. Then she said, "Cory told me about the men he suspects in confidence. Promise you won't reveal their identities."

Mel looked at Cat. She was silent a long time before she said, "I promise I won't unless I have to. But if I need to in order to save Garth, I will."

Talisa nodded. This was the best she could expect. She turned to Alain. "I came to ask if you'll go with me to these people's homes."

"Of course," he said promptly, then added, "that's the only reason you came?"

She blinked, surprised. "What other reason would I have?"

Cat leaned forward. The candle sparked glints of gold and amber in her hair. "We think Andreas knows more than he's told anyone. When Mel asked him if he had any idea where Garth was, he acted strangely."

"Are you sure he wasn't just being overly dramatic? Cory once said he likes to play-act."

Mel thought about this, then shook his head. "No. I've known Andreas for some time, if only casually. There was nothing of that in his manner today."

"Andreas is out at the moment," Alain said. "We've been waiting for him to return. If you don't mind, I'd like to wait a little longer before we head out to find these people Cory told you about."

Talisa nodded, and tried to suppress her relief. The wait might help her clothes dry a little before she faced the cool night wind again.

They sat in silence while the old house creaked and groaned around them. The wait could only have been fifteen or twenty minutes, but it seemed endless.

Then the front door opened. A minute later, Andreas Wells appeared in the doorway. He must have been caught in the rain too, for his red cloak and dark hair clung to him.

"Mistress Thatcher! What joy it gives me to see you here." He bowed with his usual flourish before his gaze moved to the other guests.

"Andreas, I think you know Master Beller," Alain said.

"Indeed I do, and have enjoyed his songs many times." Andreas flashed a brief, bright smile, but his eyes were wary.

"I don't know whether you've met Mistress Ashdale."

"I had the pleasure of meeting her – alas, all too briefly – at The Laughing Lute." Andreas bowed again.

"I was there asking about Garth Spellman," Cat said.

"Oh."

"Andreas, all three of our visitors have come tonight because of Garth Spellman." Alain's voice was very serious. So was his face.

"Oh."

"Master Beller thinks you know more about his whereabouts than you told him."

Andreas flickered a glance at Mel, then looked away.

"*Do* you know where he is?"

Andreas said nothing.

"I wouldn't have thought you capable of holding another person against his will. Especially not someone who was helping us in our cause." Alain didn't sound angry, just tired. Very tired.

Andreas's face flamed. "I'm not!"

"But you know where he is." Cat threw the words at him like stones.

He flinched, then folded his arms and stood there, face set.

"Cory wants Garth freed. He won't accept his own release at such a cost," Talisa said.

Andreas's eyes widened. "But –"

"Andreas, this is not a game." Alain walked forward and stood facing the younger man. "Tell us what you know."

"I don't *know* anything. Not for sure. I only guessed."

"Guessed what?"

Andreas hesitated.

"Two of the men Cory thinks might be involved were talking to you the last time I was here," Talisa said. "Are they the ones who have Garth?"

Andreas's eyes darted around as though he were a deer with hunters closing in on him. Then his arms dropped. "Yes. At least, I think so. They agreed to go along with your plan for the march on Freybourg, Master Swanson, but they wanted more. They wanted to hurt the Count of Eastlands as they had been hurt. They didn't tell me that, but I could tell. Then Garth started delivering messages to them."

He looked at Alain earnestly. "When Garth didn't come here any more, I thought as you did, Master Swanson, that he had grown tired of our cause. It wasn't until Mistress Ashdale came to The Laughing Lute, asking questions, that I began to wonder."

Mel frowned. "I don't understand. Why did you think they had something to do with Garth's disappearance? That was a while ago, right? Long before Updale was arrested."

Andreas nodded. "I thought they might have had plans that Garth overheard. They're both so angry they find it hard not to say things they shouldn't sometimes. Anyway, I sent word that I'd like to meet with them. I mentioned that a girl was searching for Garth. They didn't say anything, but the way they looked at each other made me think my suspicion was right." For a moment, Andreas sounded complacent.

Then his voice changed. "I would have told you, Master Swanson, really I would. But then Mistress Thatcher came with news about Cory. I'd heard before that he'd been caught, of course, but it wasn't until then that I really felt what it must be like for him. I felt awful. And then... It was as though Freyn had sent an idea into my head. I escorted Wendell and Ennis out, and as I made my farewells, I said – casually, so they wouldn't think I knew anything – that it was a pity we didn't have someone who belonged to an important family who we could exchange for Cory. From the way they looked, I knew my words had hit the mark. Are you *sure* Cory doesn't want this?" he asked Talisa. He sounded as hurt as a small boy whose present has been rejected.

"I'm sure."

"It seemed like such a good idea," he said wistfully.

"But it wasn't." Alain's voice was stern, but some of the strain had left his face. "Now we must secure Garth's release. Andreas, can you lead us to these men's homes?"

Andreas nodded. Talisa was relieved. Despite Cory's directions, she wasn't sure about finding her way through twisting streets in the dark.

"Good." Alain looked at Cat and Mel. "It might seem like an invading army if we all arrive on their doorsteps."

"I'm coming," Cat said fiercely.

"Sorry," Mel said. "Garth's a friend, and I have a large dose of curiosity in my makeup. You can't get rid of me."

The musician sighed. "And Talisa is needed to relay Cory's wishes. Very well. We'll all go."

The night was cool, but the breeze that had risen had blown the clouds away. They walked by the light of the moon and stars. Andreas seemed to know every side street and back way that existed in Freyfall, and used them all. By the time they had gone a short distance, Talisa was totally lost. Cory had said Ennis and Wendell lived near the Berrymores, but it seemed to her that they were heading in the completely wrong direction. But in a remarkably short time, Andreas motioned them to stop. "Ennis lives on this street, Wendell the next one over."

The buildings here were as tall and crumbling as the ones on the Berrymores' street. Candles flickered in a few windows, but most were dark. It was late, Talisa reminded herself. Most people would be sleeping. There was no reason to feel menace in the darkened rooms. Nevertheless, she shivered.

"You must be cold. Your clothes are still wet," Alain said, removing his cloak and placing it around her shoulders.

"What do we do now?" Cat demanded.

"Knock on one of their doors and ask if Garth Spellman is there," Alain said. "Which door, Andreas?"

"Ennis's. He's lived alone since his wife died, while Wendell has a wife and young children. It would be hard to keep someone hidden at his place."

The building Andreas led them to had no light in the hall. They waited while Andreas fumbled with his spark and flint and lit a stub of a candle he carried in his pocket, then followed him down the hall to a door at the back. He knocked.

There was no answer. He knocked again. Still no answer.

"If he's hiding a prisoner in there, it's no wonder he won't open the door," Mel muttered.

"He knows it's me. I gave the special knock." Andreas tried once more – two long taps, two short, two long. No one answered. And, strain as she might, Talisa could hear no sound from inside.

"He must be out," Andreas said.

"Then this is the perfect time to rescue Garth." Cat was staring at the door as though she would like to batter it into kindling. Talisa had no doubt she would try to do just that if it proved the only way to get in.

"Yes," Alain said slowly. "It is. I don't imagine anyone knows how to pick a lock?"

Or use an unbinding spell, Talisa thought. If Welwyn or her father were here, or any wizard... She put her hand on the knob. It moved under her fingers. "It's not locked."

They stared at each other. Then Andreas, holding the candle high, pushed the door open and entered, with Cat as close behind as his shadow.

The room smelled of dust, and unwashed bodies, and vomit. Talisa tried to breathe through her mouth as she looked around at what could be seen in the candle's feeble glow.

Like the one rented by Rina and Bart, the room was small, with a hearth at the end and a curtained alcove. There was no window. A table and chair were pushed against one wall. No other furniture stood on the cracked, dustballed floor.

A scratching noise jerked Talisa's head around.

"It's only a mouse, I think," Mel said. "Or maybe a rat." His voice echoed.

Cat went directly to the alcove and swished the curtain aside. Talisa peered over her shoulder.

The alcove was empty.

"He's not here." Cat's voice was desolate.

"But he was," Alain said quietly. "At least, someone was. There's bedding on the floor. And someone's been sick in there."

He was right. The blankets and floor were stained. Talisa sniffed cautiously, and the stench of vomit was almost overpowering.

"It's no wonder he was sick," Mel said. He had picked up an empty bottle that stood by the hearth. "Lambwort."

"What's lambwort?" Talisa asked.

"A drug that eases pain and helps people sleep. It's common enough, and fairly cheap, but it's used sparingly. A drop will send someone to sleep, but any more and the person gets dizzy and disoriented. And sick."

Cat was staring at the soiled blankets. "All this time Garth's been here, in this filthy place, forced to take this drug, sick..."

Andreas cleared his throat. "He was probably only drugged at the beginning, when they must have feared someone would search for him, and at the end, when they knew someone was. And when Ennis was out, of course, since Garth could use magic to escape. But they wouldn't have drugged him except when it was absolutely necessary. Lambwort might not be expensive, but it still costs more than either Ennis or Wendell could afford. And they're not cruel men."

Cat whirled on him. "Not cruel! How can you say that? They've kept Garth here for over six weeks. They've forced this...this *poison* down his throat. And when they didn't do that, what else did they use to keep Garth imprisoned and quiet? Ropes? A gag? For six *weeks*... And where is he now? What's *happened* to him?"

She was shaking. Talisa put an arm around her. "Cat –"

Cat shook her off. "Don't. *Don't.*"

Talisa stepped back, feeling as though she'd been slapped.

Alain spoke quietly. "Ennis is gone, it seems, and taken Garth with him. Let's ask Wendell if he knows where they are. Andreas, please lead us to him."

After a moment, Andreas nodded jerkily. As a child, Talisa had owned a rag doll. One day its back had been punctured by a jagged stone and half its stuffing had come out. It had looked the way Andreas looked now.

It didn't take long to reach Wendell's building and walk up the four flights of stairs to his room. Again, Andreas gave his distinctive knock. There was a rustling noise inside, but no one came to the door. Andreas knocked again, then called softly, "Wendell? Mistress Dale? It's me. Andreas."

"What do you want?" The woman's voice, hushed and wary, came from right behind the door.

"Is Wendell home? I must talk to him."

"No. He's gone."

Talisa closed her eyes.

Alain stepped forward. "Mistress Dale, my name is Alain Swanson. I don't know whether you know who I am —"

"I've heard of you."

"Could we talk to you for a minute? Please? It's very important."

There was silence, then the door cracked open, revealing a woman's thin face and limp brown hair.

"What is it? I can't talk long. My children are asleep. Or they were," she added wearily as a baby started to wail. "You might as well come in."

She closed the door behind them and went over to one of the pallets on the floor, picking up the crying child and stroking its head. "Shhh. Shhh. It's all right. Hush now, my love. Shhh."

Another child stirred. "Mam..."

"Go back to sleep, Lybbie. It's only some guests come calling. They'll go in a minute." She spoke in a soft voice, so as not to wake the others. There were two more children, wrapped together in blankets against the wall.

Mistress Dale turned back to Alain. "What is it?"

"Do you know where your husband is, Mistress Dale?"

She looked away. "No."

"We think he and his friend Ennis have taken a young man named Garth Spellman prisoner and are demanding that Cory Updale be freed in exchange for Garth's release. We don't want your husband punished, but we must find Garth."

"He's not here."

Alain's eyes surveyed the small room, the three sleeping children, the baby in its mother's arms. "No," he agreed. "But he was at Ennis's. Unfortunately, both Ennis and Garth have disappeared. So, it seems, has your husband."

She stroked the baby's soft fuzz of light hair and said nothing.

"Andreas says that your husband and Ennis want to take drastic action. Do you know what that might be?"

Her face twisted with pain. "No. He wouldn't tell me. He wouldn't tell me anything."

"But you can probably guess. You know your husband."

"No. I used to, but now... No. When we lived at home, on the farm, he was so gentle. He could do anything with the animals, they trusted him so." She stood still, staring at memories. The baby started crying again and she resumed her stroking. "But ever since we came here... He's so angry. Oh, I don't blame him. I'm angry too. But his anger frightens me. I don't know what he'll do anymore."

"Who is he angry at? The Count of Eastlands?"

"Mostly at him, but also at the queen and army and everyone who helped the count or didn't stop him. I sometimes think he's angry at the whole world these days. Even me." She laughed, a laugh that was half sob.

Alain paused, then asked, "When did he leave?"

"This morning."

"Did he say when he'd return?"

"No."

"And – forgive me, Mistress Dale – do you and your children have enough to live on while he's gone?"

She laughed again. "Oh no. But then, we haven't enough when he's here either. We haven't had enough to live on since we came to Freyfall."

He reached into the purse at his belt. "Please accept these for the children's sake."

She clutched the coins he handed her and nodded. By the wall, one of the children started coughing. She glanced over, frowning.

"We'll go now. May Freyn be with you."

She looked back. "Would it really be so bad? If this young man *could* be exchanged for Cory? I know it bothers Wendell something fierce that Cory might be killed. It bothers me too. Cory's a good person. And he didn't set the fire."

Your husband and Ennis did. And you were the one who warned Cory they would. Talisa was sure of this, but all she said was, "Cory doesn't want that exchange."

Mistress Dale shook her head. "I don't understand."

At that moment, Talisa didn't either. She didn't understand at all.

They left. The baby's thin wail followed them all the way down the stairs.

GALIA

"**O**UR LESSON TOMORROW WILL HAVE TO BE a little later than usual." Melton Granton, Galia noted, did not ask whether this would be convenient for her.

"Oh?"

"I'll be testifying at a trial. I don't think my statement will take long, but I should stay to discover the outcome. Not that I foresee any possibility but the right one. Still, I won't rest easy until I know the man is judged guilty and punished accordingly."

Galia stared at him.

"I'm sure the lesson tomorrow will go as well as the one today. I must thank you. I believe I am truly beginning to understand the way your magic works." The wizard bestowed a smile on her, then left.

Trial. Cory Updale's trial? It must be.

Galia walked to the window. The evening sun made the

stone wall surrounding the college glow as though warmed from within. She looked over the wall to the tree-lined lane beyond. There was no one in sight.

Talisa had been gone for two days now. If she didn't return tonight, she would miss Cory's trial. She would be so unhappy.

Galia stood staring out.

If Talisa couldn't be present, then she would go in her stead. She would report what happened.

It would hurt Talisa, hearing what happened. Melton Granton had said the outcome was sure, and he was probably right.

Talisa would want to know anyway.

The sun sank lower. The wall looked cold and grey. Galia turned and left.

If she knew Freyan spells, she could turn invisible. That would make following Master Granton and Master Ford so much easier. As it was, she had to stay a long way behind them. It was lucky she had keen eyes. Hawk eyes, Arlan used to say.

The building the wizards entered was one of five that faced the palace on its hill. Made of the grey stone that dominated the city, it was smaller and less imposing than its neighbours. But the soldiers at the door made up for any lack of size in the building. Galia approached one of them hesitantly.

He had to look a long way down. "Your business?"

"I am here for the trial. Cory Updale's trial."

"Are you a witness?"

"No"

"Bit young to be here, aren't you?"

"I am older than I seem," she assured him.

"Hmm. Well, as long as we don't have parents come searching for a missing daughter, or your mistress hunting for an absent apprentice."

"You will not."

He moved aside. "Go in, then. It's to your left."

The room she entered was large and high-ceilinged, with a marble floor and a series of wooden benches. Like the ceiling in the Eastlands' house, this one was painted, but not with a pleasant pastoral scene. A stern-faced judge sat in the middle. His right arm pointed to a man who was throwing off his manacles while a woman waited with open arms. His left pointed to a man being dragged towards the gallows. Galia looked away hastily and slipped onto a bench at the very back. The wizards were seated near the front, just below a platform that contained four chairs. Other people sat throughout the room: green-uniformed soldiers, a man in brown homespun looking around in awe, a woman with smooth brown hair and, beside her – Galia started. What was Master Spellman doing here?

She gaped at the wizard for a minute before her gaze moved on to two women sitting together. One was crying into her handkerchief.

A door at the front opened and two men entered. One was a soldier. The other was Cory. He was led to a chair on the left side of the platform. The soldier stationed himself beside him. Did they think Cory was so dangerous that the manacles on his wrists and the soldiers at the door weren't enough?

She would tell Talisa that Cory had looked calm. He did, though he blinked now and then as though the light coming in through the tall narrow windows bothered him. She wouldn't tell her how pale he was, nor how his brown eyes were smudged with weariness.

The door opened again. A soldier marched in, raised a trumpet to his lips, and played. Was it only her imagination, or did the trumpet sound a long note of sad farewell? Her eyes moved to Cory, but his face hadn't changed. Then Galia had to scramble to her feet as three men in rich, sombre robes walked in and took their places on chairs in the centre of the dais.

"This court will hear the case of Cory Updale, accused of treason, arson and murder. May justice be done in the name of Freyn and of our beloved monarch, Queen Elira." The judge in the middle had a deep, resonant voice that carried effortlessly to the back of the room. It sent shivers down Galia's spine. Or maybe it was his words that made her cold.

The chill spread, icy-fingered, as the trial progressed. A soldier stood at the front and explained how the rear of the barracks in Freyfall had burst into flames last fall, and how two men had died in the inferno. The woman with the handkerchief sobbed loudly. She was still crying when she rose to tell how her husband had died, and how she and her children had suffered since his death. The woman who'd been sitting beside her told the same story, of a lost husband and grieving family. There were no tears left in her, she said.

Sometime during her testimony, a man came in and sat down at the far end of Galia's bench. He huddled there, head down, shoulders bowed. Galia glanced at him, then away, as the man in brown homespun rose to make his statement.

"Tell us what you know of the fire, Master Fletcher," said the judge in the centre.

Master Fletcher cleared his throat. "I was coming home after visiting a friend when I saw a glow in the sky. I hurried towards it, thinking maybe I could help. As I turned the corner onto the street where the barracks were, a man came rushing past."

"Do you see that person in this room?" asked the judge on the right.

The man in homespun looked at Cory. "It's him. Cory Updale."

"You're sure?"

"Oh yes. I'd seen him often enough, yes, and heard him too. He was always talking about how wrong it was that folk had been kicked off their land by the Count of Eastlands, and how something should be done about it."

"And you listened to such talk?" asked the judge on the left.

Master Fletcher shuffled his feet. "Well, I...The talk was around. Not just from Updale, though he spoke out more loudly than most. It was hard not to hear it. But I'm a loyal, law-abiding man. I'd never go along with such foolishness."

"More than foolishness," the middle judge said sternly. "Never mind," he added as the witness opened his mouth. "You may step aside."

The man at the end of her bench still had his head down. Galia glanced at him now and then as a captain reported on the army's search for the arsonists, and how they had started hunting for Updale after Master Fletcher had come forward with his information. Yes, they had checked with others, and yes, Fletcher's account was true. Updale was well known as a firebrand who often spoke about the injustice of the eviction. No, they had not been able to capture him, though they had made vigorous enquiries and tracked down all his friends and acquaintances. The captain's voice was soft, his words hard to catch. Galia's eyes wandered around the room. So, she noticed, did Cory's. Was he searching for friendly faces?

His attention was caught when the name of the next witness was announced. There was no difficulty hearing Melton Granton. He spoke clearly, loudly, and with the confidence of absolute conviction. He had been in Uglessia last year, helping Uglessians increase their knowledge of wizardry. Talisa Thatcher had been away when he first arrived, but had returned at the beginning of winter. He had known she had brought a Freyan companion with her but had never met the man until the day an assembly was held to decide whether to proceed with a plan to increase the production of kala. It was a plan that he, Melton Granton, had proposed, one that would have benefited both Uglessians and Freyans, and he blamed Cory Updale for its defeat. It was after this that he had learned, through Talisa's sister Welwyn, that Updale had fled Freya where he was suspected of setting fire to the barracks and causing the death of two men.

"The Uglessians knew this but sheltered him anyway?" The judge in the middle leaned forward, frowning. There were mutters in the room.

Melton Granton pursed his lips. "I don't believe the majority knew, though the Thatcher family certainly did. I hesitate to speak badly of my hosts, but they behaved most reprehensibly in this matter."

If eyes could have thrown knives, Cory's would have.

"You informed the army of the man's presence in Uglessia when you returned to Freya, I understand."

"I did."

Leonard Ford corroborated his fellow wizard's testimony. Then came the captain who had gone to Uglessia and captured Cory. Galia shifted in her seat. The wood seemed to be pressing into her back and buttocks.

Cory's eyes were roving the room again. They froze on – No. Not on her, as she had first thought. On the man at the other end of her bench. His head was raised now. His face was weathered, his mouth a thin straight line. She had seen sick people with mouths like that, as they clenched their lips on pain. The two men stared at each other.

"Master Konrad Spellman, please."

Galia's attention jerked back to the front of the room.

"Could you tell us what you know of this man?"

"Little until the other day. My grandson has been missing for some time. Until ten days ago, we thought he had left home voluntarily. When we realized he hadn't, I used a finding spell. The image I got told me he was alive, but it was very confused. I believe he is drugged." The wizard paused, then continued evenly. "Five days later, we received a message stating that Garth would be freed only if Cory Updale was released."

There was a stir in the room. It quieted as the judge on the right, a heavy-set man with a balding head, asked, "What did you do then?"

"I came to Freybourg to talk to Master Updale."

"And?"

Konrad Spellman looked at Cory for the first time since he had begun to speak. "He said he knew nothing of my grandson's disappearance. I believe him: there was no opportunity for him to be involved. He also said he would not accept his freedom on such terms. I am not so sure I believe that. I asked him to name those he thinks may be holding Garth, and he refused." Konrad stopped. His hands were clenched.

The central judge glanced at his colleagues, then back at the witness. "Thank you, Master Spellman. May Freyn smile on your search for your grandson."

Konrad Spellman bowed his head. "Thank you."

"It is late," the judge continued. "We shall break for our midday meal and reconvene two hours from now. At that time, Master Updale may speak, as may anyone who wishes to testify on his behalf."

Galia had no money to buy food. She could have gone outside, she supposed, to enjoy the sunlight and fresh air. But somehow that seemed a betrayal, when Cory could not. She stayed, wriggling on the hard bench now and then. The man to her right remained too. His head was bowed once more. Galia glanced at him from time to time, wondering whether to speak, but his hunched shoulders shut her out.

It seemed that more than two hours passed, but eventually Cory was led back in, the trumpet blew, and the judges resumed their seats. Cory's name was called.

"You have heard the evidence against you. Do you have anything to say in your defence?"

"I did not set fire to the barracks. I did not cause the death of two men." Cory's voice was just a shade too loud, a shade too defiant.

The judge raised his eyebrows. "Yet you were seen near the barracks on the night of the fire. You are known to be a rebel – a firebrand, as Captain Birch called you."

"I have spoken against the forced eviction of tenants from the Count of Eastlands' land, yes, and against those who would turn a blind eye on people who have no homes, no food, and no hope. I am proud to have done so. I would do so again, if I were free."

Galia tried to imprint the words on her mind. Talisa would want to know just what Cory said. She would be proud.

"But I believe there are other ways than violence to change what must be changed. I did not set the fire."

"Why were you seen hurrying away from it?"

Cory hesitated. Was it just the sunlight, streaming in through a window onto his face, that made his glance flicker for a moment to the back of the room?

"Well?"

"I... Someone told me that people were going to set the fire. I went to try to stop them, but by the time I arrived the building was already in flames."

"Someone told you," the judge repeated. "*Who* told you?"

Cory said nothing.

"Who were the people who set fire to the barracks?"

Still, Cory was silent.

The judge sat back. "Master Updale, you say you did not commit this murderous act. You say some mysterious person informed you about it, and that other mysterious people did it. Yet you won't say who they are. Tell me, is there any reason why we should believe you?"

"No," Cory said. Again, was it the sunshine that made him raise a shackled hand to his eyes? "Except that it's the truth."

"Then why won't you give us the names?"

Cory dropped his hand. "Because those who set the fire are not bad people. They were driven to the act by the wrong done to them, to their families, to their friends, to everyone they saw around them. I do not believe they intended the death of the two soldiers."

The sun made the room warm. Galia's hands were sweating. She wiped them on her dress. It was the same dress she had worn two days ago, and still bore smudge marks from where she had wiped the earth from her hands. She looked at the marks. She did not want to look at Cory. Not now. Talisa would not want to know how he looked, how white, how...trapped. Like a sea otter she had once seen, caught between rocks.

"I see," said the judge. He did not sound as though he saw anything. "Is there anyone here to speak for you?"

"No."

"Is there anything more you wish to say before we pronounce sentence?"

"Only... Master Spellman said he didn't believe me when I said I wouldn't accept my freedom at Garth's expense, but I won't. I will not tell him who I suspect of holding Garth because that might harm those who should not be hurt." The words came slowly, carefully, as though Cory was picking his way along a beach littered with sharp stones. "But I hope Garth's captors know that I pray, with all my heart, that they set him free no matter what happens to me."

"A laudable prayer," the judge said. "It would, however, be far more laudable – and believable – if you told us who the culprits are."

Cory shook his head.

The judges didn't even leave the room. They huddled together for less than five minutes. Others muttered to one another.

The judges must have given the trumpeter a signal, for he blew his horn again. The room quieted.

"Please stand, Master Updale."

Galia glanced up from her dress, then down again.

"The evidence is overwhelming against you. You were seen on the night of the fire running away from the barracks. You are a known troublemaker. You fled Freya when suspicion turned your way. You claim that others set the fire, but will not say who they are. It is the judgement of this court that you are guilty as charged of treason, arson and murder. At high noon two days from now, you shall be taken to the gallows and hanged by the neck until dead. May Freyn have the mercy on you that this court could not provide."

She should glance up. Talisa would not want to know how Cory looked at this moment, but she might need to.

He looked blank, as though he'd been hit one too many times. Or as though he had fallen down a cliff. As Arlan had fallen. The only difference was that Cory was not dead. Not yet.

The judges rose. Everyone rose. The trumpet blew. The judges swept out. The guard led Cory away.

There was nothing to do now. Nothing but sit and watch the others leave. Konrad Spellman was frowning. The woman beside him had her head down. Galia wondered whether she was crying. The woman with the handkerchief wasn't. "I thought I'd feel better now," Galia heard her say to the woman beside her as they passed. "But I don't. I just feel...empty."

"I know," said the other woman.

Melton Granton was coming. Galia turned her head away so he wouldn't recognize her, and saw the face of the man at the end of the bench.

He looked torn. As though a giant hand had taken his face and wrenched it apart.

No one should look like that.

The wizards were gone. Slowly, the man to her right rose. He was not old, she thought, despite his weathered skin. But he walked like an old man as he headed for the door.

Galia sat for a moment. Then she got up quickly and hurried after him. She did not know why, but she knew she could not let this man out of her sight. She would follow him and see where he led her.

CAT

NOT SLEEPING WAS BECOMING A HABIT, Cat thought, as she stood, staring out the window in Annette's sitting room. A bad habit. It made her nerves scratchy. At lunch today, she had snarled at Elina when the maid served her. The woman had burst into tears.

"I'm sorry," Cat had stammered.

Elina had shaken her head. "It's not you. Mistress Fairway gave me such a talking-to this morning, all because I'd moved some letters in Master Spellman's study when I was dusting last week, and they fell to the floor and weren't found until today. The way she talked, you'd think I'd *meant* to lose them." She'd sniffed and wiped her eyes.

"I'm sorry," Cat had repeated. She was. This was her fault. The housekeeper might be annoyed at Elina's carelessness, but it was because she was angry at Cat that she had turned on the hapless maid.

Mistress Fairway's usual coolness had plunged into new icy depths when Cat came home late the other night. Cat had knocked while Mel hovered behind her, waiting to make sure she got in safely. When Mistress Fairway opened the door, she had glanced from Cat to Mel, then back, as though...as though *we'd been doing something improper*, Cat thought. Her face burned whenever she recalled that look. Even Mel had been quelled.

"Freyn's Night, Cat – Mistress Ashdale, I mean. I'll be in touch." He had given her a quick smile and escaped. To give him credit, he had turned up yesterday to ask if she had heard any news, and if there was anything he could do to help.

If she had asked Talisa to come home with her, Mistress Fairway would not have had an excuse to look at her that way. When they'd left Wendell's, Master Swanson had said it was too late for Talisa to find an inn. He'd glanced at Cat and waited, obviously expecting her to issue an invitation, then told the Uglessian she could stay with him. Cat winced. Talisa had looked hurt by her silence, just as, earlier, she'd flinched when Cat had jerked away from her touch. But she *couldn't* have invited Talisa here. Talisa loved Cory. She would not be welcome in the Spellman house. She should have explained, Cat thought, explained, too, that she'd been unable to bear Talisa's comforting arm for fear she'd break down. Well, she'd felt too raw at the time for explanations, and it was too late now. Cat turned and walked to a small table beside the chair she'd been sitting in before getting up and walking to the window for the tenth time in an hour. Sitting still made her want to throw something. Something breakable, preferably. She picked up the letter she'd received yesterday from Annette and read it yet again.

Dear Cat,

I hope you are well, and that the servants are looking after you properly. We have seen Cory Updale. He will not tell us who he thinks holds Garth. He did say he would not accept his freedom on such terms, and I believe him, though my father-in-law has his doubts. Perhaps he will still send us word, or tell us at his trial, which will take place two days from now. That is perhaps just as well for the young man. I could not help but shudder when I entered the prison. It was so dark and grim. But then, I shudder too when I think of Garth kept captive and drugged, perhaps in a dark room of his own. I'm sorry. I didn't mean to sound so discouraged. There is still hope. I do believe Cory Updale means well. Also, he says that he doesn't believe those holding Garth will offer him any harm. I pray he is right. We will be staying here a few days more, in case he does send word. May Freyn keep you.

Annette

There had been no other news, though Master Swanson had promised to let her know if they heard anything. Yesterday afternoon, she had taken the long walk to his house, only to find it empty. She had waited two hours and seen no one, except one old man who'd wandered by, mumbling to himself.

They *should* have sent word. They should be as worried about Garth as she was. They were all to blame. Andreas was responsible for Garth's present plight, if not his initial imprisonment. If Garth hadn't become entangled in Master Swanson's plans, he would never have been made a captive in the first place. And he had met the musician because Talisa had asked him to find Cory for her.

Well, they weren't as worried, that was obvious. No purpose would be served by going to the house by the river again. It was up to her.

Think.

She had. She had thought until her mind felt bruised.

Think some more.

She walked back to the window, pressing her forehead against the glass. It had been warmed by the sun and did nothing to ease the pain in her head.

Ennis and Wendell had gone somewhere and taken Garth with them. Where had they gone? *Why* had they gone?

They planned to do something drastic, Andreas had said. Wendell was angry, Mistress Dale had said.

Angry at whom? The soldiers? The queen?

Yes. But mostly at the Count of Eastlands.

She heard someone enter the room behind her. "Where does the Count of Eastlands live?" she asked, without turning around.

There was a pause, then Mistress Fairway said, her voice frigid, "In Freybourg, I believe. Why?"

Freybourg. If she left now, she could reach it before sundown. She could go to the count's house. Warn him. Wait for Ennis and Wendell to show up.

"Why?" the housekeeper asked again.

Cat didn't answer. Instead, she turned around and said, "I'm going away for a while. I don't think I'll be gone long, but if the Spellmans return before I'm back, please tell them... No. I'll leave a note."

Mistress Fairway took a step forward. "You're leaving? At a time like this?"

"I –"

"Are you going with that man I saw you with the other night?"

For just a second, Cat considered this. Would Mel go with her? Would he be helpful? Then the words struck her.

"Of course not! Though if I were, it wouldn't be any of your business."

"Not my business? And how do you think I'll explain this to Master Spellman?"

"You have no need to explain anything," Cat said. She tried to make her voice haughty, but it sounded more as it did when she fought with her cousin. "As I told you, I will leave a note."

The housekeeper's face was mottled with rage. "So you think a note is all that's needed? Master Spellman has been kind enough to offer you his hospitality. Now, at a time when he's worried nigh to death, you take it into your head to go off to Freyn knows where, leaving a note behind. Have you *no* gratitude? No sense of shame?"

"Don't you dare speak to me like that!"

"Not dare? Master Spellman took me in when I had nowhere else to go and gave me work. I've been his housekeeper now for thirty years. I know how much he grieved when his only son died, how much it upset him when his grandson refused to study as he should. And now... This is the worst of all. For you to add to his worry and care... It isn't right and I will say so, whether you think it my place or not."

Cat stared at her. The woman was shaking with the force of her emotion. Cat's anger died.

"I'm sorry."

Mistress Fairway gaped at her.

"I'm sorry," Cat repeated. "I should have explained. I'm going to Freybourg to hunt for Garth. I think he might have been taken there."

Mistress Fairway frowned. "You asked where the Count of Eastlands lives. What does he have to do with this?"

"The men who have Garth hate the count because he took their land away. I think they've gone to Freybourg to...Well, to do something. And I think they've taken Garth with them."

"You don't know any of this."

"No," Cat admitted. "But I have to do *something*."

"Yes," the housekeeper agreed slowly. She thought for a moment. "You'd better have a good horse so you can ride quickly. Master Spellman keeps his horses in a stable on

Bartholomy Street. I'll send a message with you so the man who runs it will let you take one of them. Go and pack. I'll meet you at the front door."

Cat gazed after the woman, feeling as though a poisonous snake had withdrawn its fangs and offered to share its food with her.

But this was no time to stand here in wonder. Cat hurried to her room, packed the few things she thought she'd need, and dashed down the stairs. Mistress Fairway was waiting for her.

"Here you are," she said, handing Cat an envelope. "May Freyn smile on your mission." She hesitated, then added, "And on you."

TALISA

"**T**ALISA!"

Talisa swung around. She stared at the sea of carts and carriages, shoppers and stalls, heart thudding. *Danger*, warned a voice inside her.

Nonsense. She was letting Andreas's conspiratorial manner affect her too much. But her heart refused to quiet as her eyes searched the crowd.

Then she saw the giant of a young man striding towards her, flaxen hair streaming down his back.

"Thannis!"

He came up to her, wearing a grin as wide as the street. "It's good to see you."

"And you. But why aren't you at the college?"

His grin disappeared. "They kicked me out."

"They did *what?*"

"Master Wisher said the college didn't need trouble-makers who couldn't keep their tempers."

255

"Oh."

They stood in silence, an island in the middle of the busy river of people. A man brushed by and gave them an irritated glance.

"We can't talk here. Come with me."

Talisa led Thannis to the kala shop where she was to meet Alain and Andreas. It was bright with spring sunshine. They sat at a wooden table by the far wall.

"Tell me."

Thannis shrugged. "There's little to tell. As I said, Master Wisher told me I had to leave. He didn't even want me there one more day."

"I'm sorry," Talisa said, feeling inadequate.

He sighed. "I should be well on my way to Uglessia by now, but somehow, when I reached Freyfall..." He stopped.

She waited.

"I'm not looking forward to returning home and telling everyone what happened."

"They'll understand."

"Oh yes, they'll understand. They'll understand that I'm a hot-headed fool. They've always known that."

Talisa touched his arm gently. "I'm sorry," she said again. "Where are you staying?"

"In an inn not far from here. It's cheap, but I'll have to leave soon if I'm to have enough money for my journey home." He shook himself. "Enough of me. What about you? Did you succeed in your errand?"

"No."

She stared at the kala in her mug. It looked strong and smelled of herbs. The smell of home. She took a sip, then started to talk. At first, the words came slowly. Then they poured out like liquid from a punctured waterskin.

"What now?" Thannis asked when she finished. "Will you return to Freybourg?"

"Yes. I'll be heading there tomorrow, though not by myself." Talisa hesitated. Andreas had stressed the need for secrecy. But she was talking to Thannis, after all. She glanced around. Three of the other tables were occupied, but no one was paying them any attention.

"Alain Swanson – Cory's friend who I told you about – is leading a march to Freybourg. He wants to show Queen Elira and her court just how many of her people need help. I'm going with them."

"And you're leaving tomorrow?"

"Yes. It was meant to be later, but plans had to change." She ran her finger along the edge of the table, and remembered doing the same thing yesterday morning at Alain Swanson's house.

SHE'D COME DOWNSTAIRS late after a night of fretful sleep, broken by nightmares of Cory, bound and gagged in a dark pit. Andreas and Alain were talking quietly as she entered the kitchen. The musician cut some bread and cheese for her.

"Thank you," Talisa said. "And thank you so much for letting me stay here last night."

Alain smiled. "You're welcome. We're discussing what we can do to discover where Ennis and Wendell have gone. Andreas will make enquiries among those who know the two men. Hopefully –"

There was a knock at the front door. Alain stopped, frowning.

"I'll get it." Andreas walked into the hall. There were no brave flourishes in his manners today, Talisa noticed.

A moment later he was back, leading a boy with bare feet and a dirty face who could be no more than eight or nine. "He says he wants to see you," Andreas reported.

"That is, if you be Master Swanson," the boy said.

"I am," Alain assured him. "And you?"

"I be Sully. Sully Shepherd. My mam sent me with a message for you."

"And what is your message?"

"My mam, she cleans house for a soldier man – a captain, she says. While she was dusting furniture, she heard him and another soldier man talking. They was saying there was rumours of a big uprising, and it was going to be stopped before it started. My mam says one of the soldiers said he'd heard they was going to arrest the ringleader, a man named Alain Swanson. The captain – my mam's captain – said they should have done it long ago."

Alain had gone very still. "When was this?"

"This morning. My mam was real worried. She wanted to run out of the house then and there to warn you. But she knew if she did, she'd lose the job, and it's the only one she and my da have between them. Then I came to the kitchen.

I sometimes do, when I see she's alone in there, cleaning the hearth. The others all let her do the dirty jobs, see, but it works out fine. My mam says she don't dare take food home for my da and me, but if we slip in when she's alone she can get us a bite to eat. Da wasn't there today – he heard there might be work unloading a big boat that's just docked. When Mam saw me, she gave me the message. Someone had told her where you live, see, and she said I was to come straight here if I was to make sure the best man in all Freya and the hope for all us poor folk wasn't to be clapped up in gaol just at the worst time. I didn't even have time to eat nothing," Sully said regretfully.

"We had better remedy that." Alain rose. "Sit down and I'll get you some cheese and bread."

The boy looked at the chair, but shook his head. "You have to leave and be quick about it too, my mam said."

"We'll be gone in five minutes," Alain promised. "That will give you time for the bite you missed. Andreas, go pack our spare clothes. Sit," he told Sully.

The boy needed no more urging. The bread and cheese went down so quickly Talisa wondered that he didn't choke over them. His teeth were crooked and too big for his mouth.

Alain turned to Talisa. "Did you bring anything here with you?"

She shook her head. "I left my things with Terrin in the stable."

Andreas had returned more quickly than she would have believed possible. He carried a bag and had two lutes slung over his shoulders.

"If the army plans to stop us before we start, then we'll start sooner than expected," Alain declared. "We'll head for Freybourg two days from now."

"But that will destroy all our plans," Andreas protested. "How can we let everyone know about the change?"

"We will tell key people, and have them tell others."

Andreas still looked worried.

Alain turned to the boy. "Finished? Good. You'd better run off before you're spotted here. Tell your mam you did your task well, and give her my heartfelt thanks. My thanks to you as well." He bowed formally. Sully giggled and scrambled to his feet.

"You'll see me when we march to Freybourg," he promised. "We're all going, my da and mam and me."

"I'm delighted to hear it. By that time I'll have a new song, one about a boy who delivered a warning with courage and speed."

Sully's mouth dropped. He stared at the musician for a moment, then closed his mouth, grinned, and darted away.

"What will you do, Mistress Thatcher?" Alain asked. "Return to Freybourg?"

"No," Talisa said slowly. She picked at her finger. She'd been running it along the rough wood of the table while she thought, and now she had a sliver. "You'll need help spreading the news. I'll stay in Freyfall the next two days to do that, then leave with the rest of you."

"Are you sure?"

She nodded. "It's what Cory would want me to do." And

surely – *surely* – his trial wouldn't take place before she got to Freybourg.

"Thank you," the musician said gravely. "Your help will be invaluable. Do you have a place to stay the next two nights?"

"I'm sure Cory's sister and brother-in-law will put me up. That's no problem. But you'll have to give me simple directions so I can deliver the message. I find it very easy to get lost in Freyfall."

"I'll make them so easy a blind person could follow them," Andreas promised.

TALISA RETURNED FROM HER MEMORIES as the door opened, letting in two familiar figures. Alain and Andreas glanced around, then walked towards Talisa's table and sat down on the wooden bench.

"Master Swanson, Andreas, I would like you to meet my friend Thannis. Thannis, this is Master Alain Swanson and his apprentice, Master Andreas Wells."

Alain murmured a greeting, but Andreas frowned darkly.

"It's all right, Andreas. I've known Thannis all my life. He won't take any tales to the Freyan army."

"How did you make out?" Alain asked after he and Andreas had been served kala.

"I found all the people on my list and gave them your message. Thank you, Andreas. Your directions made it easy."

"And what did they say to the change in plans?" Alain asked.

"A few sounded dismayed that they had such short notice, but they all promised to come – and to spread the word."

"Good. Andreas and I met with similar results. Now there's nothing left to do except get a good night's sleep so we can rise before dawn."

"May I come with you?" Thannis asked.

The musician hesitated. "You're not Freyan. There may be danger, though I hope the queen and her court and army will understand that we come in peace, and act appropriately. But anything may happen. Why risk harm for a cause not your own?"

"Talisa is going," Thannis pointed out.

"That's different," Talisa said. "I'm going for Cory." And for Rina and Bart, she thought, and for a street singer she'd seen last autumn, bare feet blue with cold.

"This is important," Thannis said. "It's something I would like to be part of."

Alain regarded him soberly for a moment, then smiled. "We will be honoured to have you with us."

"You'll have to control your temper," Talisa warned Thannis.

"I will," he assured her.

"Good." Talisa rose. "I should go. It's a long walk to the Berrymores' home."

Andreas jumped up. "If you'll allow me, it will give me great pleasure to escort such a lovely lady." Andreas, it seemed, had regained his old flamboyant gallantry.

"You," Alain told his apprentice, "have work to do."

"I do? But I've delivered all my messages."

"There are others you must talk to. People who may have some idea where Ennis and Wendell are. Remember?"

Andreas looked deflated, but Talisa smiled. Amid all the turmoil, Alain had not forgotten Garth.

"ARE YOU GOING ON THE MARCH to Freybourg, Bart?" Rina asked.

Talisa looked up from her dinner of noodles and beans. Rina was leaning forward, her brown eyes – eyes so like Cory's – intent on her husband's face.

"No," Bart said shortly.

"Why not?" Rina challenged.

"Because it's a waste of time and energy. It will accomplish nothing."

"You can't know that."

"When have the great ones of Freya listened to poor people? Why would it be different now?"

"Poor people have never before gathered together in such numbers," Rina pointed out.

"Even so. It's not that I don't wish the marchers the best of luck," Bart said, flicking a glance at Talisa. "But I see no reason to join them. Anyway, I don't want to be away from you at this time."

Rina was quiet a moment. The evening sun streaming in through the window flecked her brown curls with gold and turned her skin amber, softening the circles that lay like dark bruises under her eyes.

"If you don't want to be away from me, you'll have to come," Rina said. "I am."

Bart's fork clattered onto his plate. "You're *what*?"

"I'm going on the march."

"You can't!"

"Yes I can."

"But the baby. It's due any day now."

"It's due three or four weeks from now," Rina corrected him.

"And what if it comes early? What if this foolishness starts it coming? What if it harms our baby?"

Rina was silent again. Talisa sat, hand clenched on her fork, watching her, watching Bart.

"I don't think it will harm our baby," Rina said at last. "But if it does...What sort of world do we want our child to grow up in? Do we want him or her to live in this building, this street, other streets and buildings like this?"

"It won't. We haven't been toiling away so hard for nothing. We'll move soon. You know that. We've planned that for the last six months." Bart paused, then added more gently, "I know Cory believes in this. But going won't help him."

There was silence. Talisa stared at her plate. The noodles looked like long, flabby worms. She put her fork down.

"I know," Rina said at last. "But if..." She stopped, took a deep breath, and continued. "If Cory dies, I want to know I've done this for him. But it's not just that. Even if we manage to pull ourselves out of poverty, I don't want to raise our child in a world where others are as poor, or poorer, than we've ever been." Rina's voice was shaking, but she went on. "Sometimes you have to hope, even when it's easier not to. Even when it's easier to give up and accept life the way it is. If you can't hope, you can't do anything. Bart, I have to *try*."

It was very quiet. Talisa looked up. Rina and Bart were staring at each other. Finally he sighed, a huge exhalation of breath like a sudden gust of wind.

"All right, Rina. My common sense says you're wrong, but...I'll try. I'll go on this march with you. I'll stand with you and Talisa and Master Swanson and all the others who really think they can make a difference." A wry smile twisted his lips. "I'll even try to hope."

GALIA

THE MAN FROM THE COURTROOM WALKED quickly. As she scurried after him, Galia regretted, for the second time that day, not knowing the Freyan spell of invisibility.

He stopped at a corner and looked around.

Galia ducked behind a cart filled with wood and hoped he hadn't seen her. A woman passing by paused when she saw her crouching there.

Don't say anything, Galia begged her silently.

The woman walked on, shaking her head. Galia peeked over the edge. Her quarry had vanished. She hurried out from behind the cart just as the driver came out of a shop. By the time she rounded the corner, the man was disappearing around another bend in the road. She almost ran to keep him in sight.

Gradually, the buildings grew smaller and further apart. She had never been in this part of Freybourg before, but thought that she was approaching the western outskirts of the city, far from the College of Wizards on the east side. Fewer and fewer carriages and pedestrians went by.

Then there was nothing but fields in front of her. Galia stopped beside the last building, a low grey house with a red roof that looked as though it might once have been a farm-house, and watched the man head down a dirt track that wandered between newly ploughed fields.

If an explanation was demanded of her, what could she say? In town, she might have pleaded innocence. She was going the same way he was, that was all. Such an excuse would be impossible from now on.

Why *was* she trailing him, anyway? Because she thought Cory had recognized him? Because he had looked like a man with a rat gnawing at his stomach? So? Maybe he was a friend of Cory's.

Perhaps she should go back. Her shadow was long. It must be getting late.

He left the track and headed straight for a grove of trees to his left.

Trees. There would be cover there. She would wait until he disappeared among them, then go after him.

He walked slowly now. It seemed a long time before Galia dared leave her post and follow him. As she did so, she noticed a child's face staring at her from the window of the house. She waved.

Her feet kicked up dustballs as she walked. The smell of ploughed earth was fresh in her nostrils. Her shadow went before her.

It was not a large grove. There were willows and aspens, and low bushes that caught at Galia's skirt as she tried to slip past. In places, the trees were so close together that they trapped fallen branches.

He must be in here somewhere. If he heard her, would he hide behind a tree, then spring at her and growl, "What are you doing?"

Galia stopped and rubbed her hands on her skirt. It wasn't too late to go back. It was cooler here than out in the open. A small breeze rippled the hairs on her arms. She shivered.

She had come this far. It would be silly to turn back now. Slowly, keeping her eyes on the ground, she crept forward, trying to avoid betraying twigs and leaves.

"Well?"

The voice was so loud, so close, that Galia jumped. Her heart jumped too, and when it came down started thudding with quick, painful drumbeats.

"Not good." A different voice this time. Low. Muffled. The voice of a man finding it hard to talk.

Two voices. Two men, talking to each other. Not to her. The drumming slowed.

"What do you mean?"

"You know I was at Updale's trial." Again, that voice sounded muffled.

"Of course I know."

"Then why did you ask what I meant?"

There was silence. Close by, a thrush began to sing. Another, further away, took up the song.

"I suppose you mean he was found guilty. Well, we expected that."

"So we did." Silence again, then the muffled voice added, "He's to hang two days from now, at noon."

Why was she here, eavesdropping? These were friends of Cory's, filled with pain at the thought of his death. She started to inch backwards, then stopped as her left foot stepped on a twig.

Ahead of her, someone moved. She froze. Then she heard a boot thud into something, a log, perhaps. The first man said, "Freyn's curse on them all!"

"And on us?" The words were so low Galia could scarcely hear them.

A pause, then, sharply, "What do you mean by that?"

"It's not just the army and the queen and the judges that's to blame for his being hanged, is it?"

"We had no choice. We couldn't speak up, not if we wanted to accomplish what we set out to do. Anyhow, we're trying to help him."

"Updale said he didn't want our help."

"What?"

"He said he doesn't want to be freed on such conditions. He wants Garth Spellman released no matter what happens to him."

After a moment, the first man grunted. "Crazy."

"Maybe."

"He always was a fool. He could have stayed with us rather than join with that mad musician who thinks he can change the world with no bones broken."

The other man said nothing.

"It's no fault of ours. Updale could've told what he knew any time."

"But he didn't."

"No." The voice was as heavy as the earth hitting Arlan's casket.

Galia stood motionless, trying to still even her breathing.

Neither man said anything for several minutes. The thrushes continued to sing. The wind sighed. The sun spun golden threads on the leaves to her right.

"I suppose we might as well eat," the first man said finally. Galia heard his steps again, rustling sounds. "I just wish we could light a fire and have some decent food for a change."

"A fire'd draw attention."

"I know that. I'm not stupid. That doesn't mean I can't wish for more than bread and onions. Here."

"Have you fed the boy?"

The other grunted again. "I've tried. He doesn't seem interested. Just lies there and stares at nothing, as though he's gone daft. D'you think he'll ever be the same? When he's not being given lambwort, I mean?"

"Why shouldn't he?" Anger sharpened the second man's voice.

"I don't know. It's just... He seems witless half the time, and sometimes moans and tosses like he's fever-taken. I just wondered, that's all."

"So maybe I've given him too much. I'm no healer, am I? If I were, I'd have healed my Elspeth when she fell sick of the summer fever and died, and her not past her thirty-fifth birthday. Not a day's sickness in her life, not till we got thrown off our farm and came to the city and had to live in a room without even any windows to look out of. That grieved her something fierce. I always thought, if we'd been able to afford a room with a window, she wouldn't have sickened so."

"It wasn't your fault, Ennis." The first man's voice was gentle.

"I know that. Do you think that helps? The only thing that will make it better is when I see the Count of Eastlands' house go up in flames."

Galia was so tense she was trembling. She tried to unclench her teeth, relax her muscles.

"That won't be long now. It will be the dark of the moon tomorrow. I figure that'll be the perfect time," the first man said.

"Yes." The word was a sigh of satisfaction.

"There's a shed at the back that'll go up nicely. Even better, I saw some windows open on the ground floor. All it will take is a lit rag or two tossed through them."

"When did you see all that?"

"This morning."

"This morning? While I was at the trial? And who was guarding the boy?"

"Calm down. He's in no state to go anywhere. Anyhow, I tied him up, didn't I?"

A grunt was his only answer.

It was too dim to see the ground at her feet. The sun must be very low in the sky.

"Only thing is...What do we do with the boy after that?"

"Let him go, of course. It doesn't look like anyone's willing to make a deal to free Updale, even if Updale'd agree to it."

"But he knows who held him, and who set the fires, not just the one that'll light up the sky tomorrow but the one at the barracks. It was his hearing us talk about the fires that made us take him in the first place. We don't dare let him go."

"No? Then what do you suggest we do with him?"

The other was silent for a long time. "Look, Ennis, I know it doesn't matter to you much, what happens to you after we set the fire. You haven't cared about yourself since Elspeth died. But it's different for me. I've got my wife still, and four children too. What'll happen to them if I'm taken and hanged?"

"What do you suggest we do with him?" Ennis asked for the second time.

"Freyn knows I don't like it any better than you. I wouldn't let myself see it when we first took the boy, and if an exchange could've been made, I'd have gone along with it for Updale's sake. But now...There's no other answer. We'll have to slit his throat."

She had to get help. Now.

It was so dark. She must be careful. Very careful.

Slowly, holding her arms at her sides, she turned around. Took one step. Another. Careful. Don't make a sound.

But oh, she must hurry. What would happen to the boy if she didn't?

Another step. Another.

An unseen twig snapped beneath her foot. She stopped. Stood still. *Please. Mother of the world, please.*

"What's that?" Ennis's voice. Sharp. Alarmed.

"Just some animal, I reckon. Nothing to worry about."

Her breath came out in a silent whoosh. She took a few more steps. A low branch whipped her cheek. She put a hand over her mouth to stifle her gasp. More steps.

A bush snagged her skirt. She stopped to untangle it.

A hand grabbed her shoulder. Held her fast.

CAT

CAT GAPED AT THE HOUSE IN FRONT OF HER. She had expected something larger and grander than the Spellman home, of course. The Count of Eastlands owned an immense tract of land. But this was a *monster* of a house, huge and intimidating.

She shouldn't be intimidated. She was here to do its owners a favour – and, in the process, find Garth. But she would have felt happier if she hadn't been covered with the dust of the road. She had arrived in Freybourg a scant hour ago. After finding an inn, she had come straight here without stopping to wash or eat. The innkeeper had almost, but not quite, managed to hide his surprise when she asked for directions to the Count of Eastlands' residence.

There was no sense standing here. It was late, and her errand was urgent. She brushed dust off her cloak, pushed her hair back from her forehead, and marched up to the door. The sun, flaming on the horizon, touched the brass knocker with fire.

The man who opened the door looked down his aristocratic nose at her. "Yes?"

"I would like to see the Count of Eastlands, please."

"The Count of Eastlands is occupied at the moment."

"Oh. Well, may I please come in and wait?"

There was a fractional pause. "May I enquire as to the nature of your business?"

Cat considered this. "I think it's best if I tell him myself. It's very important."

"The count is a busy man. If your business is so important, you may write a note and tell him where you can be contacted. When he's at liberty, I will convey your message to him. He will send for you if he wishes to see you." And that, his tone implied, was as likely as it was that cows would sprout wings and fly.

Cat opened her mouth to argue, then closed it. This man was even more rigid than Mistress Fairway. She would get nowhere with him.

"Thank you," she said meekly. "Could you give me a pen and paper, please?"

As she had hoped, he didn't close the door as he turned to get the items from a small table near the door. Cat rushed in, ran to the foot of the grand staircase, and yelled as loudly as she could, "Count! Count of Eastlands! I need to talk to you! It's urgent!"

Her shout certainly had an effect, though not the one she wanted. It was not surprising, perhaps, that such a house needed an army of servants. Nevertheless, Cat was amazed by the sheer number of men and women who poured out of doors and down the stairs. The man who had opened the door grabbed her by the collar and shook her.

"How dare you? Out you go. Immediately."

"I need to see the count. He might *die* if I don't," Cat said desperately.

She was shaken again. Roughly. "Threats now, is it? Baker, fetch some soldiers from the barracks."

A large young man headed for the entrance.

"No! You don't understand!"

No one listened. They milled about. Those who had arrived first told the latecomers what was happening.

"What is the meaning of this turmoil?"

The voice from the landing above cut through the noise like a hot knife through butter. Cat twisted her neck around and saw a man in chocolate-coloured satin, holding a linen napkin. Two young men and a woman dressed in sea-green silk stood beside him.

"Is it so impossible for my family and me to enjoy a civilized meal? What is all this commotion about? Who is this girl?"

Cat spared a quick glance over her shoulder and noted with relief that Baker had stopped.

"Will someone please close the door," the count said irritably. "There's a cool draft coming in."

Baker obliged.

"Now, Hall, who is this girl and what is she doing here?"

Hall let go of Cat's collar long enough to bow respectfully, then grabbed it again. "My apologies, My Lord. This person came to the door asking to see you. When I told her you were occupied, she asked to leave a note and then, while my back was turned, she burst in and shouted at the top of her lungs."

"So I heard," the count said. "Well, get rid of her, whoever she is."

He sounds as though I'm a cockroach to be squashed, Cat thought.

"I was sending Baker to bring some troops here, My Lord. This girl uttered threats against you." Another shake.

"What?" exclaimed the woman in the sea-green dress.

Cat looked at her. "I didn't threaten him," she said loudly. "I came to *warn* him. There are men who want to hurt him. Perhaps kill him."

"Who? How do you know?" the Count of Eastlands demanded.

Cat took a deep breath. "If I can talk to you in private, I can explain. That is, after all, why I came," she added pointedly.

The count hesitated.

"She might be telling the truth. You should listen to her," the countess said.

"My dinner –"

"It can wait. Anyway, we'd almost finished."

"Very well. Bring her to the rose salon, Hall."

Hall tightened his grip on Cat's collar. "Yes, My Lord."

Cat was half dragged up a flight of marble stairs and deposited in a small, elegant room furnished with rose rugs and chairs.

"Sit down," the count said, waving at a chair across from him. Cat sat.

"Now, young lady –" the count eyed her up and down and changed his mode of address –"young woman, please do us the courtesy of explaining what this is all about."

Cat flushed at his tone. "The men I came to warn you about were tenants on your land before you threw them off." If he didn't like *her* tone, it was just too bad. "I think they've come to Freybourg to try to get revenge. They took Garth Spellman captive and –"

"Wait." The count held up his hand. "Just who are you?"

"My name is Cat – Catrina Ashdale."

"And what is your relationship to these men?"

"None. I've never even met them."

"No? Then what, may I ask, is your involvement in this affair?"

Cat dug her fingernails into her palms. Calm. Stay calm. "I'm a friend of Garth Spellman. I've been staying with the Spellman family for the last little while."

The count looked her up and down again. "You expect me to believe that?"

Cat was so furious she couldn't speak.

"Father, that's not fair," one of the young men said. Cat glanced over at him, and realized he was around her age. His face was tinged with pink.

His intervention helped Cat gain control of her temper. "If you require proof that I know the Spellmans," she said icily, "I have a note from their housekeeper instructing a stable owner to lend me one of Master Spellman's horses. I needed the horse so I could ride here as quickly as possible and warn you." She hoped her last words would shame the man.

They didn't. He merely held out his hand. She took the note from her cloak pocket, walked across the room, handed it to him, and returned to her chair. The boy's face was now the colour of a peony. The other son, who looked a bit older, was frowning.

"I heard that some ruffians were using the Spellman boy to try to get a prisoner released," the countess said.

The count finished reading and set the note aside. "Yes, that's common knowledge. Go on," he told Cat.

She did, trying to keep her voice from shaking with anger. "Two days ago, some friends of Garth's and I heard where Garth was, but when we went there, both he and the men holding him were gone. Those who know the men say they're very angry about their eviction, and want to do something about it."

The count frowned. "Many of my former tenants seem to feel they have a right to complain, which only shows a sad ignorance of the law on their part. What are the names of these particular wretches?"

"I don't know," Cat lied. Even if she hadn't promised Talisa she'd keep their identities secret, she couldn't bear the thought of soldiers showing up at Mistress Dale's door.

"And that's all? You have no proof of their intention to harm us?"

"No," Cat admitted. "But I'm sure they've come to Freybourg to take action against you, and brought Garth with them. If you –"

"Enough. We have wasted too much time already."

"You can't dismiss her story just like that," the countess protested. "We may all be in danger."

"I have been told too many fanciful tales in the past, by those seeking favour, to believe everything I hear."

"She might be telling the truth, Father. And if she is, we owe her our thanks." The older son smiled at Cat. The younger nodded emphatically. His face was still red.

"I'm sure that's what she would like us to think," the count said.

Why had she come here? Why had it even crossed her mind to warn this hateful, arrogant man?

Because of Garth. And she must stay because of Garth. Cat took several deep breaths.

The countess frowned. "We don't know that. We must take precautions."

"Oh, very well. If it makes you happy, I'll send word to Colonel Bows to have two of his men patrol the grounds for the next fortnight or so. Will that satisfy you all?"

Three heads nodded.

"No!" Cat cried.

"No?" The count raised his eyebrows. He glanced at his family, his look saying more plainly than words, "What did I tell you?"

"These men have Garth. Couldn't you just have your servants keep watch? When you capture them, promise to let them go if they'll tell you where Garth is."

"So that's it," the countess said. "The girl's in love with the Spellman boy. It's as plain as the nose on her face." She smiled at Cat. "Don't fret. I'm sure when the ruffians are caught, they'll divulge your friend's whereabouts."

Cat ignored the blush she knew stained her face. "They'll have nothing to gain if they're already prisoners. You *must* catch them and bargain for Garth's freedom. You owe it to me. I warned you." She tried to make her voice strong, but it shook.

"No." The count rose. "My wife may be right about your motives. Be that as it may, we can make no deals with miscreants. Now, we really must return to our dinner. Casper, perhaps you could escort this young woman downstairs and bestow on her a small acknowledgement of the trouble she has taken."

"Of course." The older son rose.

Cat rose too. "I can find my way out, thank you. And the only acknowledgement I want is Garth's freedom. Freyn's Night."

All the way back to her inn, she thought of the many things she wished she had said to the Count of Eastlands.

"No one here of those names."

"You're sure?"

"Yes."

It was the tenth inn she'd tried, and the last on the list her landlord had given her. Emerging into the bright noon sunlight, Cat blinked hard to hold back tears.

There are other inns, she reminded herself.

Yes, but none that Ennis and Wendell could afford.

Perhaps the Countess of Eastlands was right. Perhaps Ennis and Wendell would disclose Garth's whereabouts when they were captured.

If they were captured. If the presence of two soldiers didn't scare them away.

A carriage pulled by a pair of glossy chestnuts clattered past. The horses resembled the one she'd ridden to Freybourg, Master Spellman's best. It had accepted the challenge of a fast journey with zest. But the horse's speed had not helped. Nothing had.

There was only one thing to do now. It was, she admitted, what she should have done when she first arrived in Freybourg. She had no power or influence, but Konrad did.

A smiling maid led her to a suite of rooms on the top floor of The Swan's Nest and knocked on the door. Annette opened it. She stared for a second, then threw her arms around Cat. Cat returned the hug. Smiling more widely than ever, the maid closed the door and departed.

Annette drew back. "Cat, it's so good to see you. But what brings you here? Is there news?"

Cat looked around the small parlour. "Is Master Spellman here?"

Annette shook her head. "He requested an audience with Queen Elira. Word came an hour ago that she would see him. You *do* have news, then?" A starving woman with food in sight could have been no more eager.

"I think I know who has Garth, and that they're in Freybourg, but I don't know where. Why did Master Spellman request an audience?"

"He wants to ask her to delay Cory Updale's execution."

"Execution?" Cat echoed.

"He's to be hanged tomorrow at noon."

"Oh." Cat swallowed. Talisa must feel...devastated. She swallowed again. Then another thought hit her. "Is Master Spellman afraid that the men who hold Garth will...will harm him when Cory is killed?" The moment she asked the question, she wished she hadn't.

Annette looked away for a moment, then back. "A delay will give us more time to find Garth. Also, my father-in-law has doubts about Master Updale's guilt. He wants the execution postponed so further enquiries can be made. But come. I'll show you to a room, then send for something to eat."

It was over an hour before Konrad Spellman returned. Cat took one look at his face and knew the results of the audience were not good.

He stopped when he saw her. "Catrina. What brings you here?"

"She has some news," Annette said. "But first tell us what happened."

He sighed. "Nothing. Queen Elira listened to me. She was very sympathetic about Garth. She even agreed that it was quite possible that Updale was innocent, but said that if he were, all he had to do was name the guilty parties. I think she's under some pressure. The army is very intent on showing it's caught and punished the man who set fire to its barracks and killed two of its own, and some of the courtiers are equally intent on setting an example to show what happens to those who speak out against them."

"She won't delay it even for a day?"

"No."

"Then we must work very quickly to find Garth," Annette said. "Cat, tell us what you know."

Cat did. Konrad listened, frowning deeply. When she ended, he said, "You say you've checked all the moderately priced inns in Freybourg."

"Yes."

"And there was no sign of them. So how can we find out where they are?"

Cat said nothing. She had hoped he would have an answer. In the silence, she heard a carriage draw up in the courtyard below.

"What about Master Updale?" Annette asked hesitantly. "Would he know where these men would stay in Freybourg?"

Konrad considered this. "He might. It's worth a trip to the prison to ask him. Will you accompany me, Annette?"

She shook her head. "There's nothing I can do that you can't. And the prison makes me shudder."

"I'll go," Cat said.

CAT COULDN'T BLAME ANNETTE for not wanting to visit the prison. It was so dark, and her footsteps wakened cavernous echoes as she walked down the long corridor. The smell was the worst. The prison reeked of sweat and urine and dust. Old dust.

The guard halted in front of a cell. "Visitors, Updale."

The young man sitting on the cot at the back of the cell looked up. His face stiffened when he saw them. Slowly, he rose and walked forward.

The guard handed the candle to Konrad. "Call if you need me." He left.

"I can't tell you anything more," Cory said. "I'm sorry, but I can't."

"We're hoping you can," Konrad said. "Tell him, Cat."

Cat began her tale. She was soon interrupted.

"Andreas? He wouldn't be involved in anything like this."

"Yes he would," Cat said, and continued.

Pain flicked across Cory's face when she described the bottle of lambwort and the vomit-covered blankets, and again when she reported their encounter with Wendell's wife. She hadn't wanted to, but she liked him.

She finished with an account of her fruitless search for Ennis and Wendell.

"Which brings us to the reason why we're here," Konrad said. "We hope you have some idea of where they would stay in Freybourg. Wait," he added, even though Cory had made no move to speak. "I know you don't want to betray these men. But you've also shown concern for my grandson. There's no choice now. If we're to get Garth back, you *must* tell us what you know."

Cory looked at him for a long moment, then nodded. "Yes. But..." He stopped, frowning. Cat held her breath.

"I'm sorry. I can't remember either of them mentioning anybody in Freybourg. It's unlikely they would know anyone here. They came from the hills, like me. Their families had lived there for generations."

"You must be able to think of *something*." Cat pleaded.

The frown deepened. "A deserted building or abandoned shed, perhaps. I'm not surprised you didn't find them at an inn. I doubt either of them could afford even a cheap one."

"That doesn't help much." Frustration grated in Konrad's voice.

"No. I'm sorry. I hoped... Perhaps they will let him go. At least they know I want Garth set free."

"But they don't!" Cat wailed. "They'd gone before Talisa could deliver your message."

Cory almost smiled. "They do know. And you were right. They are in Freybourg. One of them was at my trial."

"*What?*" Konrad leaned forward. The candle flame leaped.

Cory nodded. "He was sitting on the bench at the back. A small brown-skinned girl was at one end, and he was at the other."

"I saw them on my way out," Konrad said. "I have a vivid recollection of him. He looked the way people do when an illness claws at them. A good friend of yours?"

"An acquaintance."

"But your sentence caused him such pain?" Konrad cocked his head. "I wonder why."

Cory didn't answer.

After a moment, the wizard continued, "It is possible that I received a good enough impression of him to use a finding spell. I can't locate my grandson, but I might – I just might – be able to locate his captor."

FIVE HOURS LATER, he was still trying. He had retreated to his bedchamber to concentrate. Annette and Cat had said little in that time. Neither had suggested dinner. Now Cat stood at the window. The city was quiet. The sun rested on the horizon.

Find him. *Find him.*

At least she could still hope. There was no hope now for Cory or Talisa. As they had left his cell, Cory had said, "If you see Talisa again, tell her..." and stopped.

"What?" Cat had asked.

After a moment, he'd shaken his head. "No. There's nothing more to say."

Nothing. The word echoed and echoed in her mind.

Behind her, she heard Annette's dress rustle as she stirred in her chair. Then the door of Konrad's chamber opened. Cat whirled around.

"I've found him."

"Where?" Annette asked before Cat could.

"In a grove to the southwest of the city. There were two men, the one I saw in the courtroom and a larger, younger man. I was surprised to see Galia there too."

"Galia?" Cat stared at him.

"An Islandian girl who I met at the college a week or so ago. She was at the trial, but I have no idea why she was there or how she came to be a captive."

"Garth?" Annette asked. "How...how is he?"

Konrad paused. "Physically, he looked unhurt, though thinner than he should be."

And his mind? Cat wondered. She couldn't ask.

"Now to rescue him," Konrad said briskly.

"You can't go alone," Annette protested.

"I won't. I don't want the army involved. There might be fighting, and Garth could get hurt. But I have a friend here, a Colonel Blade, who retired early. He's a good fighter – and an intelligent man, which is even better. I'm sure he'll help. And if I know him, he'll bring along his groom, an able man who also used to be a soldier."

"I'm coming too," Cat said.

He looked at her.

"I grew up on a farm. I know my way around fields and woods."

He continued to look at her.

"I'm coming," she repeated. "You can't stop me."

"Probably not," he agreed. "Very well. Get your cloak and we'll be off."

TALISA

THE RISING SUN TOUCHED THE WATERFALL with fingers of rose and gold. Talisa looked at it with awe. It seemed like something that came from another world, the world of the spirits perhaps.

But then, everything seemed different today, transformed by the waves of people who had been pouring into the square even before the stars began to pale in the night sky. And perhaps there was more to be awed at in their presence than in any torrent of water.

Talisa saw a bent old man with a cane, a tiny, toothless woman clothed in an assortment of rags. Rina was not the only woman heavy with child, and several babies bounced in sacking on their mother's or father's backs. Small children clutched the hands of ones yet smaller. It was a motley crowd, united only by poverty and hope.

Bart was surveying the crowd too. "Some of them will

have trouble making it," he predicted. "It'll take us a good day and a half at least."

"That's why I'm here," Thannis said.

Bart looked at him. "You should be able to carry at least three," he agreed. A smile tugged at his lips. "I should be able to manage one or two myself."

A ripple of music drew Talisa's eyes to Alain Swanson, who stood at the front, lute in hand. He struck a few chords, then threw back his head and started to sing "A Merry Life on the Road Have I." Those in the lead took up the song and passed it back, until the whole assembly was singing. Halfway through the first verse, Alain swung around and started off. Through King Leopold Square they went, down Portby Road, and around the corner into West Way Street. The bridge to the west bank lay ahead.

Talisa gasped. In front of the bridge, with a troop of horsemen behind them, was a line of archers. Bows were drawn, arrows nocked, ready to fly.

The music came to a jagged halt as person after person saw the menace. Talisa's fingernails dug into her hands as she watched Alain sling his lute over his shoulder and walk forward.

"What is the meaning of this?" he called.

The line parted enough to allow a tall roan horse to pass through. After a few paces, it stopped.

"I think that is my question, fellow," the horseman said coldly. "Why is this mob here?"

"No mob, but a group of Her Majesty's loyal subjects going to Freybourg to pay her a visit."

Talisa doubted that those at the back could hear what was said, but everyone was quiet except for a lone baby who started to wail.

"Why?" demanded the officer.

"To ask her, out of her concern for her people, to better the lot of those who need her help."

"It scarcely needs a few thousand beggars to talk to her." Beside her, Talisa felt Bart stir angrily. "Tell the mob to return to their homes before they get hurt."

Alain tilted his head to one side, like a dog puzzled by its master's words. "How is Queen Elira to know how many seek her help, unless we all go to see her?" he asked reasonably. "And as for our returning to our homes – we have only just left them. It would be foolish to return now, when we have barely begun."

"It would be more foolish to stay and be riddled with arrows."

Alain was silent. Whispers swept through the crowd like wind through tall grass.

Talisa's eyes darted around. If arrows flew, where could they run? If everyone fled, some would be trampled. Especially the children. The old people. And there were the horsemen behind the archers, ready to charge into them with slashing swords. She felt sick. Bitter as it was, they must give up.

When Alain spoke again, his voice was conversational. "Tell me, Major, are you acting on orders?"

The soldier hesitated.

"No? I didn't think so. What will happen to your career, I wonder, when the queen discovers you have massacred thousands of her people, including women and children, who were doing no harm but merely wished to speak to her?"

Silence. The whispers had stopped. The roan tossed its head.

Alain continued. "On the other hand, what will happen to your career if she and your superiors hear that you have acted with sense and good judgement, and allowed us to proceed? We are peaceable. None of us carry bows, or swords, or even daggers. A few of the luckiest among us have knives to cut our meat, but that is all. If my words do not entirely convince you of the harmless nature of our assembly, then I invite you to come with us. We will be glad of your company, and you and your men will benefit by hearing some fine music along the way."

A minute passed. Two. Then the major turned and shouted, "Archers, return to barracks. Horsemen, prepare to ride out with this mob."

Alain had done it! Incredibly, he'd saved them without giving in. Talisa's breath whooshed out. She hadn't known she was holding it.

Alain struck up the chords again. The song was ragged at first, but by the time they had crossed the West Way Bridge, everyone was singing lustily. Only the deaf could fail to hear them as they walked through the streets on the west bank.

The day was warm and sunny, with just enough of a breeze to keep insects at bay. There was talk, and laughter, and music – fine music, as Alain had promised. The soldiers rode up and down the line. "Like sheepdogs," Rina said. Bart snorted. "More like wolves, ready to spring."

They walked in the grass by the side of the road when they could, but sometimes steep banks or farmers' fences made that impossible. Then riders and carriages were forced to slow. One plump middle-aged man was so enraged that he descended from his carriage and shouted abuse at the crowd. He only stopped when a soldier rode up and told him he'd suffered no harm – yet. Talisa turned away to hide a smile.

They stopped beside a quiet river for their midday meal. Talisa sat on the grassy bank and marvelled at some children chasing one another around the meadow. "They've been walking all morning. Where do they get the energy?"

"They'll be wanting to be carried before long, I warrant," said a woman close by.

She was right. By early afternoon, most of the little ones were too tired to walk any more. Talisa hoisted a small girl onto her shoulders, as many others were doing. It was no trouble. She was disturbingly light for a five-year-old.

"How are you doing?" Bart asked Rina as he lifted a boy.

"I'm fine," she assured him. "This is almost as good as being back in the hills."

There was less laughter and less singing as the afternoon wore on, but there were no complaints and no real mishaps until late in the day, when Talisa heard a sharp cry behind her. She turned.

A girl who looked to be about twelve sat on the roadway, holding her foot in both hands. Blood gushed from it.

"What happened?" someone asked.

"A piece of sharp metal, looks like. She must've stepped on it," someone else said.

A woman bent over the girl. "Oh, Edda. Here. Let me see."

"It hurts, Mam, it hurts." Edda's face was white with shock.

"Shush, love. I know. It will be all right. I'll just wipe away the blood so I can see what's to be done." The woman tore off a ragged strip of her shift.

Talisa winced when she saw the long, jagged gash that was wide as well as deep. It needed a healer.

It was a simple healing. If she had even a speck of wizardry, she could have done it. But she didn't.

Someone did, though, and he came now, with two children clinging to his neck and an old man clinging to his arm. Thannis deposited his riders gently, then knelt beside the girl. New blood covered her foot.

"I have a little knowledge of healing," he told Edda's mother. She nodded and made room for him.

Within a short time, the bleeding had stopped, the wound was sealed, and the foot wrapped in a clean cloth.

"How is she?" asked Alain, who had joined the ever widening circle around Edda.

"She'll be fine," Thannis said. "But she shouldn't walk on it for the rest of today. Maybe not tomorrow, either."

The girl was too big to be carried easily. Alain surveyed her, then looked at an approaching green-coated horseman.

"What's going on?" the major demanded.

"This girl stepped on a piece of metal and cut her foot."

The major looked down at Edda from his seat on the tall roan. "It's to be expected if she's fool enough to go around in bare feet."

"Arrogant ass," Bart growled, but not loudly enough for the man to hear. There were other mutters.

"It's difficult to wear shoes when you don't have money to buy them," Alain said mildly. "She will be unable to continue on foot. Can she ride behind one of your men?"

"What?" The major stared at Alain as though he had asked for a chest of gold.

"Or behind you, perhaps."

This time the major was speechless.

"I'll be glad to offer the lass a ride, sir," said a middle-aged, fatherly looking soldier who had just ridden up.

The major looked relieved. "Very well. But I hope this will be the last such request," he told Alain.

"I hope so too."

Edda's mother helped her daughter settle herself behind the soldier, then walked alongside as the horse started off at a slow walk.

The sun was low when they stopped for the night. Some sank to the ground and sat, too exhausted to move, while others gathered sticks for fires or collected water from a nearby stream. By the time the sun disappeared, hundreds of fires dotted the meadow.

"I wish I'd brought food we could cook rather than bread and cheese," Rina said.

"Never mind. We're lucky to have a fire." Bart stretched his long legs out to it.

They *were* lucky, Talisa thought, gazing into the flames. It might have been a disastrous day. Instead, it had been a good one. Tiring, but good. She had even spotted Sully as she was carrying water from the stream, and called Alain over. The musician had sung his new composition, about a woman who'd risked her job to give a warning, and the brave boy who'd brought it. Sully and his mam and da had listened, beaming, as had their neighbours, while the soldiers' fires flickered in the distance. Talisa smiled, remembering, then inched closer to the warmth. The wind had picked up with the coming of night.

Thannis was looking towards a nearby fire. "Does he never get tired?"

Talisa followed his glance and saw Alain talking to the people there. "He's worked for this for two years. Perhaps now that it's actually happening, it gives him strength."

"He handled the major with a fine hand this morning, didn't he? And this afternoon. I would have lost my temper."

Talisa laughed. "I thought you weren't going to do that ever again."

"Well, I'm going to *try* not to."

Alain came over to them. "All well here?"

"Yes," Thannis said.

Alain smiled at him. "Thank you for all you did today. Supporting the old man, carrying the two children, healing the girl's foot. To think I tried to persuade you not to come! What a loss that would have been."

It wasn't only the light from the flames that gave Thannis's face a pink glow. "Thank you for letting me come. I feel as though I'm *meant* to be here."

Alain regarded him gravely. "Perhaps you are. Perhaps we all are." His eyes moved to Rina. "And you? It has not been too hard a day? I see you are near your time."

"It was tiring," she admitted. "But not too much so. Like Thannis, I'm glad I came."

"She believes this march will do some good," Bart said.

"You don't?"

"It won't get us our land back."

"No," Alain agreed soberly.

Silence fell. Somewhere, an owl hooted. Talisa looked into the flames, hearing Cory's voice, talking of his home in the hills.

Another memory stirred. "The high hills are uninhabited. Couldn't land there be given to those who used to live on the Count of Eastlands' property?"

Bart shook his head. "Life's too harsh there. Nothing would grow."

"Usit would."

Thannis leaned forward. "Talisa's right. Our legends tell us that Uglessians settled there over five hundred years ago. They found life easier there than in Uglessia. That was before Freyans drove us out."

Another silence, this one sparked by hope. Then Bart shook his head again. "The land's sure to belong to someone, even if it is unoccupied."

"The crown, probably," Alain said. "If Queen Elira

agrees to lease it to those who would settle there... It's a thought. A good thought." He smiled at Talisa.

She smiled too. "If this works, Cory will be filled with joy."

Cory. His name echoed in the silence that followed her words.

A twig snapped in the fire, and a spark flew up and landed at Talisa's feet. She stared at it.

"There is still hope," Alain said. "Ennis and Wendell may yet confess, for it seems likely to me they are guilty. And perhaps there will be more sympathy for people like Cory after this march."

No one answered.

"When the march is over, I will do anything I can to help him. His death would be a loss to the world. He is a compassionate and courageous young man – as well as a very talented carver."

"An idealistic young fool, in other words." Bart threw a pebble into the flames.

"That's another way of putting it," Alain agreed. He laughed. "Perhaps that's why I like him. I've been called that myself – except for the young part." He rose. "Better go to sleep soon, so we can get an early start. I'm hoping we'll reach Freybourg by midday tomorrow." He left.

They wrapped themselves in their blankets and lay down. The wind had strengthened. The fire felt good on Talisa's back, but her face was chilly.

Sleep would not come. She rolled over and stared up at the sky. There was no moon, but the stars were bright.

She wouldn't think of Cory. She *wouldn't*. She needed to sleep.

Tomorrow, she would see him. After they had all gathered in front of the palace, after Alain had spoken to the queen, she would go to the prison. She and Cory would be together, or as together as they could be with bars between them. She would tell him everything about the march to Freybourg. He would want all the details. How happy he would be if Queen Elira said she would work to improve the lot of those who were poor – and surely she would. Pray to all the spirits of the mountains that she would.

It would be good to see Cory. But it would solve nothing. It would do nothing to set him free.

Slow tears oozed out of Talisa's eyes and down her cheeks. The stars blurred.

It was a long time before she slept.

GALIA

THE BOY BESIDE HER – GARTH SPELLMAN, Ennis had called him – mumbled something.

Galia glanced at him. He was lying on his side, facing her. His dark eyes were open, but they didn't seem to see her. Or anything. Was Wendell right? Had the drug destroyed his mind? Maybe she should go inside it and see.

Later. There was urgent work to do now. Grey light had begun to colour the sky. The men were still sleeping, but for how long?

She twisted her wrists. How many times had she done that since the rope had first been tied around them? Fifty? One hundred?

Twisting hurt. Her wrists were raw and speckled with blood. But she must get free. She twisted again. Surely the bonds were looser.

No. They weren't. Her struggles seemed only to draw them tighter.

If she didn't escape, what would happen to her?

Last night, she had been too frightened to think. The hand clutching her shoulder had seemed to clench her mind too. She lay still, remembering.

"So there was someone here," said her captor. "Good thing I haven't lost my skill at tracking wild things in the woods, even if I have been too long in the city. What are you doing here?"

She couldn't speak.

He shook her. "Come on, out with it. Who are you and why are you here?"

She swallowed hard, but still couldn't speak.

"Wendell?" Ennis called.

"Got her," Wendell called back.

"Her?" A pause. "Well, bring her here."

Wendell's hand shifted from her shoulder to her elbow. "Come on."

She stumbled over roots and stones as she walked, blinded by the darkness and her fear.

There was a little more light in the clearing, enough to make out the dim outline of Ennis's face. "Who in Freyn's name is she?"

"Don't know."

Ennis came closer and inspected her. "I've seen you before," he exclaimed. "Weren't you at the trial?"

She nodded dumbly.

"You followed me, didn't you? Why?"

"I...I don't know."

'You don't know?" He reached out and grabbed her shoulder. His hand wasn't as large as Wendell's, but his grip was just as hard. "*Why?*"

"I don't know," she repeated. She tried to explain. "It was the way you looked. And the way Cory looked at you."

His hand dropped. He stood silent.

"What do we do with her?" Wendell asked.

After a moment, Ennis said, "Tie her up for tonight. We'll decide tomorrow."

"She heard what we said." Wendell's voice was heavy.

"Yes."

Neither man said anything more. Ennis dug some rope out of his bag and tied her wrists and ankles. She sat there, watching the men eat bread and onions. They didn't offer her any. She didn't mind. She couldn't have eaten anyway. Now and then, she glanced at the boy on the ground, but it was too dark to see him clearly.

The men exchanged a few low words, but nothing that gave her any hint of what they intended to do with her. After a while, Wendell placed a cloak on the ground, picked her up, and deposited her on it. He was surprisingly gentle. He dropped a shirt over her. It was big enough to almost cover her, and warm, though slightly smelly.

She had waited until she thought Ennis and Wendell were asleep, then started wrenching her hands this way and that. Over and over. Over and over.

AT SOME POINT during that endless, futile night, she must have slept. Now there was little time left.

There was an unbinding spell that Freyan wizards used. One of the teachers – she couldn't remember which one – had taught it to Galia's class. Poor as she was at Freyan magic, she could have worked this spell if she had bothered to learn it.

Perhaps there was a sharp stone she could use to cut the rope. Thank the Mother, Ennis had tied her hands in front of her, not behind her back.

After some searching, she found one. But she couldn't bend her hands far enough to reach her wrists when she held the rock, and when she placed it on the ground and tried to saw the rope, it rolled away.

Somewhere, a bird began to sing. Galia glanced at the lightening sky with dismay. The men would soon be awake. Her chance for freedom, perhaps for life itself, would be lost.

No. No, no, *no.*

Her ankles. She might not be able to reach her wrists, but she could reach her ankles. Freed legs were far more important at this stage than freed arms.

Garth moaned as she bent over to retrieve the stone. *Quiet,* she begged silently. As though hearing her, he stilled.

Cut, she willed the stone. In the Mother's name, *cut.* Were any of the strands frayed? No. She didn't think so. She kept working, rubbing the sharp edge of the stone against the centre of the rope, even though the motion chafed her raw wrists.

Some strands broke. She drew in a gasping breath, then looked quickly over at Ennis and Wendell. They didn't stir.

Sleep. Just a little longer. Sleep. She sawed more fiercely.

And then, suddenly, she was free.

She sat for a moment, letting the thudding drum of her heart calm, then straightened slowly. Muscles screamed. With great care, she rose to her feet.

There was a rustling sound. She froze. But it was only her fellow captive, moving restlessly.

She took a step. Two. Stopped.

If she left now, what of Garth? Ennis might want to let him go after they burned the Eastlands' home, but Wendell didn't.

The sooner she left, the sooner she could bring help. And the Eastlands family needed to be warned.

But the men would know she would be back. They would flee. And they might find it safer to get rid of Garth before they left. Permanently.

She stood motionless while the first pink fingers of dawn touched the sky. Then she turned back.

Garth wasn't bound. He was free to go with her, if she could persuade him to do so.

Could she risk a whisper? Her eyes moved to the sleeping forms. Wendell stirred. Her heart jumped. Then he was still.

No whispers.

She must go into Garth's mind. Gently, she reached out.

She almost drew back. She had never felt a mind like this. Lumpish. Like congealed porridge.

But there was something there. Something moving. Moving sluggishly, but it was moving. She could not talk to it directly. But she could implant an image. An image of him rising, walking with her. Away from the camp. Walking through the woods. Quietly. Carefully.

Rise. Walk. Rise. Walk. Over and over again. Rise. Walk.

Something flickered, stirred. In his eyes. In his mind.

Rise. Walk.

And he did. Slowly, oh so slowly, he pushed his blanket aside and rose. Took a step towards her.

Then his eyes widened. He stopped.

He was looking over her shoulder. She turned.

She had been concentrating too hard on Garth. She had forgotten to watch the sleeping men.

Sleeping no longer. Both were on their feet, staring at her.

"How in Freyn's name did she manage that?" Ennis asked. "She not only freed herself but got the Spellman boy moving without so much as a word."

"She's more powerful than she looks," Wendell said. He walked towards her. Instinctively, she backed away.

"Don't be a fool," he said. "You know you can't escape."

She did. She stopped.

He put his hand on her shoulder. "We'll have to tie you again. Sit down."

She sat. He found the broken rope and shook his head. "Not enough." Glancing at her, he whistled. "Come look at her wrists, Ennis."

Ennis frowned when he saw them. "She's rubbed them raw."

"Might as well untie her hands and use the rope on her ankles. We'll be around all day to make sure she doesn't escape."

Ennis nodded. "Her wrists won't hurt so much then."

They weren't cruel. They could be kind. But that didn't mean they were less dangerous, Galia reminded herself, as Wendell gently unwound the rope from her wrists and fastened her ankles. Nevertheless, the tight knot in her stomach relaxed a little.

Ennis took Garth's arm and reseated him on the blanket. Garth gave no resistance.

The men took some food from their bags. "Not much left," Ennis commented.

"Doesn't matter. We won't be here after tonight."

Where would they be? Where would *she* be?

Wendell offered her a slice of dried meat and a hunk of bread. Despite her tight stomach and dry mouth, she devoured them. She hadn't eaten since yesterday morning. It didn't matter that the meat curled at the edges and the bread was stale. The water Wendell gave her was even more welcome. Garth drank from Ennis's flask, but turned his head when Ennis held out food.

"I'm not giving him any more lambwort," Ennis said.

Wendell frowned. "What about his grandfather? If the boy's mind's clear –"

"I will *not* force any more of that Freyn-cursed drug down his throat!" Ennis looked at Garth, then away.

"Anyway, his mind's so clouded it will take ages to clear. If ever."

Wendell shrugged. "All right."

The men ate, then sat in silence. Galia sat. Garth sat. The sky brightened to a perfect, cloudless blue.

Would they miss her at the college? She had been gone a whole day. Surely someone would notice. True, she had missed both classes and meals before. But never so many. Raven... Surely Raven would notice.

She could try a mind call to Raven. She had never been skilled at mind-talk over a distance, but perhaps...

She gathered all her mental energy and called. Paused. Called again. Again.

After a while, she gave up. She would, she was sure, have felt Raven's response if he had heard her cry for help.

It was a long day. At one point, the two men talked in low voices. They kept glancing at her and Garth. What were they saying? Were they...Were they planning to kill them?

She might never go home again, never see her mother or father or sisters or brothers or little Mala. She wanted to hold Mala in her arms, watch her grow into a girl, then a woman.

Why had the Wise Women taken her away? Why had the Dreamer said she must come to Freya?

If only the men would look away long enough for her to untie her feet, she would run. Even if they came after her, even if they caught her, she would have *tried*.

And Garth? Would she leave him behind?

Yes. She had been foolish to waste time this morning trying to rescue him. She glanced at him. He was sitting as he had been the last time she looked, but his eyes were now on her face. They were brighter than they had been earlier. Steadier.

No. She couldn't leave Garth.

Not that it mattered, one way or the other. The eyes of the two men constantly flickered her way. There was no escape.

It was hard to breathe. She felt as though she were drowning. Drowning in a dark cold sea. If she let the sea evaporate, seep into the air and sky around her, she wouldn't drown. If –

No! Control. She must control her emotions. She must not let them rule her. Use your power, do not let it use you, the Wise Women had told her, over and over again.

She dug her fingers into the earth and breathed deeply. The sky remained a pristine blue.

She sat. Garth sat. They all sat. And waited.

They waited until the sun was a red haze on the horizon. Then Wendell stirred. "It's time."

"Yes."

Wendell glanced at the captives. "What do we do with them?"

Ennis said nothing. Wendell was silent too for a long time. Finally, he spoke. "I guess... I don't like it. But I guess there's but the one thing to do. At least it'll be quick."

Mother, no! Please. Please, Mother. No! Galia closed her eyes.

"No." Ennis's voice was so low that at first she thought it was an echo of her prayer.

"What do you mean, 'no'? We've talked –"

"We've talked, yes."

"Look, Ennis. It's not that I like this any better than you. But they know too much. And like I said, I've got a wife and children to think of. What happens to them if I get myself hanged?"

"So you'd kill them."

"Don't sound like that, as though you're better than me! I told you I don't like it. But what choice do we have? Anyway, the Spellman boy's had it easy all his life. Bet he's never lacked for food, no, nor warm clothes either. Not like my little ones. You didn't see any wizards worrying about *them* when Eastlands threw us off our farm, did you? Why should I worry about a rich boy like Garth Spellman?"

"And the girl?"

Wendell was silent for a moment. "She's different, I admit. She's older, but there's a look about her that reminds me of my Bella. But still, we can't just let her loose. It was her own fault. Why'd she have to come snooping around here anyway?"

"Because of Updale."

There was silence. Galia watched the sun disappear and wished she could cry. Her eyes might not feel so hot then, her throat so tight.

"I've been thinking, Wendell. All day I've been thinking, and I don't like what I've thought. Ever since I lost the farm, and then my wife, I've been set on revenge."

"And you're not now?"

"Oh, I'd still like to see the count's house go up in flames. And if he was to go up with it, I'd shed no tears. But what's the cost, Wendell? We wanted to get even with the army that helped kick us out, didn't we, so we lit the barracks. And what happened? Two soldiers died, and Updale is to hang for what we did."

There was something in Ennis's voice that dragged Galia's eyes away from the sky to his face. It looked the way it had yesterday afternoon. Torn.

"You didn't sit in that courtroom. I did. I had to watch and listen to those soldiers' wives talk about their husbands' deaths. Yes, and they had children too. And Updale... If I had a son, I'd be proud if he turned out like that young man. Two lives lost and a third to be lost because I was burning to get back at those who had done harm to me and mine. And now you say we should kill two more people?"

"Ennis –"

"You talk as though Garth Spellman was an enemy of ours. But he was working with Alain Swanson to try to change things. He's no enemy. Nor is the girl. I can't stand to see them killed, Wendell. And if you try to kill them, I'll stop you. Freyn help me, I'll stop you, even though we've been good friends for the last twenty years."

The two men stared at each other. "I'm bigger than you," Wendell said.

"I know you are."

They continued to stare. Galia forgot to breathe.

"Wendell, I know you want to go free, for the sake of

your family, and I don't blame you. Why don't you go off on your own to set the fire? When you've done it, go to Freyfall and get your wife and children. Then go somewhere. Anywhere. Change your name. I'll stay here and guard these two. When you've been gone a couple of days, I'll set them free. That'll give you enough time to get away, Freyn willing."

"And what'll happen to you?" Wendell's voice was hoarse.

Ennis looked away. "Like you said yesterday, it's different for me. I've no wife or young ones to worry about."

"I don't like it."

Ennis looked back. "I don't either. But we've only got two choices, and I like this one a lot better than the other."

There was an endless moment of silence. Then Wendell said, "All right, then. If you're sure."

"I'm sure."

She could breathe again, Galia found. It felt good to breathe.

THERE WAS NO MOON, but there were many stars. Galia gazed at them and tried to find The Fisher. At this time of year, it hung in the western sky at home.

She wasn't at home. But now she dared hope she would be, one day.

It was at least two hours since Wendell had slipped away, moving as silently as he had last night when he'd captured her. An hour ago, Ennis had offered them more bread and meat. This time, Garth had eaten a little. He had even said, his speech so slurred it was difficult to make out the words, "Than u."

She had said thank you too, and tried to put all the gratitude she felt into her voice. Perhaps she had succeeded. Ennis had smiled.

She wished he would untie her feet, if only briefly, so she could shake them and get blood back into them. She didn't ask. Ennis had done enough.

Stones rattled in the woods to their right, as though someone had stepped on loose rocks. Was it Wendell? But he wasn't coming back here.

Ennis sprang up. A knife flashed in his hand. He stood, head cocked.

More stones. He moved, quickly. Out of the clearing, into the bush.

Who was there? What was happening?

A hand covered her mouth. A voice murmured in her ear. "Shhh. Don't worry. You're safe." Arms lifted her. A shadow bent over Garth, lifted him. They were carried into the trees to the left. She was let down gently. "Don't make a sound," said the voice. A moment later, she felt the rope drop from her ankles and saw a dark outline move soundlessly away. But there were others with her. Garth. The figure that had picked him up. Another, smaller shadow.

Galia's heart was pounding so hard that it hurt. It's all right, she told herself. He said you're safe. But who was he? And what –

There was a sudden, scuffling noise. A muffled cry. Then a man's voice shouted. "We've got him."

"Good," called the tall form, then said more quietly, "let's return to the clearing." He and the shorter figure led Garth back. Galia followed. Her legs shook.

Two men emerged from the woods, pulling Ennis.

"Don't hurt him," Galia said. Her voice was so small that she cleared her throat and repeated it, more loudly. "Don't hurt him."

The man beside her turned sharply to look at her. She recognised the hawk-nosed face of Konrad Spellman. "He would not let the other man kill us," she explained.

The person on Garth's left said, "He hurt Garth. He kept him locked up and drugged." It was a girl's voice, and it trembled with anger – and fear. The girl turned to Konrad. "How is he?"

"I don't know," the wizard answered. "Garth? Garth, can you hear me? Do you know what's happening?"

The boy's head moved from left to right, then back again. "Gran...Granfaffer? Isit–" The words slurred together. He stopped, mumbled something completely unintelligible, then tried again. "Isht you or an...anoer dream?"

"Oh Garth," the girl said, and burst into tears.

Garth's head turned to her. "Cat? Don...don...cry." She cried harder.

"I think he will be all right," Galia said. "Ennis did not give him the drug today, and he has been getting better. But it would be wise to have Raven see him."

"An excellent idea," Konrad said. "But how did you come to be here?"

"I followed Ennis from Cory's trial. Then Wendell caught me and – Oh!"

"What is it?" asked one of the men holding Ennis. Ennis had stopped struggling.

"We have to hurry. Wendell left two hours ago to set fire to the Count of Eastlands' home."

"Don't worry," Konrad said. "Cat warned the count that something like that might happen, and he posted guards. They may already have Wendell in custody, just as we have this fellow. Good job, Blade," he told the shorter of the two men.

Galia saw the flash of the other's smile. "It was a good night's work," he agreed. "But a great deal of the credit goes to Farrier."

"They always fall for the trick of the thrown stones," said the taller, thinner man. "Almost feels like we're back in the army, eh, Colonel?"

"It does. Come on, you." The colonel pulled at Ennis's arm.

"Don't hurt him," Galia said again.

"He won't be hurt if he causes no trouble."

They left the clearing and entered the woods. Ennis and his guards went first, then Galia, then Garth, supported on either side by his grandfather and the girl – Cat, Garth had called her. Galia wished she had someone helping her walk too. She was so tired that every root became an obstacle to trip over, every bush a thicket of thorns. After she almost fell for the second time, Konrad left his grandson and came to her side.

"May I?" he asked, taking her elbow and guiding her through the woods. Behind them, Galia heard Cat singing softly.

Then they were out in the open, with only a few fields between them and Freybourg. Away from the shelter of the trees, the wind that had only been a murmur became a cool lament. It blew from the west straight towards them. Galia shivered, and thought of her bed at the college. Soon, soon, she would sink into its softness, pull the clean blankets around her, snuggle into them, sleep...

"What's that?" someone demanded.

Galia dragged her head up. The men in front of her had stopped. They were gazing towards the city, where dancing red lights illuminated the night sky. She stared. They all did.

It was Ennis who provided the answer. "Guards or no guards, it looks like Wendell managed to set fire to Eastlands' house."

CAT

GARTH WAS SAFE. HE HAD RECOGNIZED HER. He had responded to her song, humming a few notes of the refrain the second time round. Soon he would be well. He *would*. Nothing else mattered.

She was sorry about the Eastlands. But she had warned them. If they hadn't listened, or if the guards had been inadequate, that was not her responsibility.

"The fire must have spread," Master Farrier said. "The sky wouldn't be so red if just one house was blazing."

He was right, Cat realized. And the red glow was growing. It gave so much light she could see her companions' faces clearly.

"The wind," Konrad said. "It's strong, and getting stronger. Who knows how many buildings will burn before the night's done."

"The bucket brigade will be out," Colonel Blade said.

"Little good it will do," Master Farrier said grimly. "Not

with the fire having taken hold the way it has, and the wind blowing like this."

Colonel Blade glanced sharply at his groom, then looked at the sky again. He dropped Ennis's arm and turned to the wizard. "Can you make a spell to bring rain?"

Konrad shook his head. "There were no clouds all day. By the time I found them and brought them here, it would be too late. The wizards at the college must be trying. Working together, perhaps..."

The doubt in his voice sent a shiver down Cat's spine. She still had a firm grip on Garth's arm, and felt him shiver too. Was he cold, or did he understand what they were saying?

"I thought wizards could change things at a moment's notice."

"Wiz...wizshards mus work wish th' mater...materals ach hand," Garth said.

Cat's smile nearly cracked her face.

Konrad's smile was just as wide. "I'm glad you were listening to my words all those years, Garth." Then his smile faded, to be replaced by a small, thoughtful frown. "That's how magic works for Freyans. It seems to be different for Islandians, who have a more personal approach to the power they wield." He turned to the girl beside him. "Galia, I know you're tired. I know you have had a frightening day. But do you think you can give Freybourg the rain it needs so desperately?"

The girl, who had been staring at the sky to the east, started as though jolted awake. "Rain? I –" She broke off and thought for a moment. "Two hours ago, I could have. Now... I do not know."

"Why could you have done it two hours ago?" Konrad asked.

"Because I was so sad. I thought I would not see home, or...or *anything*." Her voice wavered. She looked so small, Cat thought. "It would have been easy to let my sadness touch the water in the air and ground and become clouds. If I had not stopped myself, it would have happened without my even wanting it."

Konrad was silent a moment, then asked gently "Could you recreate that feeling so that rain can come?"

Galia went rigid.

"No!" Cat cried. It was all too easy to imagine how Galia had felt. "How can you ask her to make herself as miserable and frightened as she was then? It's *wrong*."

Galia gazed at her. Then she smiled, a smile as warm as the sun had been at midday.

"Thank you," she said softly. "You are right. I do not want to feel as I did then. But it will be for a short time only." She took a deep breath. "I will try."

Cat had been present when wizards cast spells. She had seen their bodies go still and their faces intent. She had heard the words of power tremble in the air. This was nothing like that. True, Galia was still for a minute or two. Then her face contorted. As though she'd been struck by a physical blow, Cat thought. Or great mental anguish. Loss. Fear. Cat's hand tightened its grip on Garth, but he didn't seem to notice. His eyes were fixed on Galia's face, which remained distorted for a long moment. Then Galia's shoulders slumped and her face went slack with misery. Cat wanted to wrap her arms around the girl, but knew she mustn't. She looked at those around her. They were all watching Galia. Master Farrier had dropped his hand from Ennis's arm, but Ennis didn't try to escape. He stared at the Islandian as intently as the others. Minutes passed.

"Look," Master Farrier said. Startled, Cat glanced at him. He was pointing at the sky above Freybourg.

A black cloud had formed. As Cat watched, it grew larger and larger, darker and denser.

Then, as though a knife had been plunged into its heart, rain gushed from it onto the flames below.

It was a short walk to the city. There was no rain as they trudged down the dirt track, nor as they entered the western outskirts. As they approached the centre of town, though, they were met by a faint trickle as the black cloud, like a punctured waterskin, let out its last remaining drops. People passed them, singly or in groups.

"Is the fire out?" Colonel Blade asked one such group.

"It is," a man answered. "Didn't take long after the rain started. What a deluge! A couple of my friends went off to a tavern to talk about the night's happenings, but sitting around in wet clothes has never been my idea of fun. I'm heading home to dry off."

"Did the fire do much damage?"

"There'll be a few folk without homes, but there's not as much harm done as we feared. For a while there, we thought the palace itself would go up. Some sparks landed on the roof of the east wing, and we weren't at all sure we could douse them before they spread. Then the rain came."

"Thank Freyn," said another man. "Half the city or more might have been burned if not for that rain."

"Must have been the wizards' doing, I figure," said a third. "Sure wasn't a sign of a cloud before that one formed right above the fire."

The group passed on, talking and laughing in short, excited spurts.

Garth had not spoken since his one remark about magic, but he appeared steady and alert. Cat didn't think he needed her support any more, but she held his hand anyway. Tightly. He didn't seem to mind.

Konrad, Cat noted, still kept a guiding hand on Galia's arm. Cat was glad. The girl had looked completely drained after she'd formed the cloud. Colonel Blade and Master Farrier had resumed their hold on Ennis.

Cat stepped into a pool of water, splashing the bottom of her skirt. She laughed, feeling like a child walking through puddles. Garth glanced at her. She smiled and squeezed his hand.

The palace looked untouched. It stood on its hill, wings outstretched like a great swan protecting its fledgling young. But it had been unable to protect the buildings below it. Cat and her companions came to a stop and stared at the damage. The walls were intact, though scarred with scorch marks, but their roofs had caved in and their doors crumpled.

"If only the roofs had been made of stone like the rest of the structure," Colonel Blade said.

Galia pointed. "There is the courthouse."

Its door was completely gone. In the light of the torches held by the people milling around outside, Cat saw a great charred beam of wood lying slantwise in the hall. As she watched, a shower of stones fell from above.

Master Farrier shook his head. "It's not safe. It may have to be torn down and rebuilt."

"And to think Wendell did all this," Ennis said. His voice held a note of awe. Colonel Blade glanced sharply at him and tightened his grip.

"At least no one would have been in these buildings when the fire came," Konrad said. "But what about the houses that went up in flames?"

They walked on. The rain might have drowned the fire, but it couldn't quench the acrid smell of smoke. Cat tried not to breathe through her nose as they approached the heart of the destruction.

Again, the stone buildings still stood. But as she got closer, Cat saw that the fire had gutted many of them. Some seemed in danger of crumbling from within.

The street was crowded with green-uniformed soldiers, black-robed wizards, refugees from the burnt houses, volunteers come to help and curious onlookers come to gawk.

"Stand back!" someone shouted. A second later, a large cornerstone crashed onto the street. People screamed and scrambled back as one entire side of the building came rushing down in an avalanche of stones. Cat flinched out of the way as someone almost stepped on her toes.

"There's too many people here," Colonel Blade said. "Someone will be hurt. I'm going to talk to whoever's in charge. Farrier, guard our prisoner." He dropped Ennis's arm and strode over to the officer who had ordered everyone back.

"Raven!" Galia cried suddenly, and tore off. Cat followed her with her eyes, and saw a tall man with a silver streak in his black hair. She and the others walked after the Islandian.

"Raven," Galia called again.

He turned from the soldier he was talking to, a burly, blunt-featured man. "Galia! I'm glad to see you. I've been worried about you – though less so since the rain came. At least that told me you were nearby." A smile lit his lean, long-nosed face. He was a man in his late middle years, Cat judged, with brown skin like Galia's and hair and eyes as dark as the bird he was named for. His eyes scanned the group. "And Konrad. I'm happy to see you as well."

"Are many hurt?" the wizard asked.

"Yes, but not badly. Smoke inhalation and broken bones from falling debris mostly. There may still be some trapped inside, though. I was talking to Captain Carter here about whether his men could check this place without undue risk to themselves."

"From here it looks as though it should be safe enough," Master Farrier said.

Captain Carter smiled. "Ah, Farrier, is that you? You always had a good eye for the structure of buildings. Come inside and take a look at these stairs. It's them I'm worried about. We think there may still be some of the servants trapped on the top level."

Master Farrier hesitated. He glanced about, then, obviously feeling there were enough people to keep an eye on Ennis, he dropped his hand with a muttered, "Stay here," and accompanied the captain through the gaping door.

"Were any of the Eastlands family hurt?" Galia asked Raven.

"No. Apparently they'd been warned, and posted a couple of soldiers. The guards didn't see the man who threw a burning rag through an open window, I'm told, but they were vigilant enough to catch a glimpse of him when he was sneaking away. One of them ran after him. Stuck a knife into his back, poor man." Raven sighed and rubbed a hand across his forehead, leaving a charcoal streak behind. "By that time, the fire had caught hold, but at least there was time for everyone to escape safely. Unfortunately, the wind blew sparks from the house onto adjacent buildings."

So Wendell was dead. And what of his wife, who had stood in her dark room with a crying baby in her arms and a coughing child on the straw mat by the wall? What would she do now?

Garth stirred and murmured something. When she glanced at him, she saw that he was watching Ennis. She looked at Ennis too. He was staring at Raven, his eyes wide.

"Poor Wendell," Galia said.

"Wendell?" Raven asked.

"The man who set the fire. The one who was killed."

Raven raised his eyebrows. "You know him?"

Galia nodded.

Raven studied the girl's face. "Obviously a great deal has happened to you. You'll have to tell me about it when tonight's work is done."

A soldier walked towards them, shouting, "Go home! Everyone who has no business here, leave. Now. You're in the way. Go home."

"That probably includes us," Konrad said. "Unless I can help, that is. I have some rudimentary skills as a healer."

Raven shook his head. "I think every healer in Freybourg is here, including all the teachers from the college."

"Speaking of healing... I won't bother you now, of course. But I hope you can inspect my grandson tomorrow. He's been given drugs for some time. I think he's all right, but I would feel more at ease if I were sure his mind has not been damaged."

"Of course," Raven said promptly. "I'll come as soon as I can. Where are you staying?"

Konrad told him, then added, "I suggest I take Galia there tonight. She's had a hard day. My daughter-in-law will look after her well."

"A good idea," Raven agreed.

From the corner of her eye, Cat saw Ennis take a step backwards. Then another. She opened her mouth to cry a warning.

"No," Garth murmured, and squeezed her hand.

She stared at him. What did he mean, no? Ennis had kept him a prisoner for almost two months. He had kept him tied up, drugged. He might have destroyed his mind. He should be punished.

Galia had turned. She was staring right at Ennis. She said nothing.

Cat swivelled her head, watched Ennis take two more steps backwards, towards the dark shadows of an adjacent building.

She opened her mouth again, then caught Galia's eye. The Islandian shook her head.

Galia had said Ennis had saved their lives.

Perhaps. But only after he had put them in danger. Only after he had mistreated Garth.

"No," Garth breathed again. "Thersh Wende's fam...famly."

Wendell's family. A woman who looked old beyond her years. A crying baby. A coughing child. Two other children. In a building that smelled of dust and decay. Was that why Ennis was escaping into the darkness? To look after Wendell's family?

Cat closed her mouth and kept it closed.

THE SHEETS SMELLED OF SOAP and fresh air. Cat snuggled more deeply into them and pulled the blankets higher.

Then she remembered and sat straight up, opening her eyes to sunlight bathing the room with gold. It must be well into midmorning.

Garth was back. He was well. She was sure of it. She bounced out of bed. The sooner she was dressed, the sooner she could see him. She went to the basin and splashed water onto her face.

The girl in the other bed stirred and opened her eyes.

"I'm sorry," Cat said. "I didn't mean to disturb you."

"It is all right," Galia assured her. She yawned. She still looked tired, but not as exhausted as last night, when she'd had trouble finding enough energy to undress and get into bed.

Cat pulled on her dress, then waited impatiently while the other girl dressed.

"Do you think Colonel Blade will catch Ennis?" Galia asked.

The colonel had been upset when he'd returned last night to find his captive missing.

"I'm sorry," Cat had said. "We forgot to keep our eyes on him."

Colonel Bade had sighed. "Well, he can't have gone far. I'll look for him."

"I don't think he will," Cat said now. "There were so many people standing around and walking away that Ennis could easily lose himself in the crowd."

Galia smiled.

The others were already sitting around a table in the small parlour when the two girls entered. Garth leaped to his feet. "Cat!"

"Freyn's Day to you both." Konrad lowered his cup of kala and rose to draw two chairs up to the table.

"I'll send for more oatmeal and kala," Annette said. There were still dark circles under her eyes, but the eyes themselves were smiling, and her cheeks were pink. She hadn't cried when Garth walked in last night, just enfolded him in her arms and held him for a long time.

A bowl of hot porridge was soon in front of Cat. She ate hungrily. Even so, she managed to raise her head frequently to glance at Garth. Every time she did so, she found his eyes on her. Her heart sang.

But oh, he was pale. And thin. So thin.

"You missed Raven," Konrad announced.

Cat's head jerked up. She stared at him, then at Garth.

Garth smiled. "Raven says I'm fine."

She hadn't realized how worried she still was until that moment. It was as though a thin cloud had hung in front of the sun. Now it had blown away, and the world was bright.

"It was kind of Raven to come so early," Annette said. "He must be tired after all his work yesterday."

"Grandfather said he wouldn't be at ease until Raven inspected my mind to make sure it wasn't damaged."

Konrad regarded his grandson. "So you caught that? I wasn't sure how much you were taking in."

"Most things, by then. Earlier..." Garth frowned and looked down. His finger drew circles on the table. "I'm not sure. When you came... I knew you were there, but it seemed like a dream. The last little while has all been like that. I never knew what was real and what wasn't. And most of the time, I felt so sick I didn't care."

Cat thought of the vomit stains. Her hands clenched into fists.

"And before that?" Annette asked gently. "Was it very bad?"

Garth raised his head and smiled at her. "No. Ennis forced lambwort down my throat when he went out. He and Wendell were afraid I would use magic to escape, even though I told them I got spells wrong half the time. But Ennis mostly stayed home. I hated always being in that one small room. And I was hungry. But then, so was Ennis since he gave me half his food. But I wasn't hurt. The worst thing, apart from worrying about what everyone must think of me, was the *boredom*. The only thing I could do was talk to Ennis."

"And what would you and Ennis have to say to each other?" Konrad asked.

"He told me about his farm, and his wife. And we argued a lot, about what was the best way to make changes."

"I see," Konrad said.

Garth hesitated, then said, "I didn't like the methods he and his friends had chosen, but I do think things must change. I've been...Well, I was trying to help bring that about. That's how I met Ennis and Wendell, and accidentally overheard their plans."

"I know," his grandfather said. "Cat told us."

"I had to," Cat said. "I'm sorry."

"It's all right."

Konrad sighed. "I don't agree with you, but we won't argue about it now. I'm just glad to get you back. But tell me, why did you write us that letter? If you hadn't, I would have searched for you."

"They said they'd kill me if I didn't."

She should not have let Ennis go. She should *not*.

"They didn't know about Cat. I hoped that when she didn't hear from me, she would come looking for me, the way she came looking for her father. And she did." Garth smiled at her. Then his smile faded. "I hope Master Coyne will take me back. He must be very angry."

"He is," Konrad said. "But he'll take you back when he learns the truth."

"Are you sure?"

"He told me that you and Talisa Thatcher were the most promising apprentices he'd ever had, and that it was a crime you were forsaking your studies."

Garth's mouth stretched in a grin as broad as the River Frey at its widest.

Annette poured more kala for them all. As she set the pot down, she laughed. "We're just finishing breakfast, and it's almost noon."

"Noon!" Galia's hand shook so badly that kala spilled onto her fingers.

"You've burned yourself," Annette said. "I'll get some water."

Galia didn't seem to hear her. She was on her feet, her face white. "Cory. I had forgotten. He is to be hanged at noon."

Cat gasped. She had forgotten too.

"Cory?" Garth asked.

"Cory Updale," his grandfather said. "I gather you know him."

"Yes, but... Hanged? I thought he was safe in Uglessia."

"A lot's happened while you've been in a stupor."

"But he's innocent."

"Can you prove it?"

"Yes. I heard Ennis and Wendell talking. They set the fire."

Galia nodded. "I heard them too."

Konrad looked from one to the other, then rose. "I tried to persuade Queen Elira to postpone the execution until further investigation was done. She didn't listen to me yesterday, but she may now. Come along. There's no time to waste."

As they emerged into the sunlight, Konrad said, "She may not want to see me again, but she won't refuse to meet the girl who saved the city."

SHE DIDN'T. No sooner had Konrad sent in their names, and an explanation of who Galia was, than Queen Elira came sweeping into the antechamber. Talk ceased. Everyone scrambled to their feet.

The queen came straight to them and clasped Galia's hands. "So you are the one who created the blessed rain. I am so glad you are here. I had sent to the college to ask which of its learned wizards had saved Freybourg. My messenger returned with the news that it was none of them, but rather the Islandian girl who is staying there this year, Freyn be thanked. But come into my audience chamber, where we can talk in peace."

Cat wondered how much the waiting courtiers resented them as they followed Queen Elira. But perhaps there was no resentment. They must be grateful to Galia too.

The queen seated herself and waved them to chairs. She looked tired, but otherwise very much as Cat remembered her from Midsummer a year ago, though today she was dressed in a brown walking dress, shot with amber.

"You use your power well, Galia, unlike some of our own wizards. I hear it was Master Granton at the college who created the wind last night in a foolish display of his new knowledge." The queen's lips folded in a tight line. Galia's eyes went wide.

"Enough of that," Queen Elira said, smiling at Galia again. "You must tell me about yourself. But first, welcome to you all. Master Spellman, it is good to see you again. And you, Mistress Spellman. I am delighted that your son and grandson is safely restored to you. I remember him well from last Midsummer." Queen Elira turned to Cat.

"And you, Catrina. I understand you are once again engaged in foiling conspiracies. The Count of Eastlands told me it was a girl named Catrina Ashdale who warned him that there were those who meant him harm."

Cat smiled but could think of nothing to say.

"Your Majesty is most gracious," Konrad said. "Forgive me if I am abrupt, but our business is urgent."

Was she wrong, or did the warmth in Queen Elira's eyes vanish, to be replaced by wariness? "And what business is that?"

"The business of Cory Updale. His execution must be stopped."

The queen frowned. "Master Spellman, we spoke of this yesterday. I told you that stopping, or even postponing the execution, was not possible."

"I know. But since then there is new evidence."

Garth leaned forward. "Your Majesty, the men who kept me prisoner often spoke in front of me, forgetting I was there. It was they, not Cory, who set fire to the barracks. It weighed on their consciences, I think – both the fact that men had died in the fire and that an innocent man had been blamed."

"And who are these men?"

"Ennis Waters and his friend Wendell. I'm sorry. I can't recall Wendell's family name."

Was that true, Cat wondered. Or was Garth reluctant to give Wendell's name because that might lead to Ennis's capture?

"Wendell also set fire to the Count of Eastlands' home last night," Konrad said.

"So I understand. I have spoken to Colonel Blade. He tells me that the other man, this Master Waters, escaped."

"Unfortunately, yes."

Was there *nothing* Queen Elira hadn't found out? No wonder she looked tired.

"Unfortunate indeed. It would be good to question these men. No," she added, holding up a hand as Garth opened his mouth, "I don't doubt your word. But I am still not convinced of Cory Updale's innocence. From all accounts, he never denied that he knew who the arsonists were, yet wouldn't name them. To what extent was he involved?"

"I heard Ennis and Wendell too," Galia said. "Garth is right. They felt very badly, especially Ennis, because Cory was going to die for something they had done. They would not have felt that way if he had been involved with what they did."

"No?" The queen lifted her eyebrows. "I'm not so sure. How did you come to overhear them?"

"Ennis was at the trial. So was I. I do not know why, but I followed him when the trial was over, and came to the trees where he and Wendell were. I heard them talking before they caught me, and afterwards too."

"Your Majesty, surely there is enough evidence to demand that Updale's hanging be stayed," Konrad said.

The queen hesitated.

There was a knock on the door. The man-at-arms opened it and exchanged a few words with the liveried servant outside. Then he turned back, took a couple of steps forward, and bowed deeply.

"Your Majesty, forgive me for interrupting. But a soldier just rode in with the news that a great mob of ragged people is approaching the city. They are less than an hour away."

TALISA

THE SKY WAS FLUSHED WITH PINK WHEN Talisa opened her eyes. A Freyan sky, she thought. At home, mountains gave the sky less time to reflect the sun's comings and goings.

Then the noise around her made her throw her blanket aside and rise. The camp was stirring.

There was no time for fires, despite the chill bite of the early morning air. They ate quickly, washing the food down with water from the nearby stream. Talisa swung her pack over her back.

"Thannis, Thannis, we want a ride." The girl and boy he had carried yesterday came running up. The boy grabbed his hand and danced around him.

"Mam said we weren't to bother you," the girl said. "But you don't mind, do you?"

"Of course not." Thannis knelt down, a willing victim, and the two climbed on his shoulders.

Talisa glanced over at the child she'd carried yesterday, but the girl was holding her mother's hand and looked refreshed from her night's sleep.

Talisa wished she felt refreshed too. But the tears she had shed the night before seemed to have lodged in her mind and heart. Rina looked equally weary.

"Are you all right?" Bart asked.

"Yes."

"You're sure?"

She sighed. "I'm tired, that's all. I fell asleep with no trouble, but then I woke up and couldn't get back to sleep for a long time. It didn't help that the baby kept kicking."

Bart was silent. Behind them, Talisa heard the children giggling.

"It was strange," Rina said. "Soon after I woke, I saw a red glow in the sky in the direction of Freybourg. As I watched, the glow spread. I wondered whether the whole city was on fire."

"At least, locked up as he is, Cory can't be blamed for setting this fire," Bart said.

Talisa winced.

Rina's head dropped. Bart took her hand. "Sorry."

She nodded. For a while, they walked on without speaking. The whole assembly was quiet. Perhaps they were all tired, Talisa thought. She was glad to see that Edda was mounted behind the middle-aged soldier again. The sun was behind them, but reached long fingers out, splashing gold onto the leaves of the hedge that marched beside the road.

Rina's head was still down, Bart's lips pressed tightly together. Talisa took a deep breath. She couldn't relieve their fear, any more than she could ease her own, but at least she could distract them. She began to sing, softly at first, then more loudly as faces turned her way. She was on the chorus of her second song, a familiar Freyan ballad, when Rina's voice joined hers. Then Bart's. By the time she was halfway through the third song, most of the people around her were singing. Even Thannis, who didn't know the words, hummed along.

They walked. They sang. The morning wore on. Then, towards noon, the people in front of them stopped.

"What's happening?" Thannis asked as he came up beside them, the two children still riding his shoulders. The old man was clinging to his arm again today.

"I don't know," Rina said.

Bart was staring ahead. "Look." Talisa squinted in the direction he was pointing.

"The palace," she said. Was it really only four days since she'd been in it, begging for Cory's life?

"We will soon be in Freybourg, friends," Alain called. He stood on a rock beside the road so he could be seen and heard. "Rest for a short while, and eat, so you will be refreshed when we enter the city."

The children Thannis had carried scampered off to find their parents, while Thannis helped the old man settle himself on a low boulder. Rina handed bread and cheese to everyone.

Alain was walking through the assembly. He stopped when he reached them.

"Freyn's Day. How are you?"

"A bit tired, but fine otherwise," Rina said.

"It won't be long now."

"I'm not sure I find that thought reassuring," Bart said wryly.

Alain's eyes fell on the old man on the boulder. "Reassuring for those who have trouble walking so far."

Bart's eyes followed his, then roamed over the mass of people sitting or sprawling on the grass. "The citizens of Freybourg will be surprised when they see our raggle-taggle procession."

"Not too surprised. I saw one of the soldiers sneaking off through a grove of trees a while back. The major wants to make sure they know we're on our way."

"Will it make a difference? That they know we're coming?" Rina asked.

Alain shrugged. "Not much. We can hardly keep our approach a secret. This will give them more notice, that's all." He turned to Talisa. "I need you to help lead a song."

She blinked. "A song?"

"A song about the poor and dispossessed. It's one I've sung before, but simplified. I want everyone in this crowd to sing it. I want us to sing it as we march through the streets of Freybourg and as we stand before the queen."

"You're hoping people will be moved by the song, I gather," Bart said. "But will they? Will they even listen?"

Alain glanced at him. "I don't know. But since the only weapons we have are our presence and our stories, we must use both."

His words made Talisa feel naked suddenly. She shivered.

Alain turned back to Talisa. "Will you teach those around you this song, then lead them as we enter Freybourg? I will lead those in front, and Andreas those in the rear, but we need a strong voice in the middle."

Talisa nodded.

He reached into a pocket and handed her a sheet. It was the song she had heard him perform at The Laughing Lute, but now the tune held only the main melodic line. The words were equally simple. She looked up. "It will be easy to teach them this. We will sing it, loudly and clearly." She smiled. "The people of Freybourg will hear this story."

THEY APPROACHED FREYBOURG SINGING. As Talisa had promised, they sang loudly and clearly. The song began:

We were the people of the hills
We were the people of the land.

The words that followed told how they had lost their land and come to the cities to find nothing waiting for them but dirt, and hunger, and cold, and sickness. There was none of the anger that had been in Alain's original version. There were no accusations. Only the facts.

And hope. Hope rang through the refrain. Perhaps it was that hope that made people walk with new energy and sing as though they wanted all Freya to hear.

But we have seen a future
Where no one lacks for food
No one's dressed in rags
And we will reach that future
If no one falters
No one flags
A future world of caring
A future world of light
A future world of sharing
A future world so bright.
Yes, we have seen this future
Where no one lacks for food
No one's dressed in rags
And we will reach that future
If no one falters
If no heart flags.

A hawk hovered overhead, as though trying to catch the words. Talisa smiled up at it and sang even louder.

She could see the city now, not just the palace perched on its hill. Only a couple of fields separated them from the outlying streets.

"What's that?" piped a voice behind her. She turned. The boy on Thannis's left shoulder was pointing towards the city.

Thannis stopped singing. "What?"

"That."

The child had good eyes. It took Talisa a moment or two to make out the green-clad figures. There were a great many of them. They were moving toward the edge of the city, to where the streets met the grassy fields. Toward them.

Others had seen the figures too. Voices petered out, died. People stopped.

"That," Bart said grimly, "is the Freyan army coming our way."

"The whole army?" the boy asked with wonder.

"Probably all the troops that are stationed in Freybourg."

And there must, Talisa thought, as a hand reached into her stomach and squeezed, be a great many troops in Freybourg. The first of them had reached the field now. They were mounted. They were coming fast. They would soon be here.

There was no more singing.

The hawk spread its wings and flew away. If it had been a vulture, it would have stayed.

More and more soldiers trotted onto the grass, across it.

"We will meet them with courage! We will meet them singing!" Alain Swanson had a carrying voice. The voice of a trained musician. Even so, he could barely be heard above the cries of alarm, the clamour of fear. But when he started to sing, those close to him joined in. To the rear, Talisa heard Andreas's strong bass take up the tune.

It was her responsibility to lead the middle section. Her throat felt too tight for song, but she took a deep breath and began. The first two notes wobbled. After that, her voice steadied. On the second line, Rina added her soprano to Talisa's. Then others joined. Talisa heard Thannis's deep growl, the quavering tones of the old man, the high, thin trebles of the little ones.

They started walking forward. Slowly. Much more slowly than before. But they walked. And sang.

"I hope he knows what he's doing," Bart muttered. He and Rina were holding hands. Talisa wished someone were holding hers. Cory. Her father. Welwyn. Someone she loved. Someone who loved her.

The song helped. It gave them courage. Enough courage to keep walking, even when the horsemen came closer. And closer.

The troop that had escorted them from Freyfall – though escorted was perhaps not the right word, Talisa thought – was strung out beside them. She watched the soldier who bore Edda stop. Edda slid down from his horse.

The marchers walked towards the oncoming horsemen. The horsemen rode towards them.

Would they collide?

The singing was ragged. Talisa forced new strength into her voice, made it ring with conviction as they began the chorus.

The singing steadied, like water reaching clear ground after running over rough stones.

The soldiers were so near. So near. Talisa could see their faces. Did they betray a trace of uneasiness? A flicker of bewilderment? Or was it just her imagination? Her hope?

Closer. Closer still.

"Halt!" An officer held up a gloved hand. Those around him, those behind him, stopped. Obediently. Precisely. They looked even more formidable now. Ranged in row after row. Men and horses. Swords. The noon sun glittered.

The swords were minor suns, flashing light into Talisa's eyes.

The marchers came to a ragged halt, but continued singing. They headed into the third verse, then the refrain. The song ended.

It was so quiet, without the song. Too quiet. Only the jangle of horses' harnesses, the wail of a baby somewhere behind her, the chirp of grasshoppers in the fields.

The man who had held up his hand advanced two paces. "What are you doing here?" His voice resonated clearly in the silence. It was deep. Stern. A father demanding an accounting from unruly children. Only a father did not bring rank after rank of armed men with him.

Alain spoke mildly, but his trained singer's voice was as easy to hear as the other's. "We have come to speak to Queen Elira."

"Queen Elira has no interest in talking to a mob."

"A mob, General? Surely not. Mobs imply a threat. But it is you, not us, who bear arms."

Alain paused, then continued. "As you can see, we are a peaceful procession of men, women, and children. We mean no harm. We have walked from Freyfall to Freybourg, to ask Queen Elira for her help for the poorest of her subjects."

A horse in the front row snorted and sidled to the left. Its rider stilled it.

"Queen Elira will not see a mob. If one or two of you wish to speak to her, we will provide an escort to the palace. The rest will remain here."

"No."

The general jerked as though he'd been slapped. Several hands touched their sword hilts. Talisa sucked in her breath.

"We have come a long way. All of us. We came – and it was a hard trek for many – to speak to the queen. To show her our plight. For one or two only to see her would be a mockery of our journey. Of our hopes."

The general glanced over his shoulder at his men. More hands reached for their swords. Bart's arm encircled Rina.

The general looked back at Alain. "She will not allow a rabble like this to rage through the streets of Freybourg, terrorizing her people more than they have already been terrorized."

"There was trouble here last night?" So Alain too had seen the glow in the sky.

"A ruffian set fire to the Count of Eastlands' house. The whole city almost went up in smoke."

"I see," Alain said slowly. "Queen Elira's concern for her people is, of course, commendable. And to be expected. It is the knowledge of that concern that draws us here. I can understand, given the circumstances, why she does not want us to progress through the streets of Freybourg. Please ask her to come here to speak with us."

The general's eyes roved over the crowd. "Why should she?"

"We are her people, just as those in Freybourg are."

"The people of Freybourg are law-abiding subjects, not an unruly mob."

"Have you noticed any signs of unruliness here?" Alain asked.

The general's eyes scanned the marchers again.

"Or of unlawfulness? We have broken no laws in coming here." Alain's voice was as unruffled as it had been when he began.

"Queen Elira has said she will see one or two of you. Nothing more. If you do not wish to accept her gracious offer, then leave." The general raised his voice close to a bellow. "All of you."

There was rustling, like wind moving through leaves, but no one spoke or turned to go.

The general's hand went to his sword. "Leave now, or face the consequences."

The breath of the old man behind Talisa was a raspy wheeze. The sun was hot, but her hands were icy. So icy.

Alain raised his voice too. It floated effortlessly over the crowd behind him, the ranks of motionless soldiers in front of him. "And did Queen Elira give you orders to cut her people down if we did not leave? Has she told you that she will not come here?"

The general's silence was his answer.

"Perhaps you should ask her before you order your troops to kill a peaceful assembly of men, women, and children," Alain said, and waited.

They all waited.

The sun blazed.

The grasshoppers chirped.

"I could not ask Queen Elira to put her life in danger," the general said finally.

"There is no danger. We bear no arms," Alain said, as he

had said before. "But if you are worried, why not have us searched while you send a message to the queen?"

After a moment, the officer said, "Very well." He turned and gestured to one of his men, who nudged his horse forward. The general spoke to him quietly. The man nodded, wheeled his horse around, and rode away.

Alain turned to the marchers. "Sit," he called. "Rest a while. Offer no resistance to the soldiers who will search you for weapons."

Talisa sank onto the ground gratefully. Her legs felt shaky.

Thannis lowered his two burdens. "Run and find your parents," he told them. They did. They didn't look frightened. Perhaps they were too young to understand.

The old man was still wheezing. He wiped his sweating face on a dirty sleeve. "I've not been so scared since a mad dog came after me when I was but a boy."

They sat quietly. When anyone spoke, it was in a low mutter. Talisa watched soldiers walk through the crowd, inspecting sacks, patting men's chests and arms. Did they expect to find knives hidden up sleeves? Everyone's eyes were on them, and on the troops still mounted in silent, motionless ranks. The air was as tense as it if a storm were brewing.

Then someone began to sing. Not Alain. It was a child's voice, high and pure.

The child was right, Talisa thought. Their song had lifted their hearts before. It would now. She sang. So did others, more and more, until the whole crowd took it up.

As the song went on, Talisa noticed the closest soldiers look at them and at each other. Was it wishful thinking, or did the hard wariness in their faces ease a little?

Then five soldiers stood above them, blocking the sun. "Give us your packs."

They all handed over their bags, except the old man, who didn't have one. The soldiers inspected them, then passed them back.

"Stand up," said a stocky trooper with a dark moustache. He spoke to all of them, but his eyes were on Thannis. "What are Uglessians doing here?"

Thannis spoke before Talisa could. "I believe in what these people are doing."

The soldier grunted. He and two others approached Thannis as they would a maddened bull. He stood rock still while they patted him down. The remaining two did the same to Bart.

"All right," the stocky soldier said. They turned to move on.

"Wait," Rina said. "Excuse me, but I was wondering... My brother. Cory Updale. He's in prison in Freybourg. Do you know anything about him? Is his trial soon?"

Talisa's breath caught.

The soldiers glanced at each other. "Updale?" The stocky man frowned.

"Isn't he the one – ?" began a lanky youth.

"Yes," his older companion interrupted. He looked at Rina's anxious face, her swollen belly. Then he glanced up at the noon sun. His eyes returned to Rina. There was something in his face. Something Talisa did not want to see.

Pity.

No. May all the mountain spirits prevent this. No.

"I'm sorry," he said. "His trial's been held. He's to be hanged today. At noon."

No. No no no no no! The word was a shriek in her heart, a howl. No. No. NOOO!!

Bart's voice was barely audible. "Where?"

"Hangman's Field. It's close. On the outskirts of the city. A bit south of here."

"I must go to him," Rina whispered.

"Yes," Bart said.

"Orders are no one's to leave this area," someone said. One of the soldiers. Talisa couldn't see which one, for the haze in front of her eyes.

"I *must* go," Rina said.

After a moment, the stocky soldier said, "It may be too late, but... All right. Archer, go with them. Say I gave leave if anyone questions them."

"Yes sir," the lanky young soldier said.

Rina turned. "Talisa..."

Talisa nodded jerkily.

Archer led them through the seated people toward the open field. Rina's and Bart's fingers were tightly intertwined. Rina took Talisa's hand. Talisa was grateful.

The voices of the people seemed far away. Everything was far away. The ground. The sun. She was cold. So cold.

The singing was weak. Faltering.

It was just that everything was so far away.

She stumbled.

Rina's fingers dug into Talisa's palm to keep her upright. The pain pulled the world into focus.

The singing was still thin. Ragged.

No. Voices sang loudly, with conviction, with hope.

Yes. But further away. Around her, they teetered on the edge of silence.

They needed someone to lead them. They needed her.

No! It was a simple song. Everyone knew it. If people fell into silence, it was only because soldiers were among them.

Soldiers were throughout the crowd. Yet it was only here, where there was no leader, that voices faltered.

Anyone could lead them. It didn't have to be her.

Yet Alain had entrusted her with the leadership. Because she was a musician. Because she had a gift.

Cory. *Cory.*

This was Cory's cause. This was Cory's dream.

"Talisa, what is it? We must hurry." Rina tugged her.

Slowly, Talisa pulled her hand free. "I'm sorry. I didn't mean to hold you back. I must stay here to lead the singing."

Rina stared at her, brown eyes – Cory's eyes – wide in her white face. Then she nodded. "Yes." She leaned close and kissed Talisa's cheek. "If we have a chance, we will tell Cory...We will give him your love."

Then she and Bart were gone, running after the lanky young soldier. Talisa stumbled back the way she had come.

Thannis was listening patiently to the old man, who was thumping his stick on the ground and spluttering. He sat on a large rock, Talisa noted. Thannis must have found it and brought it over.

"It's all very well for you, young man. Three of them it was that searched you. But me? Did they even look my way, much less search me? They did not. Do they think me so feeble I can do nothing?" He thumped the ground again.

Thannis jumped to his feet when he saw her. "Talisa! Why –"

"I must sing."

After a moment, he nodded. Talisa took a breath. Another. And another.

Her throat was blocked by tears. How could she sing?

She was useless. She would not go to Cory, yet she could not sing.

She must. She *must*.

The first note wobbled. So did the second. Then Thannis took her hand and held it fast.

The third note emerged strong and pure.

She sang. After a while, she heard the voices around her strengthen. They sang their song. Their song of hope.

GALIA

QUEEN ELIRA STOOD. "AN HOUR AWAY, YOU say."

"Or less."

"I had not thought they would be here this soon. Reports from travellers on the road said there are a great many small children and old folk among them. They have surprised me. Well, it cannot be helped. Send a courier to General Rock. Convey my apologies that he and his men must be disturbed so soon after their labours last night, but tell him to muster his forces to ride out immediately and confront this mob."

"But, Your Majesty! You can't!" Garth cried.

She turned and looked at him. "Why do you say that?"

A lock of dark hair had fallen into Garth's eyes. He brushed it aside. "It's not a mob. It's just a number of poor people. All they want to do is talk to you. Truly, Your Majesty."

Queen Elira's mouth thinned. "And how do you know this?" Like dark clouds moving in to cover a sunlit summer sky, anger had replaced her earlier smiles. Galia shifted uneasily.

Garth gripped the arms of his chair, but met the queen's eyes steadily. "I know Master Swanson, who organized this march. I carried messages for him, telling people about his plans."

Cat's face had gone the colour of a shell bleached by the sun.

"Your Majesty –" Konrad began.

The queen glanced at him. "Don't worry, Master Spellman. I will not punish your grandson. He has undoubtedly already suffered for his actions. I have no doubt his recent captivity resulted from them. But nor can I rely on his statement, since he has displayed a remarkable lack of judgement."

A tide of red flooded Garth's face, but he said, his voice shaking only slightly, "Ennis and Wendell acted against Master Swanson's beliefs. He means nothing but good."

Cat had recovered some colour. She leaned forward. "Your Majesty, I met Master Swanson during my search for Garth. I am sure the group he leads is peaceful."

Queen Elira regarded them, frowning. Then she turned back to the man-at-arms. "Tell General Rock to inform this Master Swanson that I will see him, plus one or two others if he chooses. But I will not have an unruly crowd descend on Freybourg and frighten its citizens, especially after the events of last night."

"Yes, Your Majesty." The man bowed and left.

The queen shifted her attention to her guests. She looked old suddenly, Galia thought. It was as though this new emergency had loosened an avalanche of care on her.

"I'm sorry we were interrupted so abruptly. I'm afraid I must ask you to leave now. Again, my thanks for the service you did all Freybourg." She smiled at Galia, but the smile was brief, her mind elsewhere.

They couldn't be dismissed. Not now. Not yet. Galia stared at the queen in dismay. "What about Cory?"

"My dear child, we have already discussed this matter at some length." Impatience was sharp in Queen Elira's voice.

"But he is going to die in less than an hour. And he did not do it. Garth and I both heard Ennis and Wendell say they had set the fire."

The queen sighed. "As I have said, I do not doubt it. But I also do not doubt that Master Updale was involved to some extent in these men's wretched schemes."

There must be words that would convince her. There *must*. Galia struggled to find them. But before she could, Cat spoke.

"Your Majesty, you have said that you owe Galia thanks for saving the city." Cat stopped and swallowed. "Last year, you were gracious enough to say you owed me thanks for saving your life."

After a moment, the queen smiled. Faintly, but she smiled. "That is true. I have not forgotten the tawny cat that sprang to the rescue." Her smile faded. "Be that as it may, I cannot repay my debts at the expense of Freya. I believe this man to be a potential danger. I cannot risk the safety of my subjects."

Three years ago, all the way down the path to the beach, Galia had hoped, she had prayed, that she would find Arlan alive. She had known she would not, but she had still hoped. Now hope was being wrenched from her again.

Talisa, I tried. I did try.

"Your Majesty." Annette spoke for the first time. Her voice was steady, but Galia could see the effort she made to keep it so. "I went with my father-in-law to talk to Cory Updale after we received the letter from Garth's captors. I had expected to find some sort of monster. I found a young man – a boy, really – who was torn between his desire to help my son and a desire not to hurt people he knew. I do not believe he is dangerous." She stopped, then struggled on, hectic colour flushing her face. "I think... I'm sorry, Your Majesty. But I think you will be acting unjustly if you do not stop this execution."

The rug under Galia's feet was thick, as thick as the silence that filled the room. Galia stared at it, then raised her head and looked at the queen. Hoping. Praying.

Finally, Queen Elira nodded. She turned to the man who sat behind the table in the corner. "Master Scribner, write a note authorizing Cory Updale's release."

Master Scribner dipped his pen into an ink bottle and wrote. When he finished, Queen Elira went over and pressed her seal ring to the paper. She handed it to Konrad.

"The guards will have taken him to Hangman's Field at the southeast edge of the city. You'll have to hurry if you're to be in time."

They hurried. Out of the audience chamber, through the waiting room filled with brocade and satin and staring eyes, out of the palace.

But haste was almost impossible in Freybourg that day. It seemed all the city had gushed out of homes onto the streets.

"This is as bad as Freyfall," Cat gasped, dodging around an agitated group.

"News of the approaching marchers must have spread as quickly as the fire did last night," Konrad said grimly.

Behind them, a bugle blew. Someone shouted, "Clear the way!"

Cold stones pressed against Galia's back as she stood, like everyone else, against a building as rank after rank of mounted soldiers trotted by.

"There's no *need* for so many," Garth said.

As soon as the soldiers had passed, people thronged back into the street.

"We should have a bugle too," Cat muttered.

Galia nodded. She refused to look at the sun. She concentrated on walking as quickly as she could, even though her legs had begun to ache. At least her small size made it easy to slip through gaps in the crowd. She kept her eyes on Konrad's black cloak. She wasn't sure where the others were.

The crowds thinned. Shops gave way to houses.

Cat was beside her again. "We can go faster here."

"Yes," Galia said, though it didn't feel as though her legs *could* walk faster. "Where are Garth and his mother?"

"Behind us. Garth can't walk very fast, after being tied up and drugged all that time." Cat was silent a moment, then burst out, "I should never have let Ennis go." After another brief silence, she sighed. "Or maybe I should. I hope Wendell's family will be all right."

They passed the tree-lined lane that led to the college.

If they had horses, they could go faster. But it would take too much time to go to the college and borrow them.

"Do you know how much further it is?" Cat asked.

"No."

Cat looked up at the sky, then quickened her pace. Galia clenched her fists and did the same.

Konrad was about twenty yards ahead. Galia saw him veer onto a dusty track.

Cat glanced behind her, then stopped. "I don't see Garth and Annette. You go ahead. I'll wait to show them the way."

Grasshoppers chirped in the fields. Dust rose in soft clouds around Galia's feet. Konrad was well ahead now.

He would be in time. He *would*.

What if he were not? What if, by the time he arrived...

No. She would not think of that.

If he arrived too late, Talisa would be...

No.

Where was Talisa now? And Thannis?

Galia felt very small, and very alone.

Above her head, a raven croaked.

She forced herself to walk faster. It was hard. So hard. Her legs felt as though she'd been pounding them with stones. And she was climbing up a hill. Not a steep hill, but a long one. She leaned forward, into the incline.

Konrad stopped. Bent over.

She hadn't thought she could, but she ran.

His hand was massaging the back of his calf. His face was contorted with pain. "Cramp," he gasped. "Here." He held out the queen's pardon.

She felt the smoothness of the paper in her hand. The weight of the responsibility in her heart.

She couldn't run the whole way. She ran. Walked. Ran again. Her lungs burned.

Then she was at the top of the hill. Below, across an expanse of open ground –

The gallows. A simple post rising out of the ground, with another, shorter post at the top. She was too far away to see it, but she knew a rope hung from that post.

There was a cart beneath the gallows. Horses. Soldiers in green uniforms. Others, further away. A couple of women, she thought. Some men. On the cart, a man with brown hair. Cory.

Two soldiers gripped his arms, led him forward.

In a minute – less than a minute – they would fasten the noose around his neck. Hang him.

She was too late.

Cory would die. As Arlan had died. There was nothing she could do.

No! No! *No!*

Lightning flamed down. Out of the sky, which was achingly blue, totally cloudless. Out of *her*. Her anger. Her fear. Her outrage. It hit the top of the post and split it in two.

The thunder came a second later.

By the time she reached Hangman's Field, Konrad had caught up with her. He was limping slightly, but the pain had eased from his face. He went to the officer in charge. "From the queen," he said, and nodded to Galia. She held out the paper.

The man took it, but his eyes kept darting to the charred gallows. His men looked like lost sheep who wished someone would tell them which way to go. One of them was staring intently into the sky. Beyond them, a woman was sobbing.

Cory still stood in the cart. His wrists were shackled. His eyes looked like large bruises in a face drained of colour.

"As you see," Konrad said, "Queen Elira orders Cory Updale's release."

The officer's eyes returned to the paper in his hand.

All the way down the hill, Galia had been aware of three people hurrying across the field. She could see them clearly now: a young soldier, a tall, dark-haired man, and a woman with curly brown hair who was heavy with child.

"Cory!" the woman cried.

Cory's head swung in her direction. He blinked, then blinked again. "Rina? Bart?" His voice was that of a bewildered child.

The soldiers stood back as the man and woman approached the cart. "We heard...We heard you were to be hanged," the woman said. "We thought we'd be too late. But then the lightning came. From nowhere. What..." She glanced at the burned gallows, at the gawking soldiers. "What's happening?"

Cory's gaze had followed hers. "I don't... I was ready. At least, I thought I was. Then the lightning struck. And now... Now it's all to be done again." His voice shook.

Galia took a couple of steps toward the cart. "It is all right. Master Spellman and I brought orders from Queen Elira that you are not to be hanged."

The young woman gasped. The man with her stared at Galia.

Cory closed his eyes. He swayed. One of the soldiers beside him put out a hand to steady him.

Cory opened his eyes and shook his head. "I don't understand." His eyes went to Konrad. "Did the queen agree to pardon me in return for Garth's release? Is Garth...?"

Konrad came over. "Garth is safe and well. In fact, if you turn your head, you'll see him."

Sure enough, Garth and Cat and Annette were making their way down the hill.

The officer also came over. "Cory Updale, I have orders from Her Gracious Majesty that you are to be released. Unlock his bonds," he told his men.

They did. In a moment, Cory was free.

TWO HOURS LATER, Galia sat waiting along with a sea of people.

Waiting had not been hard at first. She had been so happy to see Thannis and Talisa again. Not that Talisa had noticed her at first. She had no eyes to spare for anyone but Cory. Galia had tried not to mind. Anyway, there was Thannis's bear hug to make her feel better.

A lean, dark-haired man had come up to them. "I'm glad you're both free and safe," he'd said, looking from Cory to Garth and back.

"So am I," Cory had said, face flushed with excitement. "You've done it, Alain! You've brought them here. More than I ever dreamed."

"We haven't succeeded yet," Alain had said soberly, his eyes on the ranks of horsemen. Then he'd turned back to Garth. "I wish you hadn't suffered in the cause of bringing this gathering together. I am sorry."

"I'm fine now," Garth had assured him.

Alain had smiled, then moved back through the crowd, frequently stopping to talk to groups or individuals who sprawled on the ground, talking quietly or singing.

Alain Swanson was not the only one who'd apologized to Garth. A tall young man in a red cloak too warm for the day had come up to them, shaken Cory's hand solemnly, then turned to Garth.

"I'm sorry."

Garth had blinked. "For what?"

"Andreas had no part in your capture, but he suspected who had you, and suggested that they bargain your freedom for Cory's," Cat had explained. She was sitting very close to Garth and holding his hand tightly.

"I'm sorry," Andreas had repeated. "It seemed a good idea at the time."

"It might have been if it had worked," Garth had agreed.

His grandfather, who'd seated himself on the rock beside the old man, had sighed.

"I shall make amends," Andreas had promised. "A song for your wedding, perhaps?" He'd smiled at Cat, who'd turned pink. "Now I must be off and lead my section in our glorious song. My profound respects to all here." He'd given them a sweeping bow before leaving.

The other thing that had happened during those two hours still made Galia feel warm. Annette had told Cory, "I'm so glad you're safe. We were worried we wouldn't arrive in time."

"We didn't," Konrad had said. "Master Updale would have been hanged if it had not been for Galia, who has a close relationship with the atmosphere."

"The bolt of lightning!" Rina had exclaimed. "I wondered..." She'd gone over to Galia and kissed her cheek. "Thank you."

"Yes, thank you," Talisa had whispered. Her green eyes had been misty with tears when she smiled at Galia.

It had been hard not to feel happy, even though danger, mounted on horseback, threatened them all.

But the waiting had gone on too long. People moved restlessly. Voices fell silent. Eyes strained toward the city. Tension hung in the air like brooding thunderclouds.

A child's high voice asked, "When is the queen coming? I want to see the queen."

"Good question," Bart muttered.

Then Galia spotted something. She squinted into the bright sunlight. A small group. In the distance. Riding toward them. Others had seen it too. There were murmurs, mutters.

"The queen?" Garth speculated.

"Probably," his grandfather answered.

Thannis gripped Galia's hand for a moment. "Whatever happens, don't let me lose my temper."

The party rode closer. Now there could be no doubt.

It was Talisa who began the song, rising to her feet so her voice could ring out clearly. From all around, people followed her example. By the time Queen Elira reached the line of mounted soldiers, everyone was standing. They swung into the second verse as she reined her horse to a halt. *They must be able to hear us in Freybourg*, Galia thought, and sang even louder. The chorus came, then the third verse, the chorus, the final verse, the chorus again.

The silence that followed stretched out like a vast, incoming wave.

Queen Elira finally spoke. "I thank you for your song. As you may know, I love music." Surely there was a touch of warmth in her voice. "However, I did not come to listen to singing, but to ask you why you have come to Freybourg."

Galia stood on tiptoe. Even so, she could not see above the heads of those in front of her.

"Stand on the rock," Konrad said. She clambered up.

Alain Swanson stepped forward and bowed. "Thank you for coming to see us, Your Majesty."

"You are Master Swanson?"

"Yes, Your Majesty."

"I am waiting for your explanation."

Alain was silent for a moment. When he spoke, his voice was quiet, but so clear Galia heard it easily. "We come in peace, Your Majesty. Your soldiers can vouch that none of us carry arms. We mean no harm to anyone. We came simply to ask for your help." He paused.

Galia saw courtiers and a few black-robed teachers from the college in the queen's party. Was Raven among them? He would have come if he thought there might be injuries. She craned her neck, but most of the figures were hidden by the soldiers.

Alain spoke again. "There are many people here, Your Majesty. Many of your subjects. There are men and women, old folk and children. Two things only unite us. We are all poor." Galia saw Annette stir self-consciously. "And we all have hope. Hope that you will help us."

"What kind of help?"

"Houses for those without homes. Food for those who go hungry."

"Beggars!" someone shouted. A man thrust his horse forward till it stood beside the queen's. "I warned Your Majesty, they're nothing but a band of beggars."

Anger rippled through the crowd like waves roused by a flung stone.

"Eastlands," Cory said. The name was a curse. The old man spat. Alain spoke above the rising tide of hostility. "We are not beggars. We seek only what is fair and just. Everyone here is willing to work, if there is work to be had. But too many people have swarmed into Freyfall – other cities, too, but mostly Freyfall – in recent years. People who lost the land they lived on."

"That's right!" someone behind Galia shouted.

"He robbed us of our land, he did," another voice called.

"Threw us off. Land my family had looked after for years and years."

"*He's* the one should be homeless. Then we'd see who'd be a beggar."

"Look at him. *He* don't care."

The back of Galia's neck pricked, as with a coming storm. She looked around. People who had stood so quietly, so proudly, short minutes ago, were red-faced, beetle-browed, clenched-fisted.

"He's a bad man!" A child's shrill yell.

"Out of the mouths of babes," Bart muttered. His arm was around Rina, holding her close.

At least Thannis hadn't flown into a rage. He was frowning, but it was a worried frown, not an angry one. Galia smiled at him, then looked back at the queen and the count – and the soldiers. Most had their hands on the hilts of their swords.

Alain raised his voice. "We came in peace." Were his words meant for those behind him as much as for the soldiers?

The Count of Eastlands gave a scornful laugh. "Sounds peaceful, doesn't it? There's no such thing as a peaceful rabble. I suppose you came to beg for your land back."

"Fool," Konrad said.

"Maybe he's so upset about his house being burned that he has to lash out," Annette suggested.

"You're right we want our land back," a man shouted.

"But we didn't come begging."

"Wouldn't beg. Not from you."

"It'd do us no good if we did, would it? Can't get water from a stone, nor caring from a heartless man."

Galia saw Queen Elira turn her head and speak to the count. He said no more.

But the damage was done. The jeers continued.

Queen Elira looked at Alain. Galia saw her lips move, but could not hear what she said above the surge of voices. Alain turned and called to the people. Those close by may have heard, but Galia only caught "peace" and "calm." His words might have been thrown into the wind.

A sword flashed in the sun. Another. Another, until every soldier in the front row sat with sword held high.

We are close to the edge. Very close. In another minute, we will hurtle to our deaths. As Arlan did. Galia closed her eyes.

In the distance, thunder rumbled.

"Rain won't help now," Konrad said. She opened her eyes and looked at him. He was staring at the soldiers. "I could use a holding spell, but it would only halt one or two swords. And your rain would only make people wet and miserable."

Ahead of her, a half grown boy stooped and picked up a rock. The man beside him did the same.

"If even one rock gets thrown, the soldiers will charge," Bart said.

More thunder, in a continuous low growl.

She had not even known she was creating a storm.

Control. Her nails dug into her palms. She must not give in to anger. She must not give in to despair.

The thunder died away.

Surely, *surely,* there was something she could do.

"You have a great gift," the Wise Women of Atua had told her. *"It is a gift you must use sparingly, and well, to help, never harm. Think before you use it, then use it wisely."*

Wisely. But she was not wise. She couldn't think.

"Mother, help me," she whispered. "Please help me." But no inspiration came. A sob rose in her throat.

"Fog," said an aged, cracked voice.

She looked at the old man who was sitting once more on the rock.

"You come from the Misty Isles, don't you?" he asked. "Don't hear that name so much these days. Islandia, they call it now. But they're still misty, ain't they? Surrounded by mist, they used to say."

"Yes," she whispered. "*Yes.*"

Making fog at home was easy. It came from the ocean and the land and the sky. It would be harder here. It would take longer. It might take too long.

She glanced at the soldiers, then at the people around her, some silent, edging away, clutching their children to them, others clutching stones, hurling abuse. How long would it be before they hurled stones?

"The song," Talisa said, and started singing. The others joined in.

Would it work? Would the sound of the familiar song bring back the earlier mood? Perhaps.

She couldn't worry about that. She must concentrate.

There was water in the air. In the ground. She must find it, stir it in the mixing bowl of her own emotions.

Mist was not the bitter tears of Arlan's death. It was a gentler sorrow. The ache of longing for her home and family. Sympathy for Queen Elira, who had had age descend on her today like an unfamiliar mask. Regret that Mallory had lost his beautiful house.

And mist was bewilderment. That was easy. Why had Arlan died with most of his life still to live? How could the Count of Eastlands have tossed so many people off his land and into poverty? Why were the soldiers ready to mow down men, women, and children as though they were stalks of wheat? For a moment, hot anger stabbed her. She thrust it down. Anger had no part in what she was creating.

Moisture touched her hands, her face. She opened her eyes. The sun was gone. The world wore a thin grey skin. As she watched, the skin thickened. The soldiers grew faceless, hazy. Then they disappeared. The cries of anger, the shouted insults, stopped.

"They must not panic. Neither the people nor the soldiers," Konrad said. "Keep singing."

They did. Their voices rang in the stillness.

The fog thickened. Faces close by disappeared.

"Join hands," Cat called. All around, other voices took up the cry. Galia grabbed those closest, felt the bony, crooked fingers of the old man, the firm, large hand of

Konrad Spellman. Their hands rooted her in the formless world. She sang louder.

They all did. Not just their small group. The whole gathering sang the song they had sung so often today. Their voices filled the void of silence, the void of nothingness, that the mist had made.

When they stopped, there was a ripple of laughter, a murmur of satisfaction, before they stilled again.

Queen Elira's voice floated out of the grey curtain that had descended. "A remarkable thing, this sudden fog."

"Yes," came Alain's response. "I don't understand it."

"Don't you?" There was a touch of laughter in the queen's voice. "I think I do. But we were interrupted. You mentioned lodging and food. Perhaps something can be done, at least to help those most in need. But there is nothing I can do about the restoration of land. The Count of Eastlands was perfectly within his rights."

Galia tensed. Would this statement ignite fury again?

"It's hard to be angry at a disembodied voice or an unseen face," Thannis said. He was right. There was a collective rustle as the queen's words ran through the crowd, but nothing more.

"I know," Alain said. "The Count of Eastlands did nothing that was against the law. As you said, he was within his rights. Whether he was *right* is another matter. But there is other land. Higher up in the hills, there is land that belongs to no one."

"It belongs to the crown," Queen Elira said sharply.

"Then it is yours to bestow, out of generosity to your people."

After a moment, the queen said, "It would be a hard life, farming there."

"It would," Alain agreed. "Many may choose to stay in Freyfall, especially if they have food and a roof over their heads. But I think many others will choose to go to the hills they love."

"You propose, then, that I give this land to those who want it?"

"I do."

There was a long silence. Then the queen laughed.

"You ask much, Master Swanson. But your requests make sense. I do not like to see my people hungry or home-less. I am well aware that it is the pressure of so many people thronging into the cities that has caused the present problem. We shall have to consider the matter further, and work out the details, but...Your plan does have merit. For now, I would suggest that those assembled here rest overnight, then return to Freyfall tomorrow. Food can be distributed to those who need it." She raised her voice. "It would help if the fog were no more."

Galia took the hint. In a few minutes, the fog disappeared.

EPILOGUE

THE CHILD CROUCHED BY A TIDE POOL, HER dark curly head bent in absorption. She didn't look up when Galia stopped beside her.

Galia knelt and studied the pool too. The water shimmered with colours far more brilliant than those in the ocean just beyond. Like the sapphires and emeralds and amethysts she had once seen displayed in a shop window in Freybourg, Galia thought. Only far more lovely. And filled with life.

"There's a starfish." It had been a long time since she had seen a starfish.

The child's head jerked up. "You're not Mama." Her dark brown eyes were round with surprise.

Galia smiled. "No. Were you expecting your mama?"

The child nodded but said nothing. She continued to examine Galia. Then her eyes moved to the boat pulled up on the beach a short distance away.

"You came on the boat."

"Yes."

"Did you sail it all by yourself?"

"No. Two others came with me. They climbed up the hill to the village. I decided to walk down the beach." It was the sight of the dark head and small body that had decided her, but Galia didn't mention that.

The girl nodded. "Are you a Wise Woman?"

"I'm not very wise. Not yet, anyway. I do know some magic, though." A pebble was digging into her knee. She shifted her weight. "Why did you think I might be a Wise Woman?"

"Grandmama said the Wise Women should be coming soon, to look after the sick folk and the sick animals."

"Your grandmama is right. Raven and Sari have come to do just those things. Raven will help the sick people, and Sari the sick animals."

"Oh." The child absorbed this. "What can you do?"

"I can change the weather."

The wide eyes went even wider. "Are you going to change our weather now?"

Galia looked at the pale blue sky, feathered with clouds. "Probably not."

"Why did you come then?"

For a moment, Galia was quiet. Then she said, carefully, "Would you tell me your name?"

"Mala."

She had expected this answer. The age was right. And the girl had Brianne's pink cheeks and rounded chin, and Arlan's arched eyebrows. And Galia's hair and eyes. All the same, the name caught at her breath. She couldn't speak.

"Why did you come?" Mala repeated.

"To see you." Her voice was husky. She cleared it. "To see you, and your mama and grandmama and grandfather and aunts and uncles."

Mala stared at her.

Galia smiled then. "I'm your Aunt Galia. You won't remember me, but I remember you, though you were just a baby the last time I saw you."

Mala frowned. "Aunt Peris said you were far away in another country."

"I was, yes. I was in a land called Freya, at a school called the College of Wizards. But when the school closed for the summer, I sailed back to Atua. Then Raven and Sari and I came here."

"Are you going to stay here?"

Galia hesitated. It was not too late to change her mind. The Dreamer said she had fulfilled the purpose for which she had been sent to Freya. The Mother said she had learned enough that she could go home, if she wished.

All those years away, she had longed to be here so bitterly that it sometimes made her stomach ache. And now...

Galia turned her head and looked out, beyond the foamy froth of waves breaking on shore, to the distant horizon where sea and sky merged. If she returned to the college, she would have to go beyond that horizon, to reach Freya. And then sail up the River Frey to Freyfall and, after that, travel overland to Freybourg.

But the journey would not be lonely. Along the way, she could stop to visit people she knew. Galia smiled, remembering.

Two days after the confrontation in the field outside Freybourg, Kerstin and Jem Brooks had arrived. "We came as soon as we received Talisa's letter," Kerstin had said. "All the way here, I was afraid we'd be too late. And so we were. Thank Freyn our help wasn't needed."

They were connected, she and Kerstin Brooks. Raven had told her that.

"The Dreamer who saw you at the college was not the Dreamer on Atua. It was Kerstin Brooks."

Galia had stared at him. He'd smiled.

"She sent a request, along with the invitation to the council last Midsummer. In a dream, she had seen you at the college, and knew you were important for the future of Freya. She asked that you come with the delegation." He'd paused, then smiled again. "If it had been anyone other than Kerstin, we would have ignored the request. But Kerstin has been so intertwined with Islandia, ever since she was a girl, that we do not ignore her."

"I hope you don't mind," Kerstin had said, with a small, anxious frown. "It was wrong to uproot you from your home. But I knew that your presence here was vital for Freya. And for Islandia," she'd added thoughtfully. "For all three lands. We are all interconnected now."

"I don't mind," Galia had said. And, to her surprise, it was true.

She had made friends. Friends she treasured. She thought of them now.

Talisa and Cory would go to Uglessia to let Talisa's family know everything was well, then return to Freyfall. Talisa would complete her apprenticeship. "I owe it to the Coynes," she'd explained.

Cory had nodded. "And to your music. As for me, I hope the carver Master Coyne mentioned is still interested in talking to me. If he will take me on, maybe he can teach me how to work in stone, for when we live in Uglessia." He and Talisa had smiled at each other.

"And by the time you return to Uglessia, we should be settled in the Freyan hills not far away," Rina had said. She'd leaned back against Bart and sighed with satisfaction, all signs of strain gone from her face.

They had all been together, crammed into the Spellmans' parlour at the inn. Cory, Garth, and Cat had sat on the floor. Jem had offered Cat his chair, but she refused to leave her spot beside Garth.

There were many people she could see on a journey to Freybourg. She could stop in Frey-by-the-Sea to visit Kerstin and Jem Brooks in their home on Wizard's Hill. She could stop at Frey-under-Hill to see Cat, who might even have a new brother or sister by then. She would definitely make use of her time in Freyfall to talk to Talisa and Cory. And to Garth and Annette and Konrad Spellman, though Annette might be busy. She had been appointed as one of the people who would oversee the plans to provide lodging and food to those in need. Queen Elira had asked Alain Swanson to be part of the group, but he had refused. "It's important work, but it's not my work. My job is making songs. I am more than happy to leave it in your capable hands," he'd told Annette, causing her to blush prettily. She had looked dazed but pleased ever since being asked to perform this task.

It had been decided to extend the exchange of wizards for one more year. Raven would be at the college. So would Thannis. Jem and Kerstin's influence, plus Konrad's, had been enough to make Master Wisher say grudgingly that Thannis could come back on condition that he never, *never* get into another fight.

If she returned, she could learn Freyan spells and possibly teach Islandian magic. Melton Granton had proved that this was possible. She might not even mind teaching *him* again. At least, not too much. He had been so devastated when he realized that the wind he'd roused, using the new knowledge she'd given him, might have helped destroy Freybourg, that his arrogance had oozed out of him like blood from torn flesh. Nor was Thannis the only one who had received a stern lecture and the threat of expulsion from the College of Wizards. Galia had almost felt sorry for the man.

If she returned. She still could change her mind.

She looked back at Mala, but the child had forgotten her question and was busy trying to catch a minnow.

"Mala."

Mala looked at her.

"You asked me whether I'll stay here." Her knees were sore. She shifted her position, then glanced around, at the path that led from the beach to the fields and houses that perched on the cliff, at the house on the headland – *her* house – which had, surely, shrunk during her absence, at the shore, ever changing on the whim of the waves. So familiar. So loved.

Above her head, a gull squawked. There were always gulls here. But then, even in Freybourg, you could see gulls sometimes.

"I'll be here for the summer. Come autumn, I'll sail back over the sea to Freya. Now, isn't it time you were home? Your mama will be worrying."

"Mama knows where I am when she can't find me."

Galia hid a smile and climbed to her feet. "Even so. Come." She held out her hand and felt Mala's small, wet fingers grasp it.

As they started towards the path, she saw people appear on the cliff top, then start down the hill. People she knew. Her mother. Her father. Peris. Brianne. Cai, though the boy she had left had turned into a man.

She smiled down at the girl beside her. "I'll be in Freya for a year. After that, I'm not sure where I'll be. But whatever I do, I'll always come back here." She breathed deeply, taking the sharp sea air into her lungs. She could see her mother's face clearly now. Tears ran down Mala's cheeks.

"I'll always come home."

PHOTO: CATHERINE MCLAUGHLIN

ABOUT THE AUTHOR

LINDA SMITH is the author of *The Minstrel's Daughter*, and *Talisa's Song*, Books I and II in the "Tales of Three Lands" trilogy. Titles from her first series, The Freyan Trilogy, were finalists for a number of book awards, and another recent title, the 2003 picture book, *Sir Cassie to the Rescue*, was highly recommended by *CM Magazine*. She has also published poetry and short fiction in a number of anthologies and periodicals, and has had her work broadcast on CBC Radio.

Born in Lethbridge, Linda Smith grew up in Alberta, and has lived in Truro, Nova Scotia; Saskatoon and Boston. Since 1984, she has made her home in Grande Prairie, where she worked as a children's librarian until 2001, and now writes full-time.

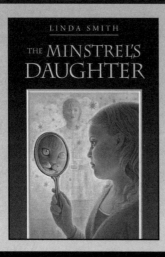
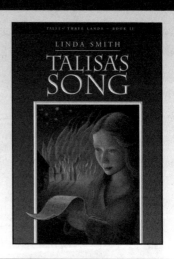